Nana blinked her c
it?"

Gape-mouthed, I speared her with an incredulous glare. "Yeah, that's it. Isn't it enough? Nana, the secretarial pool, for God's sake! I am an award-winning investigative reporter. I broke open a huge exam-cheating scandal and won every major collegiate journalism award. Then I became the first female editor of my college newspaper. I graduated Magna Cum Laude. I wanna be a writer not a secretary."

Nana twisted her lips into a smirk. "So, since you stormed out, you'll never know if you would have gotten the job."

I spat. "I wouldn't take it if he offered it."

Nana grinned. "So, you expected to start at the top?"

Duh. Yeah, Nana. Okay, so, I didn't say it out loud. Of course, Nana came equipped with the grandmother radar thing and figured out I said it to myself.

Nana tipped her head. "You ought to be grateful to the man for giving you a dose of the way the real world works."

Crap. This nana let you get away with nothing.

## Praise for Susie Black

"Rag Lady is a wise and wonderful book that will grab your heartstrings and not let go."
*~ Anastasia Abboud, author of Tremors Through Time*

"I laughed out loud throughout this hilarious book."
*~ Nancy Brashear, author, Gunnysack Hell*

" Holly Schlivnik has attitude to spare."
*~ Ellen Byerrum, author Crime of Fashion series*

"Black takes fans of her fast-paced whodunits into Holly Schlivnik's entertaining background. A witty, enjoyable read."
*~ Corinne LaBalme, author of French Ghost*

"Sassy, smart, snarky characters who come to life on the page."
*~ Terry Newman, author of Heartquake*

"A colorful cast of well-hewn characters."
*~Nellie H. Steele, author of The Cate Kensie Mysteries*

"Erma Bombeck meets Maise Moscowitz in a groundbreaking tale of shattering the glass ceiling."
*~April Willis*

# Rag Lady

## by

## Susie Black

*Holly Swimsuit Series*

This is a work of fiction. Names, characters, places, and incidents are either the product of the author's imagination or are used fictitiously, and any resemblance to actual persons living or dead, business establishments, events, or locales, is entirely coincidental.

**Rag Lady**

COPYRIGHT © 2023 by Susie Black

Cover Art by *The Wild Rose Press, Inc.*

The Wild Rose Press, Inc.
PO Box 708
Adams Basin, NY 14410-0708
Visit us at www.thewildrosepress.com

Publishing History
First Edition, 2023
Trade Paperback ISBN 978-1-5092-4997-8
Digital ISBN 978-1-5092-4998-5

*Holly Swimsuit Series*
Published in the United States of America

## Dedication

Rag Lady is dedicated to those whose wisdom and wit guided me through the hills, valleys, and unexpected curves of life:

To my mother who raised her daughters to believe they could do anything that they set their minds to.

To my dad and mentor: without the opportunity you gave me, I would not have stories to tell.

To my nana who taught me the important things: How to care, how to swear, how to drive, and most of all, how to live.

Prologue

Her expression was utterly priceless. Mea culpa. It was rather unprofessional of me to break into hysterics as a response to her question, let alone snort the coffee out through my nose. I stared down at the sodden mess. No doubt about it. The darned silk shirt was a goner. I'd be getting it back from the dry cleaners with one of those little tags with the sad face pinned to the care label saying, *"We're sorry. We tried our best, but we are unable to save your garment."*

I considered apologizing to her. I mentally tried on a couple to see if they fit. "Gee whiz, I'm sorry I shot the coffee out of my nose." Or, "Sorry I snorted coffee all over it. Please print another computer report." Yikes. I abandoned the idea of apologizing, and chose to emulate all of my bosses who *never apologized for anything.*

My young assistant, Tiffany, and I had just finished a lengthy meeting. If I squinted, she kind of reminded me a little of myself back in the day. Of course, she had bigger boobs and better posture than me. She was eager to please and anxious to learn. And she asked me, of all people, to share the secret to my success and teach her the industry ropes. Why she considered *me* qualified to teach her *anything* remained a mystery.

Heck, every time I had the answer, somebody changed the question. Nonetheless, she asked me a question, and it deserved a response. I'd been taught the only way to pay it back was to pay it forward, so naturally, I'd give it my best shot. I glanced around my office for the smartest way to start.

I dismissed the awards and plaques displayed on the wall next to my desk. No need for any self-aggrandizement. For some inexplicable reason, the kid already idolized me.

I also disregarded a photographic history of Mermaid Swimwear told by the collection of ad posters of our best-selling ladies' swimwear styles decorating the majority of my office walls. No sense in starting the story towards the end of the movie.

I turned my attention to the framed business card and hangtag collage of my career hung next to my college diploma. The map I'd used to navigate the hills and valleys, U-turns, and unexpected curves throughout my career stared down at me from my office wall. I had a success story to tell, and the best way to do it was right before my eyes.

By now you're probably asking, "Who the heck is this klutz?" Let me introduce myself. My name is Holly Schlivnik. I am a successful sales executive in the ladies' swimwear industry. I got into the rag business by accident. Or, maybe by a mere quirk of fate. Toss a coin. And they say God doesn't have a sense of humor. Ha! I am living proof God has quite a twisted one.

You'd think a bunch of tiny bikinis wouldn't weigh much…think again. Trust me, they do. Sometimes as I'm struggling to push a rolling rack filled with incredibly heavy garment bags onto a rickety freight elevator, I'm pretty sure it's God I hear cackling with divine amusement from someplace deep inside the elevator shaft.

Chapter One

Considering how little control we humans actually have over our lives, it's a miracle we ever accomplish anything on our own. We carom off the walls separating the days from nights like a herd of hairy ping pong balls trying to get a grip on the meaning of life. The dumb ones muddle through clueless, yet think they know it all. The smart ones figure out that the way your life turns out has little to do with anything you come up with.

The reality is our fate is mostly determined by genes, timing, and a large dose of dumb luck. The choices we make usually boil down to either the process of elimination or taking the easy way out. This pretty much described my life's game plan after I graduated college. In other words, I had no clue.

At the end of my college freshman year, my dad, a ladies' apparel sales rep, got a huge opportunity and moved my family from Los Angeles to Miami. Relocating from hip LA to "God's waiting room" failed to excite me, and I chose not to go.

Three years later, armed with my journalism degree and a blind idealism only the young can sustain, I was more than ready to take on the world. I'd been raised to believe life held no limitations. And nothing impossible to accomplish if I set out to do it. Stunned didn't adequately describe my reaction when it only took five minutes with the Managing Editor of a major city newspaper to shatter the world as I expected it to be.

So, what is the only logical thing for an extremely self-confident, independent girl to do? I ran across the country to put some distance between me and the stinging slap of reality and to let those who loved me make it all better and tell me what to do next. As if. No chance of it *ever* happening with my family, who kept a legal pad with the line drawn down the center for comparison decision-making velcroed to their wrists. I might plead until my voice turned hoarse, but at the end of the day, no one but me would decide what to do with my life. Cripes.

My nana had two favorite expressions: Man plans and God laughs, and nothing turns out the way you think it will. She believed things happen for a reason, even if we don't understand why. She warned me to be careful what I wished for since I might get it. That sometimes God punishes us by granting us our wishes, and other times God saves us by not granting them. And that God helps those who help themselves. As I'd soon learn, Nana had the secret of life down pat.

Once back at my parents' house, I discovered my college degree qualified me for not a single job. Since so far my next move appeared as clear as mud, talking things over with Nana seemed a logical starting place. Maybe by osmosis, I'd have an epiphany. I sure needed one. Even though it now seemed pretty irrelevant, graduate school registration loomed only a few weeks away.

Nana lived in the same apartment building as my parents in North Miami Beach. I took the elevator up three floors, and a sense of peace washed over me as I opened her apartment door. No matter how dire the situation, it always improved in Nana's cozy kitchen. The love emanated from the oven directly to my heart. I closed my eyes and breathed in the comforting scent of coffee brewing. As a little girl, I could hardly wait to be old enough to join the adults after dinner as they sat around sipping coffee and sharing the events of their days. Drinking coffee became a sign of belonging and always meant comfort in a cup.

Nana's long and narrow kitchen featured glossy stained knotty pine wood cabinets hung over white Formica counters, and a floor covered by a faux tile linoleum that fooled no one. The kitchen walls were papered with a cheery tropical floral print. The kitchen had a white gas stove with a double oven, and an older model white refrigerator with the kind of freezer on top you pulled down to open with ice cube trays you smacked against the counter to loosen the cubes.

Nana's kitchen might have been old-fashioned, but nothing was old-fashioned about her. She was not your typical Jewish grandmother. Anything but. Never judgmental, she possessed an open mind and an approachable heart on anything. Smart, funny, and fearless, she taught me life's important things: to care, to swear, and to drive. Yep, my myopic nana with the coke bottle glasses, who probably set a world record of the number of driving lessons she'd taken before finally getting her license at sixty years old, taught me to drive. Imagine taking driving lessons from Mr. Magoo.

Like the rest of the women in our family, Nana was short. Plus or minus five foot one if you squinted and your measuring stick was inexact. She wore her wavy gray hair cut in a bob. She had an average bust, flat-as-a-pancake tush, and a round tummy, making her appear perpetually pregnant. Without her glasses, she was blind as a bat.

Sharing coffee and conversation in Nana's kitchen was as comfortable as snuggling into a favorite warm cardigan on a cold, rainy day. I sat on one of the slightly cracked vinyl chairs and rubbed my hands on the round Formica table shiny with age. There was no other place where I'd be safer, lick my wounds, and figure everything out.

Nana pecked my cheek and I breathed in her scent, relishing the aroma of Tabu mixed with a dash of nutmeg. Her pale gray eyes twinkled through her thick lenses and resembled big blurry owlish marbles. As though time had stopped and we'd never been apart, she gave me a devilish wink and slid a cup of coffee and a slice of freshly baked babka in front of me.

She appraised me over the rim of her eyeglasses. "So, kiddo, I don't mind telling you. Those wrinkles creasing your kisser are gonna become permanent if you keep frowning."

I puffed the air out with my cheeks. "Right now, my life isn't much fun."

She smirked. "Life isn't fun. It's life. So, you'd better get used to it. So, why arc your panties in a bunch?"

Nana listened without interrupting as I climbed onto the imaginary soapbox and railed over my plight. "The SOB kept calling me *honey* instead of Holly, even though I kept correcting him." I clucked my tongue. "It doesn't get more disrespectful than that." My voice level rose in proportion to my outrage. "*Then* he asked if I took *shorthand!*" My coffee mug jiggled when I slapped the table. "I can't imagine *anything* more insulting.

*Shorthand*, for crying out loud."

Nana tsked her displeasure as she mopped the few drops of coffee I sloshed out of my cup with a crumpled napkin she took out of her apron pocket.

I wrinkled my nose. "Can you believe it? I told him no I didn't, and he had the nerve to say and I quote, '*Listen, honey, all the girls at this paper start in the secretarial pool*'." I jutted my jaw. "I told him my parents didn't send me to college to end up as a secretary. I snatched my resume off his desk, took the little remaining of my dignity, and walked out."

Nana blinked her owlish eyes and shrugged. "That's it?"

Gape-mouthed, I speared her with an incredulous glare. "Yeah, *that's it*. Isn't it enough? Nana, the *secretarial pool*, for God's sake! I am an award-winning investigative reporter. I broke open a huge exam-cheating scandal and won every major collegiate journalism award. Then I became the first female editor of my college newspaper. I graduated Magna Cum Laude. I wanna be a writer not a secretary."

Nana twisted her lips into a smirk. "So, since you stormed out, you'll never know if you would have gotten the job."

I spat. "I wouldn't take it if he offered it."

Nana grinned. "So, you expected to start at the top?"

Duh. Yeah, Nana. Okay, so, I didn't say it out loud. Of course, Nana came equipped with the grandmother radar thing and figured out I said it to myself.

Nana tipped her head. "You ought to be grateful to the man for giving you a dose of the way the real world works."

Crap. This nana let you get away with nothing.

She pursed her lips into a funnel. "If you're gonna make it through life intact, you'd better grow a thicker skin. You wanna be a writer? So, write. Do you want my advice? You better figure out how *much you* want to be a writer, and make sure it's important enough to fight for. And if not, find something else to believe in, or you'll live one heck of an empty life."

I sputtered with the cadence of a car engine missing a sparkplug. "I guess you missed the day they taught Jewish Grandmother nurturing."

Nana rolled her owlish eyes. "Come on. My opinions should come as no surprise."

She pointed to my chair and dipped her head. "You sit in that chair and ask me a question. I tell you what I think, not what I think you want to hear. Don't overthink everything, because whatever is gonna happen, will, whether you go kicking and screaming, or recognize the time to question and the time to accept." She waved a hand of dismissal. "You didn't get the job you wanted. Boo hoo. Amazing. The world didn't end. Things happen for a reason. The right thing will come along, and you'll know it. Sit back and let life happen."

She smiled and reached for the coffee pot. "For right now, have another cup of coffee."

\*\*\*\*

So, I took Nana's advice and downed another cup of coffee… or four or five hundred. I waited almost two weeks for *life to happen*. Since I was used to working hard instead of hardly working, and patience has never been one of my strong suits, this sitting on my tush waiting for the proverbial light bulb to go on began to piss me off.

The days blurred together and time dragged so

painfully slow it almost ground to a standstill. I vibrated with the impatient energy reserved for the young. I was raring to get going if I only had a clue where to go. Waiting for this epiphany crap didn't work for me. I'd have to give Nana the bad news. I gave it a shot, but her brilliant game plan flopped. Then I needed to get off my tush before my brain turned to complete mush, and come up with a more viable plan B. I'd soon find out how right my wise nana turned out to be.

Chapter Two

Once in Miami, Dad discovered the "huge" part of the opportunity turned out to be the size of the eight-state territory he covered, rather than the amount of existing business in it. Determined to make this career move work since he'd uprooted the family and schlepped it three thousand miles across the country, Dad became the unwitting king of the road. In a business where time is money, Dad worked twice as hard to make half as much as he'd envisioned, and he traveled more than he was home.

While my mother missed him, she secretly loved the arrangement of being married and single at the same time. My parents were the epitome of opposites attracting. Ballet and opera versus football and rock. Beef Bourguignon versus barbeque. When he arrived home, they did things Dad enjoyed. Mom could afford to be conciliatory. He always left in a few days, and then she did as she wished, guilt-free. He was never the wiser, and the method to her madness proved to be the secret to the success of their marriage. Note to self: The trick to a lasting marriage is not being together too much. Oh boy.

****

The sun had barely risen, and the temperature already hit a toasty 89 degrees that August day. The humidity rode in on the waves of the Atlantic and crawled onshore. It slung low on the hips of the city, clinging to it as tightly as a pair of sodden jeans to one's tush. With it being impossible to go outside and stay dry, let alone clean, bathing seemed rather pointless. A stab of pity pierced my heart as Dad, drenched in sweat, filled eight garment bags stuffed full with tightly-packed samples stored in his home office and then loaded them into his blazing-hot van. My heart went out to him. I did not envy his hard life.

Dad left Miami early on that hot, humid August Sunday morning working his way up the belly of the state. His route would eventually deadhead into Atlanta in time for the upcoming trade market starting the following Friday at the Apparel Mart.

****

The following Friday morning I sat at the kitchen table enjoying a bagel slathered with a thick schmear of cream cheese while drinking a cup of strong, black coffee. As I ate, I scanned the Miami Daily Press-Register, and tried to work up the courage to submit a resume.

Since it wasn't my house and I expected no calls, I continued reading when the phone rang. One ring. Two rings. Three rings. Four rings. Since the phone kept ringing, my parents must have missed the memo on the great new invention: the answering machine.

Mom shouted from the back of the house. "Hol, do me a favor and grab the phone. I just got out of the shower. Tell whoever it is I'll call them back."

I gulped some coffee to wash down the bagel and yelled back. "Okay. If I get to it before they hang up!" Five rings. Six rings. This is a one *really* persistent caller.

If it was me calling, I'd have gotten the hint and hung up by now. I put the cup back in the saucer and dropped the newspaper as I stood. I bent to retrieve the paper and hit my knee on the table on the way up. I knocked the cup over, and coffee splashed all over the table. I chased the coffee with a bunch of saturated napkins trying to blot the sodden mess before it spilled onto the floor.

All the while, the phone kept ringing. Mom shouted, "Don't worry if you miss it. If it's important enough, they'll call back." I stubbed my toe on the table base and scowled. Couldn't you say so before I banged my toe? The phone kept ringing. I shoved the chair out of the way and hopped on one foot to the other side of the kitchen to grab the receiver from the base of the wall phone.

*Still ringing.* Unbelievable. With this many rings, it must be a relentless telemarketer. I checked the clock on the stove and brushed the idea off. Nah. Way too early for telemarketers. They wait until you're in the middle of eating dinner to call. I was way beyond curious as to the reason someone was so determined. All I wanted to do was reach through the phone and strangle the life out of whoever was on the other end of the line.

Since the only way to shut them up was apparently to answer the call, I grabbed the receiver with my left hand, rubbed my aching toe with my right, and growled to the phone. "All right already! Hold your horses!" Imitating an arthritic frog, I jumped around and tried to balance on one foot. I yelled into the receiver, "*Hello!*"

A bubble of annoyance rose up from my belly as Dad complained at the other end. "Hol, why'd you take so long to answer?"

I muttered. "Oh, it's only you. Mom is in the shower. She said to tell whoever it is she'll call them back. Are you in the showroom or the hotel?"

He snorted. "Thanks for the warm greeting. Whaddya mean it's only you? Who were you expecting?"

Guilt stung my heart. I hadn't meant to hurt his feelings. I cushioned my response by jabbing him with our long-running joke. "I'm so sorry, Your Royal Nosiness, oh great God of Guilt."

The smile in his voice filtered through the phone line. "Hey, I resent that remark. I'm not nosy. I'm a concerned parent who happens to ask a few pertinent questions."

I chortled at his ridiculous answer. "Ha! You're more the grand inquisitor. You needed to ask *every date* his religious preference and his place of employment?"

Dad scoffed. "I merely tried to put the guys at ease."

I rolled my eyes. **"**And *that's* the best way to make a guy comfortable? More the best way to send him running out the door screaming as if his hair was on fire." I half-joked. "I have this recurring dream with an endless line of guys who are waiting for me. And you-with a clipboard checking off little boxes on an application form as you ask each one for their religious affiliation, college name, degree, job description, homeowner or renter, car brand, father's occupation, bank balance, and stock portfolio."

Dad huffed with righteous indignation. "Now you're being ridiculous."

I snickered. "With all the questions you ask, *you're the one* who should have been the reporter. Anyway, I'll tell Mom you called. Where are you, so she can call you back? Showroom or hotel room?"

Dad hesitated one beat, then two before replying in

an oddly nervous tone he tried to cover with sarcasm. "Actually, Miss Smarty Pants, I called to talk to you."

I stared at the phone bewildered. I couldn't imagine anything for us to discuss. Then I remembered his level of disorganization. "Okay, sure no problem. Do you need a phone number? Let me switch phones and go into the pit you call your office." Without waiting for a reply, I put the phone on the counter.

I ran down the hall to a closed door with a hand-written sign taped to it: *Enter at Your Own Risk*. No shit, Sherlock. I stared into a room as destroyed as if a hurricane made a direct hit. The room was such a disaster, the cleaning lady refused to go near it and suggested Mom hire a hazmat team. No kidding.

Women's clothing samples lay strewn everyplace: On the floor, over the chair, and one even hung from the lampshade. Stacks of folders and loose invoices sat piled precariously on the floor as high as the desk.

I swept the samples off the desk chair and reached for the phone. I grimaced and wrinkled my nose. Double yuck. A half-filled mug inscribed on the outside with the motto *I'm from Cleveland, what's your excuse?* sat next to the phone on the desk with a cigar butt and a ballpoint pen floating in stale coffee. How gross.

His chicken-scratch handwriting with the same names and phone numbers written a dozen times on various parts of the pad covered the desk blotter. "Honestly, you either need to get an address book or take your blotter with you since you use it as an account list."

Dad started to speak. "Hol, I don't...." He paused mid-sentence. "Hey, no office editorials. No one told you to go intruding into my private space. Anyway, for your information, Miss Sarcasm, I don't need a phone number. I called to talk to *you*."

I dipped my toe into the murky waters of the conversation pool. "Oooookay."

He took a deep breath. "Hol, I need your help." Holy guacamole. Did I detect desperation in Dad's voice? I brushed it off. He had the rep of a major drama Queen, so I had my doubts. Nonetheless, he tweaked my curiosity. "Okay...tell me."

A rasp scratched his ex-cigarette-smoker voice. "I've got a crisis on my hands. Your Aunt Elaine called to say our sister Blossom was rushed to the hospital this morning. The doctors say she suffered a stroke. Today is the first day of the Atlanta market, and the mart is already packed. It's going to be a huge trade show..."

Aunt Blossom was a kick in the pants. I hoped she recovered completely. But how this had anything to do with me remained a mystery. As though reading my mind, he continued. "The problem is, this market is the same time as the one in Dallas. Dallas is a much bigger market than Atlanta, and the bosses from my lines are all in Texas. I need to go to Cleveland, and I don't have anyone else except you to help me..."

I rotated my head in a one-eighty around the room to see who else he might be talking to, but I sat alone. Before he thought I'd hung up on him, I recovered the use of my vocal cords. I channeled the guy in the movie *Taxi Driver* and squeaked. "Are you talking to *me*?"

Dad answered in a measured tone reserved for small children. "I can't just throw the buyers out, put up a 'be back soon' sign, and leave."

Why the heck not?

He said, "I need you to come to Atlanta and run the market until I get back."

The absurdity of his solution could not possibly be overstated. He couldn't be serious. This must be some kind of joke. "Oh, good one. You had me going for a minute. Okay, this is amusing, but seriously, which phone number do you need? I promise not to make any more blotter jokes."

He yelled so loudly that I almost dropped the phone. *"Holly, for crying out loud, do I sound as though I'm kidding?"*

I gasped with the reality of his question. "You *do* understand that my knowledge of ladies' apparel is restricted to wearing it, right? Sorry, the answer to your problem is not me. Call your bosses, explain the situation, and if they can't spare one person to help you, my advice is to display the *be back soon* sign."

I snapped my fingers. "Forget that. There's a much better solution. You don't have to leave Atlanta at all. Let Uncle Barry or Aunt Elaine go instead." Uncle Barry is a lawyer and can make his own hours. Aunt Elaine is a stay-at-home mom married to a successful pharmacist. It's a lot easier for them to drop everything and go instead of Dad.

"I am meeting them in Cleveland. Blossom's condition is critical." Dad's voice caught. "She may not make it, and we all need to be there. This is the biggest market of the year." Dad pleaded. "Please. I've never asked you to do anything for me, but I'm asking you now. I *need* you to do this."

I wanted to help, but me as his problem's solution? He had to be kidding. "Let's say, for the sake of the argument, I'm crazy enough to do this. Who's gonna help me?"

"Mom. Who else?"

Good thing I left my coffee in the kitchen, or I'd have ruined my nightshirt. "Seriously? So, the blind will be leading the deaf?" Nonetheless, no matter how epic a disaster this solution turned out to be, I couldn't say no to my father. I sighed. "If we're the best you're able to dredge up, I guess Tweedle Dee and Tweedle Dumb will come and make idiots of ourselves. As Mom always says, I'll never see these people again."

He chirped with the enthusiasm of a robin on the first day of spring. "Great! Pick up your tickets at the Delta counter. You'd better hustle your bustle 'cuz your flight leaves in two hours. It'll take your mother at least an hour to pack."

My jaw dropped precariously close to my girls. "You bought the tickets *before* you called me? Pretty darned optimistic."

Dad's voice grew husky. "We're family. You'd never let me down." He promised. "You'll get a kick out of southerners. They are a unique breed."

Chapter Three

As the plane landed, an odd combination of excitement and dread twisted my heart into knots. My stomach turned a nervous flip-flop the way it does when the rollercoaster at Pacific Ocean Park is at the top and ready to drop into a steep dive. Little did I know I sat in the front car.

The taxi exited the interstate, and I giggled reading the many confusing street signs all beginning with *Peachtree*: Peachtree Drive, Peachtree Street, Peachtree Industrial Blvd., and so on. If the only address information available is the building is on Peachtree, it's impossible to know which one to take. The cab turned onto Peachtree Street and dropped us off in front of the Atlanta Apparel Mart.

I pointed to the huge building that took up the entire block and grinned at my mother. "If there was ever a time to go in with our right foot first, this is it." To anyone not Jewish, this makes no sense, so I'd better explain. While modern in almost every aspect, Nana believed in the power of all those weird Jewish superstitions covering every life situation including one to ensure a safe journey and good luck.

If someone left or took on something new, Nana always cautioned to "walk in with your right foot first." Why doing it ensures safe travel or good luck remained a mystery. Nonetheless, without fail, whether boarding a plane or going out my front door, I traversed it with my right foot first. Maybe not going into the ladies' room, but pretty much everyplace else. She was my wise nana. So, she must have dialed into the secret to living a safe and successful life. Why would I question her? The right foot first concept is so ingrained into my psyche that I'd be scared not to do it. This was no time for taking chances, so we pushed our way through the mart lobby doors and walked in right foot first.

****

I'd never been to an apparel mart before and had no idea what to expect. An array of lobby shops sold everything from magazines to mannequins. Porters pushed rolling racks laden with garment bags packed full of samples through the crowded lobby. A huge marquee welcomed buyers. A giant calendar of market events hung suspended from the ceiling. We stood in line and picked up our badges Dad left for us at the registration desk. A perky uniformed mart greeter stood next to the elevator bank and handed us directories as we pushed our way into a crowded car going up.

We forced our way out from the back when the car stopped on the fourth floor and followed the parade of models and buyers down the main aisle. Moving to the rhythm of loud music made for a carnival atmosphere, and I found it difficult to choose what to observe first. I was so busy taking in all the sideshows, I almost lost Mom.

We turned the corner, and the crowd's momentum stopped short in front of an enormous showroom taking up half of Dad's aisle. Twelve long rows of gold lamé fabric-topped tables stretched across the length of the room with matching bench seats. A raised heart-shaped stage with spotlights lining its rim was the focal point of the showroom. The gaudy room décor resembled a French whorehouse, not a showroom. A huge black banner with neon pink lettering spelling *Slinky Fashions* hung suspended from the ceiling with a giant toy slinky featuring a sexy, scantily clad young woman lying provocatively in the middle of it.

An overweight, sweating, clean-shaven, middle-aged man with jet black hair gel-stiff combed back pompadour style stood center stage with a halo of overhead spotlights glaring down on him. He wore a tight-fitting black tuxedo with a pink boutonniere and a gold lamé cummerbund ready to burst its seams. Feet shod in gold lamé socks and white leather tennis shoes tied with gold lamé laces completed the hawker's ensemble. He shouted into a microphone grasped in his left hand while holding a glass of champagne in his right. He jumped a little kick step as he waved the microphone, incongruous as a pimp doing either a sneaker commercial or the French Can-Can. Hard to tell which.

A black curtain draped closed behind him, and every two minutes a model dressed in a different sexy outfit undulated across the stage to pulsating disco music. The Master of Ceremonies leered at the models like a pimp peddling hookers instead of the clothes on their backs while he described the styles the girls wore.

After a model finished her walkthrough and headed back to the curtain, she stopped, shook her fanny at the crowd, turned back to face the buyers, blew them a kiss, and waved goodbye. As the model disappeared, the MC sucked an index finger as though it caught fire and yelled, "It's a hot number, don't miss it. It's sizzling!" after every style.

Too busy gaping at the carnival-like sideshow to pay attention, I backed into a guy delivering deli platters. I swung to my right to avoid falling face-first into the pastrami. I tripped into the Slinky showroom and landed in the lap of a male buyer. The man grinned wickedly, gave me an appreciative kiss on the mouth, and yelled to the MC. "Hey, Teddy. Did you just start giving away free samples?" The audience roared with delight as I jumped off the man's lap and ran out of the showroom.

Chapter Four

Dad's rectangular showroom opened with a sliding glass door. Glass windows stretched across the front of the showroom. Stenciled signs hung in the first window listing the lines he represented. Each label was scripted in the company logo. Dad's name and contact information was painted on the first window in smaller block letters beneath the company logo signs.

A window trimmer had hung merchandised groups of spotlighted samples in the rest of the windows to attract the attention of potential buyers walking the aisle. Each window featured styles from all his lines.

The second window had samples from Climax, a sexy, fashion-forward dress line in slinky fabrics that were neat, but not my personal style. How this revealing line was received by accounts in this more conservative area struck me as a likely challenge.

The third window had knit tops from two different manufacturers, UGC Knits and Sweet Inspirations. UGC had cool fabrics and space dye knits. Sweet Inspirations had innovative embellishments like faux turquoise stones that I loved.

The fourth window featured samples from Infinity, a less fashion-forward collection of short and long dresses and jumpsuits in fabrics and styles more suited for conservative tastes.

A couple sat at the middle table facing a husky man

in his late-forties sporting a Van Dyke beard. His longish, wavy black hair had been combed to the left side and needed cutting. His kind brown eyes peered out from behind Buddy Holly-style black-framed glasses. He had a chunky physique with wide hips and a protruding stomach pressed tightly against the waistband of his charcoal trousers. He wore a paisley print shirt and scuffed black loafers. He stood next to a wall grid pointing to a style hanging on it. Meet Mike Schlivnik, my dad.

He took a dress off the wall rack and draped it dramatically down to his side, the way a matador uses a muleta to get the bull's attention. With a straight back, and graceful for a big man, he pivoted to his left and brought the top of the dress under his nose. He stared at the people sitting in front of him as though daring the bull to ignore him.

A dead ringer for Elton John, the tall, thin seated man slapped the table and snorted. He cried out, "O-lay, O-lay! Tor-o, tor-o!" in a high-pitched voice. "Oh, my God, take a gander at Mike Schlivnik, the world's only Jewish bullfighter!" Elton turned to the heavyset woman seated next to him and squealed. "Doris, we need to buy the damned dress since he presented it like he's a hippie tore-o-dor!" Elton winked at Dad and pointed to the dress. "Hey, Seenor, what's the style number?" The two buyers erupted into hysterics as Dad theatrically fanned the sample and recited the style number.

While this toreador routine was now only an entertaining part of Dad's sales shtick, in his youth he actually did a stint as an amateur bullfighter. The middle-aged spread he now sported pushed the imagination to its limits trying to visualize *his* body *ever* in toreador pants.

If I hadn't seen the old posters and photos with my own eyes, I would never have believed it. I gave him credit. Self-deprecating, yet he'd made something interesting from his youth synonymous with his selling style. It was an effective shtick. With a dip and a sweep, *every* customer remembered his presentations.

Would the buyers expect a chip off the old block? Considering the effectiveness this life imitating art became for Dad, I ran through my life's film clips for something interesting, since entertainment seemed to be a sales job requirement. Alas, nothing noteworthy popped up unless you counted my years toiling at the Totten Tap Dance Academy. While I still remembered it, I doubted a sales presentation replete with the beginner's dance routine of *Out-Back-Down-Step- Step/ Out-Back-Down-Step-Step* would have the same effect as Dad's crazy shtick.

A Jack O' Lantern-wide grin of palpable relief spread across Dad's face as Mom and I walked into the showroom. "Thank God you're here." He held up the dress sample. "I have an hour to teach you the ropes."

Gulp.

Dad turned to Elton and Mrs. John and swept an arm towards Mom and me. "Steve and Doris, meet my wife, Natalie and our daughter, Holly. Holly is gonna pinch hit for me while I go to Cleveland on a family emergency."

Steve and Doris turned around in their seats to greet us. Steve flashed a smile and finger-waved. Doris gave us the once-over, as though appraising two prize auction steers before placing a bid. "Holly, you're the spittin' image of your mama. She sure can't deny you!"

I grinned. "We get that a lot." Mom and I are twenty years apart, almost to the day. My teachers thought Nana was my mother and my mother, whose youthful features made her appear more like a teenager, was my older sister. I hated those parent-school nights. I demanded my mother dress like a mom and not as a kid if she came to my class.

Steve turned to Dad. "I'm real sorry for your family's troubles. We're done here, so we better say adios and let you get to work." Steve joked. "Good thing you're such a fast talker. An hour's not much time to teach her everything you know."

My heart danced a nervous tango. I prayed not to embarrass myself too much or worse, embarrass Dad even more. Once Dad bid Steve and Doris farewell, he came around the table and enveloped us both in a bear hug. He clung to me for a few extra seconds and gave me a fierce squeeze. He held me out at arms' length and gushed. "Hol, you're a lifesaver."

I grinned devilishly. "Let's see if you still feel the same way when you come back."

Dad motioned me to sit at the middle table. "Relax and enjoy yourself. Southern people are nice and understanding. We're not putting a guy on the moon."

I slapped a brave smile on my kisser and prayed he was right. I hoped for the best while preparing myself for…to tell the truth, I wasn't sure. It remained a mystery as I tried not to let my imagination wander on its own and scare the crap out of me. How bad could bad be? With any luck, someplace between total embarrassment and complete humiliation. Oy vey!

I made notes while Dad talked. He gave me a brief synopsis of the best features and top selling styles that buyers should definitely write of each line. Then he demonstrated how to present the samples individually and by group.

He picked a random sample from the center rack and held out the hangtag. "Remember, the style numbers are coded, so you can figure out the prices. The first two numbers of the style number are the wholesale price. So, if the style number is 1962, then the wholesale price is $19.00. The size range is also on the hangtag under the style number." He turned the hang tag around. "The color swatches are stapled to the back of the hangtag. The fabric content is inside the garment on the care instructions. In this business, perception is *everything*. Act as if you know what you're doing. Even if you don't, people assume you do. The delivery is as ready by October 30th. You remember the meaning of as ready?"

I glanced at my notes and replied as proudly as if I'd invented the wheel. "It means the company can start shipping whenever the style is ready, but it must be delivered to the store by no later than October 30th." I narrowed my eyes. "October has thirty-one days. Why can't they take the whole month to ship and not get gypped out of an extra day?"

Dad shrugged. "No idea why. October 30th is the delivery date the bosses quoted me."

I dipped a shoulder. "I asked in case any buyers question it."

Dad checked at his watch and clapped. "Okay, kiddo, you've got the most important stuff. I better skedaddle, or I'll miss my flight." He handed me the showroom keys. It might have been my imagination, but I swore they burned into my palm. He kissed Mom and me, hugged us both, grabbed his suitcase, and yelled last-minute instructions to me as he ran out the door. "Be yourself, present the lines the way I taught you, and you'll write a ton of orders. Don't worry. You're gonna be great!"

Yeah, Dad. As Nana would say, from your mouth to God's ears.

I stared longingly down the aisle until Dad turned the corner. Once he disappeared, the all-alone-in the-world emptiness in my heart was the same one I had as an abandoned kindergartener on the first day of school. Mom gave me an encouraging hug. She watched his tush disappear and shrugged. "You'll do your best, but don't worry too much since…" We completed the sentence together, "You'll never see these people again."

Since my self-confidence had dropped below my socks after Dad left, relief flooded my heart when the day ended, and no other buyers walked into the showroom. Mom and I were too wiped out from the excitement of the trip to clean the showroom before we closed for the day. So, we left the place a mess and vowed to get in early the next morning to tidy up before the market began.

Chapter Five

Saturday dawned sticky and sizzling. Atlanta had the same stifling heat as Miami sans relief from an ocean breeze. A layer of suffocating humidity made the air thick enough to chew. The energy-sapping weather was much better suited for a lazy afternoon in a hammock and ice-cold lemonade than a day of work.

As a recent college graduate, my wardrobe mainly consisted of a variety of sweatshirts, T-shirts, jeans, and sneakers. I packed the few big girl outfits I owned in the hopes of appearing like, if not a professional salesperson, at least an adult.

Dad's comment about perception is everything stuck in my mind. I chose my most grown-up outfit for the first day on the job. Even if I sounded idiotic, at least I dressed appropriately. I stood in front of the mirror decked out in a solid black pantsuit with a light gray silk shell. I wore three-inch platform black leather heeled shoes only someone young or foolish enough wore, knowing they'd be on their feet all day. I rationalized the platforms as a necessity to reach the hangers on the top of the racks.

I struck a confident pose and was rather pleased with my appearance until it dawned on me that I'd chosen the same outfit I'd worn to my ill-fated newspaper interview. Good grief. I had enough to worry about without wardrobe woes as another complication. I prayed it wasn't an omen. Crap. I jinxed myself before I presented the first style. Perhaps calling Nana was the answer? Surely, she'd have one of those Jewish voodoo phrases to chant and ward off the heebie-jeebies? I checked the time and shook the idea off. It was too late to change and too early to call her. With only a few options available, I kept the tainted ensemble on and hoped for the best, vowing to walk in with my right foot first through every door…twice.

Mom wore a pale olive pantsuit with a light blue silk blouse and sensible lower heels. Her attire? Stylish and comfortable. By comparison, my outfit was better suited for an undertaker. Which was fitting, since it seemed like I was going to my funeral.

We fortified ourselves with the largest cup available of high-test black coffee strong enough to peel paint. We raced into the apparel center three blocks from the hotel seconds before the heat melted us into puddles. With the perspiration circles already forming under the armpits of my silk shell as we entered the mart, I'd be keeping my jacket on all day.

We donned our badges and arrived at the showroom an hour before the market began. With the two of us working, we straightened up the place in no time flat. But the empty display grids between the wall racks stuck out like sore thumbs. "Should we put a couple of things on these grids for display?"

Mom nodded yes. "Dad does."

The wall racks bulged with samples, but I had no idea which ones to choose. "Which styles?"

Mom turned a one-eighty around the room. "Anything with bright colors." She pointed to the center rack. "I'd pick a few of…."

Mom was interrupted by a twenty-something woman sauntering into the showroom. She wore a loud purple one-piece flame-printed jumpsuit with an ID badge stamped MODEL pinned below her right collarbone. She tottered on four-inch shiny purple patent leather stiletto heels fringed on the toes. She carried a cosmetic kit slightly smaller than my college freshman-year dorm room in one hand and a purple & white polka-dot parasol in the other.

Oversized purple sunglasses with curlicues on the edges and fake eyelashes on the tops shaded her eyes. Her jet black southern big hair was teased into a beehive. The hairdo was stiff enough from at least a can of hairspray, and capable of surviving a category four hurricane intact.

Her enormous cone-shaped breasts pointed straight out at attention. Either she was really cold or extremely happy to see someone. She was accompanied by a clean-shaven, swarthy man whose height set him at eye level with the woman's pointy nipples. If she made any sudden moves, she'd take out one of his eyes.

Her companion sported a full head of kinky black hair resembling a large pad of steel wool placed off-center on top of his head. He donned a purple, three-piece, vested shiny sharkskin suit. A bright yellow bow tie sat askew on his purple and yellow striped shirt. A matching yellow handkerchief was stuffed into his jacket top pocket. He wore shiny white patent leather shoes with elevator heels. He carried a gold walking stick. A huge diamond ring blinked on his pinky finger as he twirled the walking stick.

The woman smiled at Mom and me, flashing crooked front teeth. Neon purple lipstick highlighted her full, pouty lips. She strutted in and brayed in a loud, high-pitched voice. "Hi y'all. Is Mike here? I'm a few minutes late, but…" She tipped her sunglasses and revealed piercing azure blue eyes with false eyelashes so long and thick that they waved like hairy, black spiders as she batted them. She smiled a Mona Lisa smile as if she held a secret. She glanced down at the man and gave him one of those exaggerated winks. "We got a late start this morning, right, sugar pie? If y'all get my meaning?"

The man grinned up into the woman's boobs. He licked his lips as though about to take a bite. He marked his territory by patting her butt. She was a cross between Auntie Mame and a hooker strolling with her pimp. My eyes had a mind of their own, and I couldn't help but stare at the ridiculous pair. I bit the inside of my lip not to make one of my usual smart-aleck cracks.

The bimbo blushed and slapped her thigh. "Mike's a big ole worrywart. He's probably already roamin' the halls searchin' for me!"

I waited for a beat until confident I could speak without insulting her. I sputtered. "A-and y-you a-are w-who?"

The woman threw her shoulders back, her impressive chest out, and pointed to the badge pinned above her right boob. Still not ringing any bells, I blinked my ignorance. She stabbed an index finger into her cleavage and huffed with a combination of shock mixed with pity." You don't know who I am? I'm Cora Lee Deen. I've been Mike's market model for a good long time." She played a rat-a-tat- tat with her fingernails on the man's shoulder. "And this is my husband, Kaseem Deen."

She gave the room a once over. "Where *is Mike*

anyway? It's not like him to just disappear." She narrowed her eyes and pointed an index finger with a long-manicured nail curved in the shape of a purple-tipped talon at Mom and me. "And by the way, if y'all don't mind me askin', just who are y'all? Does Mike have an appointment with y'all?"

I extended my hand. "I'm Holly, Mike's daughter, and this is my mom, Natalie, Mike's wife. Dad left on a family emergency, and we're helping out until…."

She dropped her cosmetic kit and squealed like a stuck pig. She launched herself at me and crushed me in a suffocating embrace with my head trapped between her two enormous boobs.

She screeched, "Oh my God, you're *Holly*? Your daddy doesn't stop braggin' about you!" She jabbed an elbow into Kassem's midsection for confirmation. "That's God's truth, isn't it, Kaseem? It's like meeting a gen-u-ine movie star. Let me come right on in so we can get started. There's nothin' to worry about. Cora Lee's here now, and it's all gonna work out just fine."

After a struggle, I managed to extricate my head from between Cora Lee's ginormous, concrete-hard jugs still standing up at attention. I took a defensive step back, gasped a restorative breath, and shook my head like a wet dog.

Cora Lee slapped her long, tapered fingers across her rouged cheeks. "Oh, I'm so sorry, sugar. I almost crushed you with my new boobies." She proudly pointed to her chest and grinned at Mom and me. "Don't y'all just love 'em? I just got my boobs done." She giggled girlishly and petted Kaseem's shoulder. "I gave 'em to Kaseem for our fifth weddin' anniversary. It's a crazy cool thing. They put me out and then they pumped up my boobs with something called sillycone. I woke up, and poof. Instant big boobies. Ain't it just the cat's pajamas?"

At a loss for an appropriate response, I smiled and stepped aside to let her walk in. "It's nice to meet you too, Cora Lee."

Chapter Six

I paced the length of the showroom, relieved and yet nervous at the same time that not a single customer came in the first morning. A fair share of window shoppers stopped to admire the garments on display. But if I approached them, they waved me off and scurried away. I couldn't hit the ball if I didn't get up to bat. Maybe the word already got out. Mike left, so buyers needn't stop in. Or that his idiot daughter knew squat?

Finally, after lunch, a thin woman wearing a long-printed skirt and a solid knit top walked in. She wore her auburn hair cut in a pageboy, and wireframe granny glasses sat perched on the end of Flowery Stivic's ski-jump nose. She seemed more a Berkeley hippie than my image of a buyer. She exuded a serene air of calmness I hoped meant she'd be patient as I stumbled through my first presentation.

A tall man with thinning brown hair accompanied her. He wore a corduroy blazer with patched elbows and khaki pants. An unlit pipe dangled on his lips. He reminded me of my college advisor. She spoke slowly and drew out her vowels in the southerner style. He shyly mumbled hello with a slight Eastern European accent.

If appearances meant anything, they were as unlikely as buyers as I was as a rep. It leveled the playing field, and I calmed down enough to make it through my first presentation without humiliating myself.

Surprisingly, I actually enjoyed it.

I waited anxiously for how the rest of the day would unfold. Before long, a chubby, bearded man around thirty years old dressed in a plaid shirt and razor-sharp creased jeans walked in. Alan Gardener was a repeat customer familiar with the products, so we went through the first few lines quickly. We got to the last one, and I slid comfortably into the homestretch. This presenting products to buyers didn't turn out as difficult as I had imagined it to be. Maybe Dad was onto something, and I'd do a good job and not embarrass him.

Wait a minute, sister. Not so fast. I put the first group of Climax samples on the grid, and to my horror, Alan shook his head emphatically no. "I'm sorry. Gonna have to pass. The group's just too fast for me."

This rejection created a major-league problem. Alan just passed on the best-selling group in the line. Dad instructed me not to let *anyone* out of the showroom without buying something from it. Short of tying the guy down, this buyer would escape if I didn't do something fast.

They say a picture is worth a thousand words. I glanced over to the changing room and punted. "Cora Lee, please put on the Climax pink long halter dress with the feathers." I held up the sample. "Alan, before you pass on the style, wait until you see it on. It's been one of our best sellers."

Two minutes later, Cora Lee floated out of the changing room, gracefully swirling and twirling and dipping her way across the room. Her ample bosom raised them so the feathers on the halter dress seemed to wave on their own. My eyes widened as Cora Lee squeezed her boobs together so the feathers stood out even more. She leaned over and practically shoved her jugs right into Alan's nose. She crooned sweetly, "Don't you just *love* these feathers! They tickle my boobies!"

I held my breath. Alan blushed bright red as a ripe tomato as he pulled his head out of Cora Lee's cleavage. The guy might walk out in a huff or ask her out for a drink. Neither would surprise me.

I let my breath out once Alan grinned. "Tell the truth, I'd never buy it without seeing it on." He poised his pen, ready to write. "What's the style number?"

Fearing black and blue marks, I resisted the urge to hug Cora Lee. I grabbed the hangtag pinned to the garment. "Style number is 1550. The wholesale price is $15.00. It comes in pink, red, black, and white."

Almost out of the woods. Then he stumped me. "Which colors are you selling?"

I dragged my eyes over to Mom, but she just shrugged. I peeked at the color swatches and bought myself a moment. Time to test drive dad's theory. I might be a newbie at sales, but not as a consumer. A glance at the white swatch, and the answer came to me. "We're selling everything but the white. It might be too sheer."

Alan fingered the swatches. "You're probably right. Let's do pink and black. And the delivery is?"

I replied with the conviction of a preacher delivering a Sunday sermon. "As ready October 30th."

Alan asked, "Usual terms?"

My stomach clenched with the question. This guy had some nerve. I blushed from head to toe. "I'm not that kind of girl." I spat through gritted teeth. "Alan, my dad is gonna be pretty upset about this."

He paused and chose his words carefully, trying not

to embarrass me. "Holly, you misunderstood the question. I'm not questioning your morals. I'm asking about a trade discount. The industry standard is to give an eight percent discount if you pay the invoice before the tenth of the following month from the receipt of goods."

After only a few hours as a salesperson, I wouldn't call myself an expert. But since Dad didn't cover this, that sure sounded like a bunch of hooey to me. I narrowed my eyes. Maybe Alan figured me for an ignorant newbie, and tried pulling one over on me? I might be new at this selling gig, but I recognized a pile of crap when I smelled it. "Let me get this straight. You get a *discount*, and all you're doing is paying your bill on time? You expect a *reward* just for doing what you're supposed to do by paying a bill?" I muttered. "Too bad the telephone company doesn't do the same thing…"

Alan dipped his head. "Yep, it's God's truth. Really. Ask your dad." He glanced at his watch and stood. "I better get going, or I'll be late for my next appointment. Say hey to your dad for me, and I hope everything works out okay with his family. Tell him to call me at the end of next week, and I will have his orders ready." He stuffed his notes into a battered leather briefcase and left.

Mom sat with two conservatively dressed middle-aged women at the next table who'd been following along my presentation to Alan. The ladies wanted some help writing up their order, so I grabbed an order pad. When we were almost finished, I leaned closer to ask one of them a question regarding a color choice for the last style.

I detected movement in my peripheral vision and glanced at the front of the showroom. I dropped the order pad and gawked slack-jawed at the open showroom door. Mom and the two ladies turned around to see what I was staring at.

The only way to describe it? Someone with the physique of a giant man dressed as a woman. She loomed hugely, a mountain of a woman at least six-six and absolutely ripped. Muscular and rock-solid the way an athlete's body is. Not an ounce of fat on her. I guesstimated she weighed in around two-eighty, with the powerful arms and legs only a lifetime of rigorous workouts produces.

She came dressed incongruously in a frilly pink and white gingham check print sundress with a scalloped edge hem. Her feet were shod in the largest pair of matching pink peek toe pumps imaginable. My two feet easily fit into one of them with room to spare. I eyed them at least a size fourteen. Where does one find those types of shoes in such a big size? No place. They must be specially made.

She'd painted her finger and toenails with bright pink polish and carried a pink straw clutch purse in her baseball glove-sized hand. She sported bright pink lipstick and two round rouge spots dotted her cheeks. She wore a brunette wig combed in an upsweep. The dress fit tight across her busty chest. She had a slightly bent hawk nose, the hairy arms and legs of an ape, a five o'clock shadow, and a rather prominent Adam's apple bobbing up and down when he/she spoke.

I opened my mouth to greet her, but my brain and vocal cords had stopped communicating with one another, and not a single word escaped my lips. First, Teddy and his stable of hookerish models. Next, Cora Lee and her pimp-appearing husband stroll in reporting for work. Now this giant of a buyer replete with huge peep toe shoes waltzes in to see a line. Do *any* everyday people attend this market? Or is Dad's showroom just a magnet attracting all of society's exceptions?

Since I had been rendered speechless, the giant spoke up with a voice that ranged from the beginning of the sentence in a low masculine growl to a high-pitched girlie squeal at the end. She smiled at Mom and me. "Hi y'all. Is Mike available? I have an appointment to do Climax with him."

The princess of paradoxes daintily touched her blushing cheek and giggled in a self–deprecating, yet coquettish tone not normally associated with a linebacker and apologized. "Oh my… That came out all wrong. It sounded so tacky! I didn't mean to talk ugly." She ducked under the doorway and walked into the showroom. She swiveled her bowling ball-sized head and surveyed the room. "Is Mike here?"

She took a business card out of her purse and handed it to me. She pointed a sausage-sized finger at her cleavage. "I'm Jody from Mr. Sid's/Jody's boutique in Birmingham."

I stood up and bent back far enough to see her. I composed my face into a neutral expression, but my stuttering voice betrayed me. "H-hello, J-Jody. I-I'm sorry. M-Mike isn't a-available. H-he l-left un-unexpectedly on a f-family e-emergency. I-I'm h-his d-daughter H-Holly. P-please t-take a s-seat and I'll p-present the l-line to y-you."

I kept my eyes away from my mother and the ladies as I led Jody to the workstation table. The challenge now? Getting through the presentation without cracking up. Dad, you might have given me some warning. As if.

Not if he wanted me to stay. If he'd given me any inkling of all the strange people I'd encounter at this market, I'd have run for the first flight out of loony land. At least this one might be helpful. If a sample was too high for me to reach, Jody could easily grab it off the rack without having to get out of her seat.

Jody batted her eyes and gave me an expectant look. Let the games begin. I called out, "Hey, Cora Lee. It's showtime! Please put on the ruffled Climax feather style number 1550 in pink first."

Chapter Seven

Having incredibly low expectations, receiving only a few pity orders would have been thrilling. So, the sizeable stack of orders I collected by the end of the market stunned me. Dad's eyes widened as he counted the dollars and units in his head. He said it didn't surprise him. Hadn't he sworn I was a natural? Could I be any good at sales, or were the accolades just Dad's way of saying thanks for helping him out? It didn't matter. I was just happy I didn't disappoint him or embarrass myself.

After the market ended, I had my fill of peach pie and southern accents, and the time came to leave. A sense of accomplishment mixed with a surprising sadness for the experience to end accompanied me to Miami. Once home, I settled back into my routine of coffee and indecision. The clock ticked closer to decision day with every stroke of the minute hand. I needed to do something soon. Nothing worse than inertia to cloud up the mind. I went to the mall, hoping with diversion, an idea on what to do next would appear. Three hours later, I returned home with sore tootsies, but no wiser.

Muffled shouting greeted me as I walked into my parents' apartment.

They had closed their bedroom door, yet the volume of the argument was so loud, that it traveled from their room to the entry. Curious. They were the proverbially well-matched couple. What precipitated such a level of a shouting match with two people who *never* fought? I stood in the hallway and eavesdropped.

Dad snarled. "She's a natural-born salesman. She jumped in the way a duck takes to water. She wrote bigger orders than I ever could with some of my toughest customers. Harold from Renfrew's Casuals *actually left* her the orders. I usually have to chase him for weeks before I get them."

Mom yelled back. "I don't give a damn if she wrote a million dollars' worth of orders! She helped out during a family emergency. A one-time thing. She's going to grad school. Let her go. She wants to be a writer. Let her write. Maybe she'll be a newspaper editor or win a Pulitzer Prize. I'm not gonna let you turn her into some schlepper driving all over Georgia showing schmatas to a bunch of rednecks. Don't screw her life up with some stupid idea of being a salesman. One in the family is enough."

Holy guacamole. Like an invisible tennis match, my feelings regarding the subject bounced back and forth. Dad *must* be kidding. *Me* a road rep? Crazy talk. Yet, much to my surprise, I squelched the urge to dismiss it, and actually considered the concept. Oh, boy.

Dad taunted. "So, being a salesman is good enough for me, but not for Holly?"

Mom backpedaled faster than a circus clown on a unicycle. "You know I didn't mean it like that."

Dad snapped like a cranky turtle. "Well, ya sure fooled me. My phone's been ringing off the hook since the market ended. My customers are crazy about her. A couple of them said they'd rather work with Holly instead of me. She's an adult. Let her make up her own mind. All I want to do is give her the option. If she's not interested, so be it. And I will happily send her to grad school. Let me talk to her. She'll probably say no thanks faster than you can say schlepper. Either she'll prove you're much smarter than me, or she'll shock the hell out of us, and say yes. Are you afraid of which way she might choose?"

Mom sighed. "Honestly, I am afraid she'll say yes. As much as I hate to say it, you're right. It's her life to screw up, not mine. If you raise your children to be independent, you can't penalize them if they do as you've taught them to just because they choose a path you don't want them to go on. I'd be a real hypocrite not letting you give her the choice." Mom huffed. "Damned trouble maker. I want to strangle you."

Dad joked. "Part of my charm."

My mother's tinkly giggle signaled the end of their argument. Amazingly, they were now united on the concept. Yikes. I counted on Mom to quash the idea so I didn't have to choose. As if. Their bedroom door opened, and I scrambled out the front door. Better to let them take me by surprise. Oh. My. God. Double gulp. Who was I kidding? Too late. That ship had already sailed.

Chapter Eight

Panic strangled my heartstrings when Mom handed me the dreaded grad school letter of intent. The university seal burned into my hand as I opened it with all the caution of the bomb squad. Fanfreakingtastic. Time to put up or shut up. The letter stated that if I failed to sign and return it by the one-week deadline, they'd give my space away to another better-focused, more deserving student. All right, not those *exact* words. Self-abuse is the gold standard for keeping you down, and no one is more brutal than me.

My parents went out for the evening. I didn't want to be alone, so I took the letter with me and went up to Nana's. Maybe I'd find some sympathy and a solution to go with a cup of coffee.

I opened the door and walked into her dark apartment. Where could she be? How is it possible she's not available when I needed her? Didn't nanas come with some sort of radar, so they sensed if their grandchildren needed them? Maybe she needed a beeper? I better check into it and keep her on call.

I waited for her, figuring she couldn't be out too late. Aren't old people supposed to be early to rise and early to bed? Naturally, my nana didn't fit the mold. Lucky me. She's a night owl who tucked all the late-night television comics into bed. I stared at the front door, willing Nana to walk in. Maybe my parents were back and could tell me where Nana went. As I picked up the phone, a key turned. Finally. It was about freakin' time.

She walked in momentarily confused with me impatiently tapping my foot. She crossed the entry with her arms open to hug me. She spoke in an oddly endearing accent. A cross between a Boston Brahmin and a Brooklyn cabbie. "Hello, my adorable dahling! Isn't this a wondaful surprise?"

I pulled out of her embrace. "Nana, where were you? I've been waiting forever!" Or, so, in my addled state, it seemed.

Wide-eyed panic deepened the wrinkled creases of her face. "Did we have plans?" She tapped the side of her head. "Crap, am I going senile?"

An idiotic concept. We should all be as together as her. "No. I'm the one going soft in the head, not you." I narrowed my eyes. "So, where were you?"

Nana grinned. "In the next building over, playing in a canasta game at Katie Moskowitz's. I love Katie like a sister, but I *hate* it when she's the hostess. She tells a joke with the timing of a comic, but the woman can't cook to save her life. Her quiche is always runny and her strudel? Like chewing a sponge. And her coffee? Feh! So weak. You tip the rim and you can see the bottom of the cup through the coffee. If it wouldn't insult her, I'd bring my meal with me. Everyone loves Katie, and she really tries hard. So, no one wants to hurt her feelings. But thank God, it won't be her turn to be hostess for another month."

Nana gave me the once-over. "So sweetheart, why the long face? Did you lose your best friend?" Nana waved an age-spotted hand towards the other end of the apartment. "Come, let's go into the kitchen. We'll drink some coffee and I'll find something tricky to go with it. I always think better with a coffee cup in my hand. No matter the problem, we'll figure it out, as we always do."

Hallelujah. Surely after she'd downed a few cups of coffee, those brain juices of hers would start flowing. With any luck, I'd seem so pathetic, she'd tell me which way to go, and I could get on with my life. With a glimmer of hope, I followed Nana into the kitchen.

We sat across from one another waiting for the coffee to brew. Nana cocked a brow. "So, sweetheart, something's troubling you?"

Where to begin? I bought a few moments by idly shredding a napkin. Nana slapped my hand and pinned me with one of her glares that said to spit whatever it was out already. I stopped shredding and started talking. "I guess you heard the news about Dad's job offer by now?"

Nana smiled and clapped. "Yes, of course. He can't stop kvelling over all those orders you wrote. This is so exciting." Nana narrowed her eyes and tapped the tip of her nose with her index finger. "But from the expression on your face, I guess it's not so exciting to you? Eh?"

I dipped my head. "It is exciting, but also, kinda scary." I sighed. "Nana, up until a few weeks ago, it seemed like my life was set. I was going to grad school."

Nana frowned. "So? Nothing's stopping you from still going. Are you worried you'll hurt your dad's feelings if you turn down his job offer? If you are, forget it. You are not responsible for his feelings. He is. You must make up your own mind, and do what's best for you, not what you think he wants you to do. You can't live your life doing things to make other people happy." She pointed a gnarled index finger at me. "Listen, kiddo.

People come and people go, but you're stuck with yourself. So, the one person you'd better keep happiest is *you*."

She poured my coffee into a ceramic mug with a slightly chipped handle. Nana drank her coffee the old Eastern European style, in a glass. She put an ice cube in hers and looked expectantly at me.

"To tell you the truth, the problem is, I kinda *like* Dad's offer." I squirmed in my chair and shoved the letter from school under her nose. "Now I have two things to choose from: school or the job."

Nana squinted at me, perplexed. "Am I missing something?"

I smacked the table in frustration. "Choices Nana! I don't wanna make a mistake! This is my life on the line. I will screw it up if I make the wrong choice. It's not as though I can flip a coin." I gave her the stink eye. "And don't tell me to get out the stupid piece of paper and draw the line down the middle!"

Nana grinned. "And why do I do that?"

I rolled my eyes. "Yeah, yeah. To teach me the right way to make a decision." I shook my head. "Well, guess what, Nana? I don't want to make the decision. I was happy the decision had already been made. Now I'm not so sure. Even though I couldn't see the point to it anymore after the disastrous newspaper interview, grad school still seemed the logical next step."

I ran my fingers through my hair. "On the other hand, I'm trying to imagine *myself* doing the job Dad does. The adventuresome part of me says it's cool. No school, no exams, no tedious papers to compose. I'd be *experiencing* life instead of reading about it. *And* getting paid to do it. But the realistic part of me says, are you nuts? Schlepping those heavy garment bags all over the place day after day? And what kind of a life would I have traveling all the time?"

I wrung my hands. "I don't trust myself to make the right decision, and I'm driving myself crazy. I want someone else to decide, and tell me which way to go."

Nana peered over her glasses and clucked her tongue. "Well, too bad, kiddo. Life doesn't work that way. Let me tell you something. And the sooner you learn it, the easier your life will be. Man plans, and God laughs."

Huh? Nana might as well have spoken in Sanskrit. "Meaning?"

Nana answered in the same indulgent tone she used when I was a toddler. "It means plan all you want, but most of the time, your plans don't mean a hill of beans. To use your vernacular, shit happens. You're going along singing a song, confident life is a well-planned party. But the truth is, the road to life from birth to death isn't paved in a straight line. It's paved with hills and valleys, U-turns, and unexpected curves. And trust me. Nothing usually works out the way you think it will."

A product of the predictability of school, the control freak part of me got a tad pissy with the direction this conversation had taken. "So, you're saying we don't have any control over anything. Some cosmic big brother is making all our decisions for us and we're nothing more than robots? If that's the case, why even bother making a decision, since it really doesn't matter?"

Nana rolled her eyes. "Of course not. Don't be a twit. I'm saying to really live life and not merely exist taking up space, you must love a good mystery, love a good adventure, and love a good challenge. Kiddo, nothing in life is as constant as *change*. Keep your head on a swivel, and explore all your options. Look behind you for a sense of history, to the sides for a sense of proportion, and most important, remember God screwed our heads on facing forward for a reason. To see ahead to the *future*. To make good decisions, you can't be afraid to make a mistake. You will learn more from your failures than from your successes. Regret is the worst human emotion because it is the one we can usually do nothing about. Always be yourself, don't live your life for someone else, or in terms of someone else. Trust your gut, and believe in yourself."

When she finished, I asked, "So, what should I do?"

Nana waved that gnarled index finger at me again and smiled. "Nice try, kiddo. It's not important what *I* think. It's only important what *you* think. So?"

In a moment of clarity, I squared my shoulders and made my decision.

## Chapter Nine

The next week flew by in a blur with a whirlwind of activities. I shed my old life as though it was an extra layer of skin, and shrugged my new one on a couple of hundred times until it fit. After several animated conversations, I finally convinced my incredulous college roommates I wasn't coming back. Certainly, they had a betting pool as to how long I'd last before regaining my sanity. They weren't the only ones. I considered asking my roomies for the odds and placing a bet against myself.

Even though I'd be traveling most of the time, I still needed a place to live. I had to come home sometime, right? I had no idea what housing costs were or the area of Atlanta to live in. Once again, my full-service nana came through. At her next canasta game, she mentioned my new adventure to her card ladies. She bemoaned my housing challenge, and her friend Katie almost dropped her cards with excitement. Katie's granddaughter is a nurse in Atlanta, and she and her roommate needed a third. Then poof. With only a few phone calls back and forth, thanks to Nana, my housing problem was solved.

I spent the rest of the week getting all my other ducks in a row to change my whole life in the blink of an eye. I needed a car, and the five-year-old foreign sub-compact I left in California wouldn't do the trick. I sat in the driver's seat of Dad's van, and it was more like commandeering an aircraft carrier than a car. I couldn't reach the pedals or see over the steering wheel. Even with a pillow behind me and blocks on the pedals, I'd never be able to handle something so huge. Gagging, I settled on a leased metallic blue, boxy four-door sedan. The car was equipped with a trunk bigger than my last college apartment bedroom, and was to be picked up at the leasing company's field location in Atlanta. On the positive side, I could always live in the trunk if the roommates didn't work out.

Inside of a week, I managed to acquire a business-like wardrobe, a roof over my head, and a new set of wheels. The only thing missing? Any idea how to *do* the job. Hopefully, perception trumped a visible skill set, and at least I'd appear, if not be able to act, the part of a competent sales rep.

The plan called for Dad to spend a week with me on the road to teach me the ropes. One week of training seemed quite optimistic. Given my complete ignorance of anything but holding a sample, I'd have opted for at least a year of training, maybe two. Either Dad had a tremendous amount of misguided confidence in my ability, or he'd decided to let me swim or sink.

\*\*\*\*

Ready or not, it was show-time, and the curtain on my fledgling new career was about to go up. The departure date arrived along with a torrential storm, and I prayed it didn't portend things to come. Nana and Mom stood under unwieldy umbrellas, and I thanked God the raindrops blended in with my tears. After we'd hugged ourselves numb and standing around staring at one another getting drenched seemed plain silly, there was nothing left to do but for them to go home and me to get into the van.

As Dad drove away, I resolved to put on my big girl panties and resisted the urge to jump out and run back to Mom and Nana as he slowed for a stop sign. The two of them stood waving until the van turned the corner. I stared after them and memorized their faces as an immigrant would leaving home for the new world.

At face it was awfully silly, considering we'd be in the same time zone. Certainly much closer to one another than from Miami to LA. But as the distance grew between us, it seemed as if I *was* moving to another country. I had no inkling of what was to come. But as I soon discovered, the observation proved to be spot on. I was about to become a stranger in a strange land.

Chapter Ten

The long, boring drive up the flat middle of Florida on the monotonous turnpike would have been excruciating, but Dad started his roadrep101 tutorial from the minute we hit the highway and kept my mind off Miami until we reached the outskirts of Atlanta. He talked nonstop, and by the time we went out for my first real southern fried chicken dinner with all the fixins at Aunt Fanny's Cabin, I had a freshman understanding of the nuts and bolts of my new vocation.

The restaurant sat on the enormous veranda of a restored antebellum plantation in Smyrna, a small-town northwest of downtown Atlanta. My eyes widened disconcertingly as a young black boy, maybe twelve years old, greeted us with a menu hand-printed on a live oak board he wore around his neck.

He recited by rote. "Welcome to Aunt Fanny's Cabin, folks. Fried chicken dinner's our specialty. Comes with biscuits and gravy, macaroni and cheese, collard greens, peach cobbler, and your choice of beverage all for only $8.95."

My west coast liberal conscience screamed with outrage until he collected two fistfuls of tips from the crowded room of patrons and shoved a wad of greenbacks into his pocket big enough to buy a small island. Free enterprise, southern fried.

****

The next morning Dad unlocked our showroom and turned on the lights, but we could barely walk inside. The room was so jammed with cartons it was as if a UPS truck had exploded. Dad arranged for all the companies we represented to ship an entire set of duplicate samples to the Atlanta showroom. Considering the sheer volume of product to pack and unpack, suddenly my new car trunk seemed quite inadequate. Dad drove a van. It's a wonder he didn't drive an eighteen-wheeler.

Dad slit open the boxes with his van key and rearranged the cartons by the vendor. He worked hard and worked up quite a sweat. To my horror, he swiped his damp forehead with one of the samples he took out of a carton.

I grimaced. "You wipe your sweat off on a sample?"

Dad stared at me as if I'd grown a second head. "It's not a light-colored sample and, besides, the sweat will dry and no one will ever be the wiser."

I rolled my eyes. "Seriously? Sweat stains ruining the dress is no biggie?"

Dad pinned me with an exasperated expression. "Are you done yet?"

I pursed my lips. "Just sayin'."

Dad waved his dismissal with a flick of his wrist. "The key to being a successful rep is to do the most amount of business in the least amount of time. And the way to accomplish that is to be *organized*."

Miraculously, I managed to swallow back my guffaws. I waved an arm around the messy room. "This is from a man who doesn't possess a customer phone book and can't find a buyer's number to save his life? *You're* going to teach *me* the best way to be *organized*?"

Dad ignored the question mixed with the slight.

"Anyway, Miss Smarty Pants, to do the most amount of business in the least amount of time, you must plan ahead. Pack your samples by the line and put them in the order you're going to present them. Hanging the samples correctly is an art form and takes practice. It's important because it's the best way to learn all the product details. You must know the product inside and out. Remember, you're selling confidence, not clothing. You're selling your ability to put the customer with the right item at the right time."

He pulled a sample out of a carton and grabbed an empty hanger from one of the wall racks. "Pay close attention. This is the correct way to hang a garment. It's essential to get this right so the customer sees the styles at their best. It's different from hanging your personal clothes. Here, you're using the hanger as though it is a picture frame."

He laid the sample on the workstation table, slipped a foam liner on the two slanted sides of the arms of the hanger, and hung the dress on them. He pulled the lingerie straps around the neck of the hanger. He took the hung dress and placed the hanger on the grid and straightened the dress more.

After he repeated the process a couple of times, I took a sample and tried hanging it. Once I got it right, I tried to hang them on the wall rack, but even on tiptoes, the rack remained out of my reach. I literally had to jump to get the hanger on the rack. "This is ridiculous." I griped, "You've gotta lower these racks. I barely reached the samples with platform shoes. It's impossible wearing sneakers."

Dad shook his head. "If you lower the rack, with all those maxi dresses, they'll drag on the floor. You'll end up either tripping over them or tearing them."

I snapped. "Do you expect me to use a pole vault?"

Dad shrugged, demonstrating the way to lower the racks. "Okay. But don't blame me when you trip on the long dresses and pull the whole damned rack out of the wall."

**** 

After a quick lunch break, we finished hanging all the samples and arranged them by line on the wall racks. Then Dad pointed to a stack of folded canvass garment bags on one of the work tables. "Now that the samples are all hung, next, we're gonna pack them into the garment bags and put them on the rolling rack. This is the way to plan your trips. You pack your bags by line. For every appointment, you should be able to sell the account every line you packed."

Yikes. Fear widened my eyes to the size of coasters. What the Sam Hill had I gotten myself into?

Dad grinned. "Calm your jets. It doesn't always happen. Some stores only buy some lines, not all of them. The tough part is the beginning of the season. You must take everything with you since you don't know which ones are the best styles until you present them all. Once you work with enough buyers, you'll know which styles are the winners and which ones are the dogs you can leave here."

Dad grabbed a garment bag, pulled the samples together on the wall rack, and cloaked the garment bag over them. Then he pushed the hangers into the teeth of the clip and closed the bracket shut. He pushed the samples inside the garment bag and zipped it closed.

Then he tied the garment bag snugly in the center, and transferred it onto the rolling rack. Easy peasy.

Dad pointed to a bag. "You try it."

I pushed the hangers together and tried to cloak the garment bag over the samples, but the bag fell on the floor. I picked the bag up and tried it again, and once again it fell. I tried it a third time. Ditto. I glared at Dad barely controlling his snickering. "Will you stop and correct me? Or do I need to chant some hocus pocus secret salesman's voodoo?"

Dad pointed to the top of the bag. "Hold the top of the bag with one hand while you drape it over the hangers." Dad bit back his guffaws. "Keep holding the top of the bag while pushing the hangers in. After you clip them together, then shove the bottoms of the garments inside the garment bag and zip the bag up."

I narrowed my eyes. "I paid close attention to the way you packed the bag. *You* didn't hold the top of the bag while you draped it over the hangers, and it didn't fall on the ground. Why isn't it working for me?"

Dad held one hand over his head and the other one out to the side. "I'm taller and have a wider wingspan. I can arc the bag over the hangers, and you can't. Try it again, but this time don't let go of the top of the bag."

After a half dozen tries, I managed to get it right. Once I had the garment bag packed, my next task entailed the transfer of it from the wall rack to the rolling rack. I wrapped my arms around the middle of the bag and tried to lift it, but no go. I released my grip on the bag and regrouped.

The second time I bent my knees, launched myself up, went higher, wrapped my arms around the "shoulder" of the bag where the arms of the hangers were, and tried to lift it off the rack. The hangers lifted off the wall rack as I held the bag. I staggered under its weight, tripped over my feet, tipped backward, and fell on my ass with the garment bag on top of me. Dad collapsed into a chair, hysterical.

I cried out, muffled by the bag. "Will you please shut up and get this thing off me? Come on. Hurry up. It weighs a ton!"

Still chortling, he lifted the garment bag off and hung it on the rolling rack. I smacked away his offered helping hand and struggled to get up on my own.

Dad wisecracked. "In case you're unaware, you're a little smaller than me and not as strong. Try packing the bags with fewer samples in each bag and using more bags."

Ready to tell him where to shove his garment bags, I snapped. "You might have told me to accommodate for being shorter and not as strong, but nooooo, you let me almost kill myself. Good thing Mom isn't with us, or mine might have been the world's shortest rep career."

Dad's response bit hard. "Gee. And I'd given you more credit."

Crap. Did the grad school letter of intent date expire?

## Chapter Eleven

Leave it to Nana to find me two nice Jewish roommates who'd been friends since kindergarten, but were as different as night and day. Their spacious apartment was furnished with three bedrooms in a stucco building off I-85 on Briarcliff Road, a beautiful tree-lined, winding street between Buford Highway and the Chattahoochee River. This was an upscale area popular with young, single Jewish women.

A registered nurse who worked in the neonatal high-risk care unit at Grady hospital, kind-hearted Karen was a typical Jewish girl right out of central casting. She stood average height with wavy chestnut hair and hazel eyes wide-set above a Jewish hook nose. She was big busted with an hourglass figure. She was smart and funny, and I liked her immediately.

Ellen was Karen's opposite. She was a tall, thin woman with intense black eyes, a flat chest, and dark frizzy hair she wore loose down to her ass. With her parents footing the bills, Ellen was still in college. And apparently, in no hurry to finish. To be kind, she is best described as a work in progress, continuously changing direction and majors trying to find her path. Not sure I'd warm up to her as much as Karen, but I found Ellen exotically interesting.

As with any situation involving roommates, for the set-up to work, compromise is key. In our case, it included acceptance of Ellen's dog. Not exactly an apartment-sized creature, Max was a large, friendly German Shepard with a penchant for stretching out anyplace he wanted to. Including, as I'd find out, often across my bed.

****

The next day, Dad and I packed the sample bags and rolling rack into the van, and headed out of town: Destination Birmingham, Alabama. I sat in the passenger seat of Dad's van and punched the radio buttons searching for a station not blasting country western music or prayers. The twangy C & W singing style hurt my ears, and at the moment, I had no interest in Jesus saving me. Static from the CB radio mounted between our bucket seats made it hard to hear anything anyway. I gave up on the radio and went back to reading road signs.

We'd no sooner made the transition from Interstate 75 South onto Interstate 20 West, and a blinking yellow sign indicated the road closure of I- 20 due to an accident involving two jackknifed eighteen-wheelers. All vehicles were instructed to exit at the US 78 West turn-off in one mile.

I studied the map and pointed down the highway. "Is there another interstate? US 78 is only a two-lane highway." I fanned the map. "Is this map out of date?"

Dad kept his eyes on the road and shook his head. "Nope, it's the newest map. I-20 is the only east-west interstate connecting Atlanta to Birmingham."

Coming from southern California, I'd grown up on an extensive and complete freeway system. With traffic on the freeways congested no matter the time of day, it might take you forever to get someplace, but virtually every place is accessible via freeway.

I craned my neck out the window. "Wow, every 18-wheeler going west is gonna be on US 78 with us crawling behind them. At this rate, we'll get to Birmingham in time for Christmas." I scanned the map again. "Are you *sure* this is the only highway? How long is it gonna take to get to Birmingham? Mileage-wise, it's the same as from LA to San Diego."

Dad nodded. "It's the only east-west highway, and it is the same mileage as from LA to San Diego. But with no alternate interstate and only a two-lane highway with all those pokey trucks, it's gonna take us a good four hours. And that's if we don't encounter any other problems."

I parroted. "Problems?"

Dad grimaced. "In addition to slow traffic, any car trouble will be a major hassle. Only a few small towns offer even limited services. If you need a part other than a tire or battery, a gas station might not stock it. And keep an eye out for smokies. U.S. 78 is famous for speed traps." Dad played a rat-a-tat-tat on the steering wheel. "I better get a smokey report."

Dad grabbed the CB radio microphone and depressed the speaker button. I listened curiously as he spoke in some kind of road warrior code channeling Daisy Duke's daddy. "Breaker, breaker 1-9, this is Big Daddy Mike. Do y'all copy me? My 20 is US 78 westbound mile marker 200. I'd appreciate a bear report. Breaker, breaker 1-9 come in, good buddy."

I jumped as a reply crackled back across the airwaves. A booming voice with a thick southern accent yelped, "Breaker, breaker 1-9. Big Daddy Mike, I copy. This here's the Georgia Peach. There's a smokey sittin' in the trees on the eastbound side takin' pictures of westbound traffic at mile marker 218. Watch yourself, good buddy, the bear's mighty hungry. See any bears going into hotlanta?"

Dad depressed the power button on the microphone. "A big negatory, Georgia Peach. No bears in my part of the forest, but watch out for the looky-loos eyeballing a huge accident with a couple of jackknifed big rigs on I-20 going west. All west-bound traffic has been taken off the highway at the US 78 exit. You're gonna find one gigantic backup. Appreciate the smokey report, and y'all drive safe now, hear? Roger out."

I narrowed my eyes. "Are you speaking a foreign language? Big Daddy Mike? Who taught the lingo to you? Smokey the Bear? Your 20? Y'all? You've morphed into one of the Dukes of Hazard. Are bib overalls and a corncob pipe next? Hee Haw?"

Dad tsked his self-righteous indignation. "For your information, Miss Smarty Pants, I never watched the Dukes of Hazard." He grinned. "Although, Daisy Duke was kinda cute. Especially in those cut-off jeans shorts."

He dipped his head. "Take my advice. When in Rome, do as the Romans. Believe me, you don't want any problems with Southern cops. If you consider the high cost of traffic tickets and how they jack up your auto insurance rates sky high, a CB radio is worth the investment. By the way, just so you know, I'm not the only sales rep using a CB radio. Almost all the road reps are. At least the smart ones. You need one for safety reasons. If you're ever in trouble on the road, remember truckers are your best friends."

I gave Dad the big eyes. "Well, *Big Daddy Mike*, I don't see me with a CB radio yammering over smokey reports and my 20, whatever my 20 means. Breaker,

breaker, the California Rag Lady is calling. Seen any bears?" I snickered. "Not a great image."

Dad shook his head and shrugged. "Suit yourself, kiddo."

We crept along at a snail's pace west on US 78 as it wove its way towards Pell City, Alabama, POP. 691. I lived my entire life adjacent to a major urban area. The one-street town we rode through with a feed store, pharmacy, and post office as the focal points of its downtown appeared as a burg with a rural lifestyle completely unfamiliar to me.

The town faded to the outskirts with nothing but a two-pump gas station between us and the forest divided by the blacktop. Dad pointed out a patrol car partially hidden behind some pine trees. Dad slowed down as we drove past. The cop seated behind the wheel reminded me of the fidgety goof Deputy Sheriff, Barney Fife, on the old Andy Griffith television program. I took a closer peek inside the cruiser as Barney's nephew, Billy Bob, shot his radar gun on us. *Appreciate y'all visiting Mayberry, R.F.D. Y'all come back now, hear?* I'd pay good money to see the faces of my college roomies if they accompanied me on this trip through Hooterville.

We crawled behind a battalion of eighteen-wheeler convoys as we made our way to Birmingham. We wound around curves and drove through one small town after another, the first one the mirror image of the next. We finally made it to Anniston, west of the accident, and got back on I-20. We made up some lost time and arrived at our destination right before dusk.

****

We passed the sign *Welcome to Birmingham, the Magic City,* and drove into the heart of downtown.

Birmingham was a sprawling burg that had the homey feel of a small town trapped in the body of a big city. The commercial hub featured Loveman's and Pizitz department stores, the Parisian, and The Three Sisters Alabama Shop specialty stores. Their downtown flagship locations each occupied one of four corners of the intersection of 18th Street, the main thoroughfare, and 1st Avenue. We continued through downtown, passing Barber's Cafeteria, the art deco Alabama Theater, University of Alabama, Birmingham campus, and University Hospital.

We left downtown behind and drove southwest. We passed the skeletal remnants of the steel mills and iron ore mines that were once the engines that powered the city's growth. Given the industrial nature of the area, the series of surrounding mountains verdant with huge pine and cottonwood trees came as a pleasant surprise. We entered Red Mountain and Vulcan Park, and Dad grinned with anticipation as he slowly drove completely around the infamous Vulcan statue. He stopped to give me an unobstructed view of Vulcan's bare butt as he mooned the citizens of Birmingham from his mountain top perch.

We continued through the suburban neighborhoods of Homewood, Mountain Brook, and Vestavia Hills. These were affluent, quiet, lushly poplar tree-lined neighborhoods with an out-in-the-country feel. They featured large houses on huge lots, many with swimming pools and tennis courts. Plus, the tri-towns sported a country club, two golf courses, a walking street with outdoor cafes, and no shortage of luxury cars.

Dad slowed down and pointed out the various stores we sold. "We sell to a number of accounts in this area.

Not all our best accounts are downtown. These three towns are where the money is, and where the Jews live. Believe it or not, Mountain Brook has two Synagogues and a terrific deli. Maybe if time allows, Herman Neumann will join us for lunch at the deli tomorrow."

I narrowed my eyes. "Two temples and a deli in one little town? I'd never guess *any* Jews lived in Birmingham."

Dad gave me the big eyes. "Some Jewish families trace their roots in the south to way before the war between the states. Rich's department store in Atlanta? Jewish family, and the store has been in business since before the civil war. Do you remember Pizitz, the department store we passed downtown? Jewish family owners, and the store's been in business for over a hundred years. Loveman's, the store across the street from Pizitz? Started by a Jewish guy from Nashville around the beginning of the twentieth century. Jews played an integral part in the growth of the south from the beginning of our country. It proves how wrong pre-conceived notions are. You go into any small southern town, and if it has one clothing store, I guarantee it's owned by Jews."

I gave him the stink eye. "Oh, come on. You're telling me *Jews* live in dinky Pell City?"

Dad nodded. "Absolutely. Jews are often the power base in small southern towns. They're usually the professionals: accountants, dentists, doctors, judges, lawyers, nurses, pharmacists, and teachers. Educated and sophisticated people live in those small towns, and a lot of them are Jews. Not everyone living in a small southern town is Billy Bob smoking a corncob pipe."

My jaw dropped in amazement and it amused him.

Dad grinned. "Okay, Hol. So much for the sociology lesson of the day. Let's go over how to set your appointments up to do the most amount of business in the least amount of time for a city spread out the way Birmingham is. Figure out the number of appointments that can realistically be done in a day, how long each appointment takes, the time to and from the appointments on the schedule, how long it takes to get to the next area you're traveling to, then factor in extra time for delays, and so on. It's not always possible, but try to make the appointments by area. Try not to make appointments all over the place, or you'll waste time by having to drive from one end of town to the other and back again. After we check into the hotel, we'll plan this week's trip out so you see how it's done."

I'd never earn a living as a poker player. Fear etched my face. Dad smiled and gave me a calming pat on my cheek. "It might sound complicated, but believe me, it's not. You'll get the hang of it in no time. You'll make some mistakes. We all do. You're gonna learn a lot more from your failures than you ever will from your successes."

I sighed. "If it's meant to be comforting, forget it. Nana said the same thing. You two may be selling, but I'm not buying." The disastrous newspaper interview reared its ugly head. "I don't see any great accomplishment in failure."

Chapter Twelve

From the way the hotel staff fawned over my father, he could have been a rock star. After he handed her a sample, Sara, the desk clerk, thanked him profusely and announced she'd reserved him a great *down and out* room. Dad caught my confusion and explained. "*Down and out* isn't a description of a dilapidated room's condition. It's the description of the room's location. D*own* on the first floor, and the exterior part of the building facing *out* to the parking lot."

Dad backed the van into a parking space directly in front of our room. He pointed to our door. "Always reserve a down and out so you can pull your car into a parking spot closest to your room. It makes it easier to take in your samples at night."

The room was neither spartan nor luxurious. It featured a utilitarian décor set up for practicality with two double beds, one nightstand separating the beds with a lamp and clock radio on it, and a low boy dresser on the opposite wall. A TV on a metal stand faced the beds. A metal desk, office chair, and a telephone on the desk sat in the front of the room against the side wall.

We set the rolling rack loaded with samples adjacent to the desk. We hardly had any room to walk from the desk to the beds.

****

Hot steam poured out of the bathroom and fogged

67

up the mirrors in front of the sink. I came out of the bathroom sweating as if I'd been in a tropical rain forest. I wiped my face on a towel and fanned myself with an order book. I glared at Dad as he handed me more samples. I said, "No more room for another stitch, so hang those last ones back on the rack." I narrowed my eyes. "You do this stupid exercise *every night*? And the purpose? You schlep all the bags into the room, unpack them, and steam them out. Why bother? All you're gonna do is pack 'em back up in the morning. By the time you get to the first appointment, they're gonna be as wrinkled as they are now."

Dad motioned to the window that faced the parking lot. "You need to bring the samples into the room at night. They're safer in the room than in the trunk of your car. If they get stolen, you're outta business."

I wiped an errant bead of sweat off the side of my face with the towel. "I get the importance of bringing the samples in at night. But this steaming is a joke. I'm not gonna do it."

Dad shrugged. "Believe it or not, if you steam them at night, they're still less wrinkled the next day, even coming out of the garment bags."

This attention to neatness came from a guy whose van and office ought to be condemned by the department of health. I jutted my chin in defiance. "I'm not doing it."

Dad shrugged. "Suit yourself, but your samples are gonna be as wrinkled as if you slept in them."

I pointed towards the sample rack and smirked. "If we sell nightgowns and pajamas, our problem is solved."

****

Early the next morning, the hotel coffee shop hostess spied Dad and gushed, "Good morning, Mike.

It's so nice to see you again." She grinned as she grabbed menus out of a plastic holder behind the cash register. She started towards a booth with our name apparently on it since Dad walked ahead and sat himself down. A black busboy with cornrows gave Dad a big grin as though they were old buddies. The busboy brought us a carafe of coffee and two glasses of water without being asked.

The huge flock of butterflies that settled into the pit of my tummy created a weird combination of hunger mixed with nausea. I searched the menu for something mild I might keep down. Wanda Lou, our big busted, bleach bottle-blonde server, sidled over to our table, and gave Dad a big smooch on the cheek. Dad patted her affectionately on the shoulder and made the introductions.

Wanda bent over and enveloped me into a bone-crushing hug. "It's a real pleasure to meet ya, darlin'. Your daddy's a big ole sweetie pie. Now, what can I git ya, darlin'?"

I ordered cautiously. "Two poached eggs and dry wheat toast." I asked, "Do you have any fresh orange juice?"

Wanda grinned like a circus clown, and nodded yes as she wrote down my order. My face hurt seeing her grin so much. Could she turn it off, or did she just smile in her sleep? Dad must be one helluva tipper. No normal person is *that cheery* so early in the morning. She asked Dad if he wanted his usual. Without waiting for his answer, Wanda took our menus and waddled to the kitchen to put our orders in. A few minutes later, she came back and placed a glass and a small can of orange juice in front of me. Huh? Florida, the orange juice mecca, was only a couple of hundred miles south.

Besides, we Californians *don't* drink our juice out of a can. I stopped her as she started to pour the juice. "Wanda, you said the orange juice is fresh."

Wanda gave me the big eyes and dipped her head. "Right as rain, darlin'. It don't come any fresher. This here juice is fresh right outta the can."

So much for liquid sunshine. I took a few slugs of coffee to shake out the cobwebs. I opened a roadmap between us. I traced a route with my fingers as Dad guided me on the most expedient way to get from point A to point B.

Dad pointed to the map. "Remember to always make your appointments at the beginning of the week, and try to make each road trip in a circle. Make your appointments to the farthest place first and deadhead. Then work your way back, so you end up in Atlanta by the end of the week. When you leave Atlanta depends on the distance you're going. Sometimes you might need to leave on a Sunday if you're going really far."

I grimaced. "Gee, I hope it doesn't happen too often. It seems I'm gonna be home so seldom, maybe moving into an apartment was a waste of money. It's easier to just stay in hotels."

Dad's deep voice tinged with longing. "There's no place like home, no matter the infrequency you're there. Living the life of a gypsy is no life. You need a reason to be busting your ass on the road. Coming home is the best one."

I folded up the map as Wanda arrived carrying our breakfast plates on her arm. Wanda put the plates in front of us before I had a chance to reply to Dad. She slapped a bottle of hot sauce on the table and grinned. "Bone appetite as they say in French."

A glop of grainy gruel I didn't remember ordering surrounded the eggs on my plate. I pointed to it and asked Dad, "What's that glop?"

Dad held up his spoonful of the mystery stuff. "Grits. It's a Dixie staple. It's sort of southern cream of wheat. They serve it with everything," Dad mixed in some butter and spooned up a helping of the sandy-textured gunk. "Some folks eat it with jelly. I prefer it with butter and a dash of salt." He pointed his spoon at the lumpy stuff on my plate. "Try it. I bet you'll like it."

I loved cream of wheat and hoped the grits would help settle my stomach. I put a little butter in the center and spooned some up. The good manners taught to me as a child kept me from spitting the gruel into a napkin. The grainy-textured slop was tasteless. I might as well have spooned up hot buttered sand. I pushed it to the side and tucked into my eggs. When we finished eating, Dad introduced me to yet another reception clerk as we made our way back through the lobby to our room.

We packed the samples into the garment bags and loaded them into the van. As Dad pulled out of the hotel parking lot and drove onto the street, something inside me shifted, and nothing in my life would ever be the same.

I was pretty nervous and chattered to fill the space. "Kinda embarrassing the way the front desk clerk kept winking at you after you introduced me as your daughter. Eeek, he thought we were *together-together*. Yikes."

Dad leered and wiggled his eyebrows. "Don't you find me irresistible?"

I shrank back in horror. "No offense, but you're old enough to be my father." The tension melted away as we cracked up.

Chapter Thirteen

We finished our first store appointment by 10:00 on a sizzling hot morning already spongy with humidity. By the time we rolled the packed rack back to the van, I was ready to die. I took off my blazer-and still almost drowned in my perspiration. The pervasive southern humidity is a killer that mercilessly sucks the energy right out of you.

Coming from California, I was no stranger to heat. But at least in LA it was an endurable dry heat you baked in. I'd never get used to this humidity. You simmered to a slow boil in your own juices. The sweat poured off me at an alarming rate in salty rivulets down my back. Yet a cold chill danced the salsa the length of my spine. How would I ever survive the rest of the summer?

I wiped the sweat off my face with a loose sample I found rolled up in a ball in the back of the van. Dad smirked. "We mock all we are to be." If I'd been able to muster the energy, I'd have smacked him. Lucky for him, my arms rested on my sides limp as wet noodles. Take the samples in nightly and steam them? Oh, sure. The same time elephants fly.

We finished reloading the van and I blasted the AC up to the arctic setting. We pulled away from the curb, and I prayed for either a swift death or full recovery before we went to the next appointment. Either way was an acceptable outcome.

I almost cried as Dad turned the temperature down to the low setting. He waved me off as I opened my mouth to protest. "If you come in from overbearing heat and turn the AC completely up, you'll catch one helluva summer cold."

A swift death was more attractive by the minute.

Seemingly impervious to the oppressive heat and humidity, Dad grinned wide as a kid at the circus as he recapped our first appointment. "Congratulations! You made a pretty good presentation for a rookie. Now do you see the importance of allowing some extra time? Between the buyer answering the phone, helping customers in dressing rooms, and ringing up the sale, this one-hour appointment took a couple of hours."

Dad slapped the steering wheel. "Hey, I almost forgot. Let me teach you a little trick to make you seem brilliant to the buyers. The minute you get your samples, memorize the style numbers. Say a customer asks you the style number and you don't need to read the hangtag. Psychologically, the buyer gets the message, "*Holly knows the number by heart. She obviously sold tons of the style. It must be a hot number. I better write that one.*"

He had to be kidding. Eight garment bags full of samples jammed tight in the van times by four seasons. My eyes crossed adding up the total number of styles. Do reps carry cheat sheets? And this job is gonna be a paid vacation? Ha.

****

Miraculously, I managed to revive by the time we parked in front of a stylish, two-story specialty store located mid-block on a tree-lined street in Mountain Brook. We hung all the garment bags on the rack and Dad pointed to the entrance to the store. "Before we go inside, I want to tell you about Herman Neumann. He is a wise and wonderful man, but different from anyone else you'll do business with. Herman is a concentration camp survivor."

As a Jew and a human, naturally, the Holocaust horrified me. Our family had lost many members murdered by the Nazis in concentration camps. But I'd never actually met someone who lived through it. I wasn't sure I wanted to. It made a faceless, nameless monster real. If it's someone you care about, their nightmare becomes yours. Does a protocol exist? Do you ignore the number on his forearm, or do you say something? "Gee, your tattoo is interesting. My cousin Ronnie's forearm is tattooed with a heart from his stint in the navy." Oh, yeah. Perfect.

We wheeled the rack to the front door of the store, and I stopped. Dad recognized my hesitation and squeezed my shoulder. "Don't worry. You won't be uncomfortable. He doesn't hide it. He wears short sleeve shirts, and you'll see his ID number tattooed on his arm. He doesn't go out of his way to discuss it. But in case you noticed the number, I didn't want you to be caught off guard and only focus on it. The man is so much more than just the number the Nazis tried to reduce him to." Dad grabbed the front bar on the rolling rack and pulled it into the store. "Come on. Let's go. We don't want to keep Herman waiting."

Dad seemed to take everything in stride. For me, not so much. So far, this job wasn't all it was cracked up to be in this even stranger strange land. CB radios and good buddies with funny accents. Juice fresh from the can and grits. Now, a concentration camp survivor buyer, and the week had just begun.

We took the elevator to the second floor and rolled the rack into a well-appointed office. We were greeted by a short, chubby, balding old man dressed in a short-sleeved shirt and perfectly pressed trousers. Dad extended his right hand, but Herman grabbed Dad in a bear hug.

Dad broke the embrace and pulled me to his side. "Herman, I want you to meet my daughter Holly. Holly, this is my dear friend, Herman Neumann. Herman, Holly is working with me now. She's going to be taking over this territory. I'm here with her this week to teach her the ropes." Dad joked, "My big fear is all my customers will prefer working with Holly, and the bosses will kick me to the curb!"

Herman smiled and lifted his arm to grasp my hand. My eyes were laser-focused on the numbers tattooed on his forearm. Proof positive that monsters do exist. I shivered internally, and my eyes filled. I turned my head and fought for control. As Herman and I shook hands, I prayed my face didn't betray my aching heart.

Herman dipped his head at me and gave Dad a playful fist bump on the chin. "So, Michaela, vere haf you been hiding dis vun?" Herman's elfish smile warmed my heart. "Holly, it's vunderful to meet you. I love your Papa like un brodder, but sometimes he's a little pushy, yah?" Herman grinned mischievously. "Do you present da lines as if you're a matador too, or do you haf your own shtick?"

I relaxed and focused on this utterly charming man instead of the number on his arm. "No, one bullfighter in a family is enough."

Herman pointed his index finger at Dad. "It's about time you brought somevun into da business. I vorry about you. Mein daughter Diana is doing our accessory buying now." Herman winked at me. "You'll see. Zoon ve'll both be vorking for dem! Before you turn around, you'll be retiring."

Dad shook his head and grinned. "Nosiree. I won't be retiring for a long time. My wife wouldn't let me. She'd go nuts with me underfoot and annoying her twenty-four hours a day."

Dad walked over to the rack and opened the first garment bag. "Herman, let's get the work out of the way. And if you can spare the time, we'd love to take you to lunch at Sam's Deli. Holly doesn't believe killer pastrami is just down the block."

Herman winked at me. "Eh, you buying, Michaela? Yah? Vunderful. You got yourself a deal!"

Herman walked the length of the room to a conversation area with a sofa, two chairs, and a coffee table adjacent to his desk. He sat in the chair on the left side and turned to Dad and patted the seat to his right. "Michaela, come zit next to me und let Holly present me da lines. Zince Holly's mein rep now, ve haf to get used to vorking vit vun another. Und dere's no time better den da present." He pointed his finger at Dad. "Und I don't vant you should put in your two cents. Your opinion doesn't count now dat you are yesterday's news."

Dad sputtered like a car engine needing a new sparkplug. But he followed Herman's instruction and sat with his lips zipped. Holy guacamole. I liked this Neumann guy more every minute. Herman made my presentation easy. He was open to suggestions, but on top of the type of styles his customers wanted. With no interruptions, we got through all the lines quickly. We finished re-packing all the samples at noon. Herman suggested we leave the samples in his office and head out to lunch. The deli is a popular restaurant. Unless we left right then, we'd wait a long time for a table.

**\*\*\*\***

Seemingly out of thin air, a smiling hostess held three menus up and called out, "Neumann party of three." This was mighty fast service. We hadn't been waiting long enough to give her our name, let alone be called for a table. We followed the hostess to a four-top. She handed us menus and asked if we wanted any water.

After she delivered the three glasses of water and departed, Herman raised his bushy eyebrows and grinned. "Impressed vit da fast service, yah?" He leaned over to whisper conspiratorially. "Don't be. Bella, the hostess, is vun of mein vife's Maj Jong friends. They haf a deal. She makes sure ve never vait to be seated, und mein Sara lets her shop at our store vit a little discount."

I joked. "Too bad the phone company doesn't work on the barter system."

We stuffed ourselves to the gills and still made nary a dent in the sandwiches. Herman swept his hand towards the busy restaurant and winked. "So, Holly, vhat do you tink? Does Sam's pass da deli test?"

I patted my full tummy. "Are you kidding? This place is fabulous. I would never have believed that a great deli is in the heart of Dixie. Herman, may I ask you something? I hope I'm not being too forward, as we've just met."

Herman dipped his head. "Vay not?"

"I'm curious as to the name of your store. Did you name it after someone, or you just fancied the name Penelope?"

Herman blanched and widened his eyes as he

glanced at Dad. Odd response to a simple question. Somehow, I had apparently offended him. I backpedaled. "I'm sorry. Did I say something wrong?"

Herman smiled wistfully. "No, noting wrong. I just don't discuss it often. The store vas really named after *someting* if you vant to be technical. Let me explain. Mein sister Freda vas eight years mein junior. Even so, ve vere always close. For her sixth birthday, I saved up mein allowance und gave her a porcelain doll und she named it Penelope." Herman lifted a narrow shoulder. "Don't ask me vhy she selected dat particular name. She vas crazy over dat doll. They vere inseparable. A few months later, de Nazis rounded up our family and ve vere sent to Dachau. Ve veren't allowed to take anyting but vun small suitcase each. Vhen ve arrived, de suitcases vere searched und anyting valuable vas confiscated. Vhen the guard opened mein sister's suitcase, he found her doll. He ripped it apart, searching for hidden valuables. As you can imagine, mein sister started to raise a ruckus und mein mother tried to quiet Freda for fear she'd be shot on the spot. Vonce the guard vas finished, he threw Freda's doll on the ground und crushed it to pieces mit the heel of his boot. He motioned mein mother and sister to take their suitcases und to go into de line on de right. I never laid eyes on dem again. Mein papa und I vent to der left und vere slave labor. Papa died from pneumonia dat winter und I vas da only vone of der family dat survived."

Herman smiled. "Vhen I came to dis country and vas able to open mein store, I vanted to do something to honor de memory of mein sister." Herman tipped his head. "So, you are now probably vondering vhy den der store isn't named Freda's Fashions, yah? Vell to tell de truth, mein sister hated her name. It vas old fashioned und she vanted to change it to something more modern. But of course, mein parents vouldn't agree, so she vas stuck mit her name. Vell, she vould haf been upset to be memorialized vit a name she hated. So, I named de store after something she loved." Herman did a ta-da with his hands. "So dat es da story of da store's name."

After he finished telling the tale, it was as though all the air had been vacuumed out of my lungs. I had trouble breathing, much less able to speak. He'd answered my question, but the story only raised more questions. I waited for a beat until I trusted myself to speak without crying. "I'm curious." Dad flinched as I went on. "You came from a place with many people who hated Jews enough to exterminate them like insects. So, I'm trying to understand the reason you moved to the deep south, and not someplace more accepting of Jews?"

Herman smiled and tapped the side of his head. "Vell, it's a good qvestion mit a zimple answer. Vhen I first arrived in dis country, I came tru Ellis Island. No vun in New York vanted to help another camp survivor who threatened to take avay jobs from dem. A sign at a refugee center advertised southern Jews villing to help survivors." Herman waved an arm around the restaurant. " The Jewish community un Birmingham sponsored me, helped me learn English, start mein business, und introduced me to mein Sara. I took a chance. I trusted mein gut, und never regretted der decision."

Herman impishly grinned at Dad. "Michaela, zince you're paying, I'll haf unother cream soda."

Chapter Fourteen

All week the steamy, humid weather stuck to us like a piece of gum on the bottom of your shoe. I ended each day hot, tired, and cranky. But we dragged those damned samples into the hotel room every night. Despite it being his party, two days into the week, Dad finally conceded we did not have to steam the samples every single night. And they say whining is an ineffective tool of persuasion. Ha.

The training week proved both exhausting and exhilarating. With its highs and lows, successes and failures, joys and sadness, tears and laughter, love and family, love and friendship, forgiveness and redemption, as well as learning and discovery, I experienced most of the elements of an entire lifetime jammed into one week.

In the short time I'd been in the rag business, I'd certainly met my share of colorful characters. From transsexual customers to concentration camp survivors. I tasted the bitter and the sweet melding of all their flavors together in life's melting pot cooking the human stew.

We returned to Atlanta late Friday night and went straight to the mart. By the time we unpacked all the garment bags, I wanted to burn every sample. Dad was relaxed as if he'd been on vacation, and me? As if I'd been run over by a train. Hefting those sample bags a bazillion times and driving all over hell and half of

Georgia? This is no job for sissies. Am I a sissy? Only time will tell.

I hung the last sample on the rack and flopped my weary bones into a chair. "That was the longest week of my life! I'm exhausted. The concept of doing this again next week is almost too much to bear."

Dad shrugged. "So don't."

Huh? I stared at him as if he'd grown a second head.

Dad held out his hands. "It's quite simple. Selling is personal, and no two people do it the same way. Product expertise is the common thread, but it's your personality that determines *the way* you do the job. The way I do it won't be how you will. I don't give a rat's ass the way you get the job done, as long as you get it done. If you don't want to hit the road next week, don't. If you can get all your business done in as little as two weeks, knock yourself out. I don't care. I trust you to make decisions that work best for you, but you must live with the consequences of the choices you make."

I squirmed in my seat. Ironically, the thing appealing most to me before accepting the job now troubled me most. All my life someone else told me what to do and the way they expected me to do it. I might not have loved the instruction, but I drew a comfort level from the expectation, as it took the outcome out of my hands. Now, it was all on me, and not nearly as attractive.

Nana's warning of being careful what you wish for danced inside my head. It begged the question of what was it I wanted? I drew a big honkin' blank. Those damned annoying choices buzzed around my brain like a persistently pesky fly at a picnic. The family curse of being responsible for your own decisions reared its ugly head once again. First Nana, now Dad jumped into the act. I whined. "Give me just a little hint?"

His answer? A snort of derision. I gave him the middle finger salute.

Dad was anxious to get on the road, so he dropped me off at the apartment, and we said our goodbyes. I pushed down the panic rising from the pit of my stomach as the van's taillights disappeared into the darkness of the night. I keyed the apartment door open, hauled the suitcase into my bedroom, and collapsed. I fell into bed without bothering to change out of my sweaty clothes or brushing my teeth. I slept as soundly as the dead. I woke up the next day mid-afternoon sleep logy with a bad case of bedhead. I stayed in bed most of the weekend. After a sleep marathon punctuated by some sort of eating, by Sunday night I started to come back to life.

****

Monday morning, I waved hi and bye to the roommates who had no idea that I'd been in the apartment all weekend. A hot shower and a jolt of strong java started the gears meshing. After unpacking and repacking my suitcase, I dragged myself to the mart.

I stepped through the showroom door right foot first and gave the samples a good morning greeting of *hello girls* and a two-fingered salute. A box sat on the desk labeled *Remember It Monthly Calendars Kits*. An address book and a set of monthly calendars was packed inside the box.

Tears blended with my guffaws as I read the note in Dad's barely legible chicken scratch handwriting. *"Dear Holly, to make sure you don't pick up my rotten habits, this is a monthly calendar kit and address book. And before you ask, no, I did not buy an extra set for myself. I have a reputation to maintain. Good luck on your first road trip. You're gonna knock 'em dead! Love you, Dad"*

It was now or never. I sat at the desk, took a calming breath, and picked up the phone. An hour and a half later, I batted a thousand. I had no problems getting buyers on the phone, let alone setting up appointments. Hmm, this seemed way too easy. It was almost as though they expected my call. What did Nana always say? *Don't seek out trouble, it will find you all on its own.*

I pushed the weird sense off, placed more calls, and made the rest of my appointments. Eureka! My first solo trip was all set. I gave myself a mental back pat and wrote the appointments into the calendar book. I narrowed my eyes. Good grief. I had a full week of appointments. Was it beginner's luck, or the invisible hand of Mike Schlivnik behind the curtain directing the scene? Of course. Those poor buyers never stood a chance. For once, Dad's annoying interference came in handy.

Since the longest journey begins with the first step, I picked up one of the garment bags and packed the samples by line. I packed, unpacked, and repacked three of the bags to make them lighter. For every action, there is a reaction. I extended the horizontal bar on the rack to accommodate the extra bags. Crap. Still, nothing doing. So, I laid two of them on the bottom. It took three tries before I got them positioned not to fall off the rack once I moved it.

I grabbed the vertical front bar with my left hand and tried to pull the rack from behind me. But it didn't budge. I grabbed the bar again, this time with both hands. I bent my knees, and pulled, but nothing doing. I tamped down my annoyance. Salesmanship 101: If you can't get in the front door, go through the window. I went to the back of the rack and tried pushing it. The damned rack still didn't move an inch. Good grief. I'd never hit the road if the rack didn't leave the showroom. I made my first executive decision and took two garment bags off the rolling rack and left them lying on one of the work station tables. I slung my purse over my shoulder and hung my briefcase at the end of the rack. Pulling the rack from behind, I walked out of the showroom right foot first and locked the door. Time to rock n' roll.

****

I managed to bob and weave my way through the aisles without crashing the rack into any showrooms. So far so good. It took an eternity for one of the freight elevators in the far back corner to arrive on the fourth floor. The elevator car was so small, that if I didn't angle the rack in and set it diagonally across, the door wouldn't shut. The door creaked closed as slowly as an arthritic old man pushing a walker. The elevator crawled its way down and finally shuddered to a stop at the basement.

A flotilla of delivery trucks packed the loading dock. To the far right, shorter, narrower parking stalls held passenger cars. The dock sat high above the parked cars, making it impossible to load your samples while standing on the dock. The only way down was the steep ramp at the far side of the loading dock. The ramp led out to the sidewalk and directly into the street. I pressed the stop button to hold the freight elevator door open and angled the rack. I wheeled it out, released the stop button, and pulled the rack towards the ramp.

A tall, muscular, scowling black man wearing a gray uniform with the Apparel Mart logo embroidered onto his shirt pocket held a clipboard and stepped in front of the rack. He put his arm straight out like a traffic cop and pointed to my car. "Miss, you can't leave your car parked in the loadin' dock for more than half an hour. Security was ready to tow your car, but I remembered you're Mr. Mike's daughter, so I convinced the guard to cut you some slack this one time. Don't be doin' it again."

I flashed him my most self-deprecating smile. "Gee, I'm sorry. I had no idea the loading dock had a time limit. Thank you for not letting security have my car towed." I held my fingers up Girls Scouts honor style. "I promise. It won't happen again."

He pointed to the garment bags. "Want some help with them bags?"

I shook my head no. "I appreciate the offer, but I need to do this myself. If no one's around to help me, I'd be forced to do it."

He gave me an *it's your funeral* smirk and dipped his head to the garment bags. "Suit yourself."

I clutched the front bar of the rack and pulled it down the ramp. I bent my knees to account for the ramp's steepness, but all the bags still slid to the front of the rack. The rack picked up speed, and I couldn't keep up. The wheels nipped at my heels, and I almost lost my balance. I jumped out of the way to avoid being run over. The rack flew past me down the steep ramp, out of the building, across the sidewalk, and into the street. The rack crashed into the back fender of a double-parked delivery van waiting its turn to get into the loading dock. All the garment bags flew off the rack when it flipped over and they scattered into the street. Why the driver jumped out of the van yelling like a lunatic was a mystery. There wasn't a mark on his vehicle.

I dodged an oncoming city bus and ran into the street. I righted the rack, picked up the garment bags, and re-loaded them. I waved off the porter as he ran over to me. "Don't help me! I need to do this myself."

The porter held up his hands. "No problem. Just don't get yourself killed tryin' to be so independent, Miss."

I wheeled the rack to my car and keyed the trunk open. The top sprang open and bounced up and down a few times. I grabbed the first bag off the rack and heaved it into the cavernous mouth of the trunk. I stood on my tiptoes to get enough leverage to shove the garment bag into the corner to make room for the next one. But the wide and deep trunk made it impossible for my short wingspan to reach that far back.

I needed to get this shit in the car and get going. I glanced around, but no one seemed to pay me any attention. I swung my left leg over the trunk's bottom lip and jumped inside. I bent over the bag, grabbed the heads of the hangers, and pulled them into the back corner of the trunk, and jumped out. I repeated the process until all the bags and the disassembled rack were loaded into the trunk. I slammed the trunk closed, slid into the driver's seat, fired her up, and drove to the interstate fast as a bat outta hell.

If my heart hammered any harder, it would have pounded out of my chest as downtown Atlanta faded away from my rearview mirror. I struggled with the conflicting emotions of being anxious to get going while terrified to leave.

My appointments were set up so that I deadheaded to the farthest point at the beginning of my trip and worked my way back to Atlanta. I found it quite a challenge to hold open a roadmap with one hand and drive with the other. Then trying to read it while crossing three freeway lanes to the junction exit is more difficult still. Amazing that so many roads led to the middle of no place. And more miraculous that I didn't get myself killed trying to get onto one of them. Mental note to self: figure out the route to get to the place before you get in the car.

Chapter Fifteen

The next morning, I walked giddily out of my first appointment with a thirty-six-piece orderette for only one of our lines in my hand. It didn't add up to much, but I was as excited as if I'd written a million-dollar order.

Four days later, my last appointment was with Mavis Thornberry at the Fashion Hut, a specialty shop located in a Georgia town fifty miles southeast of Atlanta that was so small, you couldn't find the burg on the map.

Mavis gave me road instructions for a shortcut. Imitating a pint-sized Christopher Columbus, I set out into a type of the country I'd never experienced before. The closest I'd come to a farm were the produce stands farmers set up on some San Fernando Valley street corners to sell off excess crops at a discounted price to passersby. My only encounter with farm animals was a childhood trip to a petting zoo. The rural two-lane country road wound through lush green fields with crops growing right behind farmhouses and animals freely roaming the unfenced grounds.

I pulled behind a farmer in bib overalls wearing a straw hat driving a tractor, forcing me to slow to a crawl. I craned my neck out the window to see if I could get around Farmer John. To the left, a wooden shack sat back on a dirt plot. Some of the wood roof shingles were missing. Others flapped loosely in the breeze. The shack set elevated on cement blocks. Two broken wooden steps led from the dirt path up to a sagging porch in front of a wooden door askew on one hinge. An outhouse adjacent to the shack slouched like a tired old man. Smoke puffed out of the chimney from a ramshackle lean-to somebody called home.

Two barefoot black boys dressed in raggedy pants kicked a partially deflated ball back and forth in front of the house. An obese woman sat in a rickety rocker staring blankly into space. A red and black do-rag was wrapped haphazardly around her head, and a torn crimson sweatshirt with Harvard College in white letters covered her busty chest. Tight black stretch pants strained against her belly. Her toes stuck out from scuffed athletic shoes with the tips of the shoes cut open.

My eyes filled. Did we really let people live in such a way? Apparently, yes.

****

I got to the outskirts of the small town and checked the time. I wasn't late, but thanks to Farmer John, Mavis's shortcut turned out to be much longer. I drove past the town square and the county court building in the center of the square on Main Street. To paraphrase the great philosopher, Yogi Berra, it was déjà vu all over again. This burg was a dead ringer for Pell City and every other small town I'd been through.

The Fashion Hut sat nestled between the Dixie Dollar Store and a café. A bell jingled as I opened Mavis's door. I smiled to myself at the mezuzah nailed to the doorjamb. A chunky middle-aged woman with dyed fire-engine-red hair combed in a flip-style stood behind the counter in front of the cash register. She wore a short-sleeved lavender polyester pantsuit. The kind of readers you buy from the drug store sat precariously perched on the tip of her pointy nose.

Mavis raised her eyes at the sound of the front door chime and greeted me like a customer. "Hey there! Come right on in. We got lots of things to choose from. May I help you find somethin' pretty today?"

I walked to the counter and extended my right hand. "Hi. Are you by any chance Mavis Thornberry?"

Mavis grasped my hand and grinned back. "I sure am, darlin'." She squinted, trying to place me. "Have we met? You don't strike me as familiar, and I'm usually pretty good rememberin' faces."

I smiled. "No, we've never met in person, but we spoke on the phone. I'm Holly Schlivnik." Mavis gave me a blank stare. I struggled to keep the impatience out of my voice. "*Mike's daughter?*"

Mavis smiled broadly and flashed a mouthful of gleaming white teeth. "Nice to make your acquaintance." She held up an index finger. "Hold on a minute, hon. Lemme call my husband so he can fetch your samples. Are you parked in the front or the back of the store, darlin'?"

Before I could stop her, Mavis picked up the phone and talk-yelled into the receiver. "Hey, Wilbur. Whatchya doin'? Do me a favor an' get on over here. Don't care if Miz Anderson's comin' in. I need you over here now. Mike Schlivnik's daughter is in the store to present the lines, and you need to bring her samples into the store. Do too. Mike's the bearded guy from Miami. He's kinda chubby and presents the line like he's fightin' a bull? It don't matter if you remember him or not. Get your tush over here and help this gal. She's a little bitty thing, and I can't imagine how she'd get all those sample bags into the store on her own."

Mavis hung up and smiled. "Don't worry, darlin.' Wilbur will be here in a few minutes. Just give him your keys, and he'll do the rest."

I tried not to offend her, yet I wanted to do things on my own. "It's nice of you to offer, but it's not necessary. I can bring everything in myself."

Mavis swatted away my comment like an annoying gnat. "Wilbur's on his way, so just let him bring everything in this time." Mavis pursed her lips. "I was right surprised about you takin' over the territory. I kept askin' myself what kinda daddy lets his *daughter* drive all over the place by herself and totin' them bags in and outta stores day after day? Mighty peculiar, ask me."

I resisted the urge to go snarky and answer one who wants to get rich. Instead, I smiled mischievously and told the truth. "Actually, it was his idea." I rather enjoyed seeing her eyes widen big as saucers.

****

Mavis nervously thumbed through the Climax dress samples we'd pulled aside. "Holly, I'm gonna have to trust you on this line. These styles are a little fast for my customers. But they sure are stylish, and they're different from anything in the shop. Heck, they're different from anything I've *ever* carried."

Mavis pushed her glasses up and read the order form I'd handed her. She peered closer and squeaked like a new pair of patent leather shoes. "Holly, am I readin' this right? Maybe I need to stop buyin' my readers at the drug store and get prescription glasses! Climax of California *Every girl should have one*?" Mavis tossed the order book on the counter as though it caught on fire. "Holly, I fancy these styles just fine, but hon, I can't buy them."

She fingered the six-point Jewish star attached to a

gold filagree chain around her neck and huffed without an ounce of irony. "This here's a God-fearin' Christian town. I can't have my customers sayin' I'm bringin' in lines from some X rated company! Nosiree. I'd lose all my church ladies." She pointed to the tag on the side of the closest garment. "And those hang tags! Good Gawd a mighty! I'm sorry, hon, but I'm gonna hafta pass on this line."

By my LA standards, this seemed pretty mild. But since the little town was a universe away from LALA land in every respect, I tried being tactful and not insult her. "If hang tags are the problem, cut them off before you put the dresses into stock."

Mavis dipped her head. "I guess it might work. But how about those big ol' lips on the label? Mighty suggestive too."

I resisted the urge to roll my eyes. "Mavis, the label is sewn *inside* the garment. No one's gonna see it while your customer's wearing it." I smiled. "If a customer says something, tell them it's from a very friendly company. Let's write up the order, okay?"

## Chapter Sixteen

A pleasant female telephone operator greeted me on the second ring. "Goooooodaftanoon. Thank you for callin' Pizitz, Birmingham's first and finest department store. How may I direct your call?"

Geesh. Imagine having to repeat *that* same spiel a few thousand times a day? My jaws ached at the thought. I asked to be connected to Anna Wellington, and the operator happily complied.

Four rings later, a nasal voice smacking gum barked, "Anna Wellington."

Startled, I parroted back the same name. "Anna Wellington?"

Her disgust at my stupidity came loud and clear across the line. She snarked. "Seein' I answered the phone Anna Wellington, might give you the first clue it's me on the other end. Now, who the hell is callin'?"

Nervous, I babbled goofy as a star-struck groupie. "Of course, you're Miss Wellington. Who else would you be? You wouldn't have answered the phone as Ms. Wellington if you were someone else unless you were Ms. Wellington's assistant. Oh, but you'd have answered the phone Miss Wellington's office, not Anna Wellington. I am so sorry…."

She tsked. "Hold up now, hon. This here is Pizitz Department Stores. Trust me, we don't have budgets for staff." She cackled at her own joke. "I am my own

93

assistant, and a damn good one, if I say so myself." She smacked her chewing gum loudly into the receiver. "We've done a fine job establishin' exactly who I am, so the only question remainin' is who the hell are you?"

I managed to remember my name the second time around. "I'm Holly Schlivnik. Mike Schlivnik's daughter."

She magically morphed from nasty to nice the minute I mentioned Dad's name. "Oh, of course. Your daddy called and let me know you're my rep now. Gonna miss workin' with your daddy. He sure knows how to entertain a gal. The ol' boy always told *the best* dirty jokes!" Anna snorted indelicately. "And the way he presented the line. Oh. My. God. He was a hoot. Bobbin' an' weavin' as if he's fightin' a bull. He sure made buyin' his lines fun. Are you coming over to B-ham?"

I told her, yes, and we agreed on a date and time. She crooned. "See you next week, sugar. Please send your daddy my love, an' tell him I'm sure gonna miss him."

My first major store appointment! Oh. My. God. I took a victory lap around my desk as if I'd won an Olympic gold medal. Feeling pretty frisky, I picked up the phone. I greeted the next department store buyer in a much calmer voice. "Hi Barb. This is Holly Schlivnik. Yes, Mike's daughter. Yes, that's right. I took over the territory from him, so I'm your rep now. I'm coming to Birmingham next week. Is next Tuesday at 1:00 open? Fantastic. You're on the sixth floor in the back corner? Great, see you soon."

Holy Guacamole. I was two for two! Maybe I found my niche. This turned out to be easy. I worried for nothing. These big store buyers? Regular people no different than me, who put their panties on one leg at a time.

I was on a roll. I was invincible. I confidently made the next call. "Hello, Miss Braun. My name is Holly Schlivnik. I am the sales rep for UGC Knits and Sweet Inspirations. I am going to be in Birmingham next week and I…."

The woman interrupted me with a condescending tone. "Lemme stop you before goin' into your little spiel. I don't work with *any* road reps. I do *all* my buying in New York. Now if you'll excuse me…"

The buzzing of the dial tone brought me back down to Earth. So much for invincibility. Dad warned me I might encounter this. *"You're gonna run into some major store buyers who only want to work in New York. They think the New York office has more authority than us road reps. It's a bunch of BS, but it's gonna happen. Remember. Don't get mad, get even. And the only way to get even is to sell them."*

I gave Ms. Braun a therapeutic middle finger salute and vowed to make her my life's project. I went back to completing the rest of my calls. The appointment calendar filled up quickly with Dad's name as my magic genie. Would I always need a magic genie? Only time would tell.

\*\*\*\*

I packed the samples into the car trunk and headed south on I-75 to the junction of the westbound I-20. Twenty minutes later, a flashing yellow light indicated roadwork ahead on I-20 going westbound. Orange cones closed off lane after lane until we got to the US 78 exit. Obedient as a baby duckling, I fell into line behind a slow-moving semi. I passed through the series of small towns on US 78 from Atlanta to Birmingham. Ten miles into the trip, I got to a downslope straightaway. I passed the 18-wheeler and sped up. I accelerated to twenty mph over the speed limit to make up some time.

I came down the straightaway and gritted my teeth. Good grief. Now I pulled behind an old broken-down pickup plodding along at a snail's pace. A bubble-topped patrol car blared its siren and shot out from behind a clump of bushes. Dad warned me about these southern cops, but I failed to take him seriously. Crap! I'm on the road for barely a month, and already getting a ticket. I slowed down for a safe spot to pull over. No doubt I'd been tagged.

We rounded another curve and to my astonishment, the patrol car cut in front of me and pulled the pickup over. I slowed down to a crawl as the patrolman ordered a black man out of the pickup and pushed him against the hood. I stared gape-mouthed as the cop frisked the man and shoved him to the ground. The cop spread-eagled the poor guy and held him down with his boot in the small of the man's back. The disturbing image stayed with me all the way to Birmingham.

**\*\*\*\***

One of Dad's many lectures replayed in my head as I took a loose sample out of the trunk. "*Always make friends with support staff in hotels and motels. These are invisible, underpaid people who get little respect and are often forgotten. Always be respectful. Read their name tags and call them by their names instead of Hey, Miss. Make it your business to remember their names the next time you see them. Engage them in conversation and get to know a bit about their personal lives. Believe me, asking if someone's sick mama is doing better goes a long way to getting you all you need. Find out the kind of clothes the girl at the reservation desk prefers and bring her a sample every few trips. These people have the power to help or hinder you with the flick of a switch. If only one down and out room is available, and the choice is to give it to you, or some jerk who yells at the clerk for something beyond their control, who is the clerk going to give the premium room to?"*

It was still hot and humid as I backed into the hotel parking space and wedged the door to my room open with my briefcase. I hefted the first garment bag onto the rolling rack and muttered. "I'm actually doing this? How would he know if I didn't? He wouldn't. He's a thousand miles away. Of course, if I left the samples in the trunk overnight, it'd be my luck to have the car broken into. Wouldn't *that* be a fun call to make?" I wiped the perspiration dripping down the side of my face with my shirtsleeve and gritted my teeth. "I'll bring them into the room but I'll be damned if I'm gonna steam them." I put the last bag on the rack and wheeled it into the room. After I unbagged the samples, I peeled off my sweaty clothes and twirled in front of the air conditioner in my underwear for almost a half-hour. Paid vacation? My Aunt Fanny's tush.

****

I revived enough to walk to the hotel restaurant. Famished and engrossed reading the menu selections, I missed the hostess pointing me out to Dad's friends, Fred and Marion Batts. Fred tapped me on the shoulder, and a sudden wave of loneliness enveloped me. I patted the empty seat next to me. "Isn't this a pleasant surprise? If you're not meeting anyone, will you join me? I don't enjoy eating alone. I tried bringing a book, but it seemed

97

weird. I did room service a few times, but it was way too expensive." I frowned. "Besides, I missed being around people."

Fred and Marion shared a glance and sat down at my table. We enjoyed an hour of good food and company. Afterward, we walked through the lobby, and I bid them both good night, but Fred insisted on walking me to my room. He even waited until I locked myself in. Hot diggity. My own rent-a-daddy, sans all the nosy questions.

The phone rang as I closed the door. Nothing good ever comes from calls this time of night. Nana? God forbid if she's ill? An appointment cancellation? This late at night? Nah. I raced to the phone and sagged with relief at the sound of Dad's voice.

I gushed. "You'll never guess who I ran into in the hotel restaurant? Fred and Marion Batts. If I didn't know better, it seemed almost as if us being at the same hotel at the same time had been planned. I loved having company eating. Fred grabbed my check, but I wouldn't let him pay. Kinda like having you and Mom with me." I giggled. "Except I *would* let *you* pay."

Dad said, "Yeah, a real coincidence you running into them. So, when did you get in?"

"Around 5:30. I brought Sue Ann at the front desk a sample as you suggested. Boy, did you ever get it right. She gave me a great room. Down and out the way you taught me."

Dad asked, "You've been in town a couple of hours already. What have you been doing?"

Huh? I resisted the urge to say square dancing. "It's a long drive. I checked into the room and took it easy until I went out for dinner."

Dad asked, "You bring the samples in from the car yet? It's a bad idea to leave them in the trunk overnight. Remember. If they get stolen, you're out of business. It's a pain to bring them in every night. But if you consider the cost of replacing all those samples versus doing it the right way, it's a no-brainer."

He actually called to check up on me like he would a kindergartener? I clucked my tongue. "For your information, I brought all the bags into the room right after I checked in."

Dad chirped. "Fabulous. I'm glad ya brought them in first thing. You ought to get going, or you'll be steaming for hours."

Try again, bucko. "After I hang up, I'm going to bed."

The sarcasm flew over his head. "You're already done? Good for you. It's smart to get it out of the way first thing."

Remarkable. For a smart guy, at times he can be completely dense. "No, I'm not already done. I told you. I am not steaming those damned samples. Not tonight, not tomorrow night, not in this lifetime. You told me to make my own choices, and I did. You're not allowed to complain now over a choice I made just because you don't agree with it."

"You're right." Dad snorted. "If you don't mind presenting your samples looking like a herd of buffalo trampled over them, neither do I. It's your reputation, not mine."

I thumped my chest. "Say hallelujah, the Great God of Guilt gave an inch! Alert the media!"

He said good-naturedly, "Good night, Miss Smarty Pants. Say hi to Anna and the other buyers for me."

I took the mature route and stuck my tongue out. "Good night, oh Great God of Guilt."

Chapter Seventeen

I rolled my rack across the Pizitz parking bridge and walked right foot first into the store nervous as an expectant father. I made my way to the buying center on the top floor and found Anna Wellington's small, rectangular office in the back corner.

I maneuvered the rolling rack to the sidewall to clear the hallway and peered into the office. A medium-height, skinny, flat-chested woman in her mid-thirties stood behind a messy desk with an overflowing ashtray teetering near the edge.

Her deep V-neck floral print nylon dress had a short hemline that highlighted a pair of stick-thin legs. She wore a pair of slingback patent leather pointy-toed low-heeled shoes. A pencil was stuck in the top of her jet-black big hair like a chopstick.

With an opaque skin tone of alabaster white, she sported a slash of blood-red lipstick across her narrow mouth. She'd filed inch-long fingernails into points and painted them the same color as her lipstick.

She held a cigarette burnt down to the filter in her left hand and cradled the phone between her right ear and shoulder. She chewed a wad of gum as she thumbed through a three-ring binder with her right hand while talking on the phone.

I shrank back, trying not to eavesdrop, as Anna spoke in a conversational tone. "Arnold honey, I don't know what to tell you. If you don't have the goddamn dresses here before the goddamn ad breaks, you can take the damned dresses and shove 'em right up your skinny ass, since I sure as hell won't have any need for them. No, Arnold, the fabric delivery just isn't my problem, hon. I guess you shoulda planned your production better. I'm sure you'll find another home for those dresses. Arnold, lemme make this real clear, hon. If those dresses don't hit my dock by this Friday, I don't need 'em at all, because I'll be killin' your ad. And rest assured, you won't be gettin' any business from me down the road. There are plenty of other suppliers who will manage to get me my goods when I need them. Sorry, but I got a meetin' I'm late for. So, be sweet now, and have yourself a wondaful day."

Yikes. I resisted the urge to turn tail and run back to the car before she noticed me. Maybe this is one buyer I'd be happy if she shopped our lines in New York. Too late. She peered out into the hallway and waved me in. She pointed to the guest's chair with the hand holding the cigarette like a weapon. Yikes.

Anna hissed, "Asshole!" as she cradled the receiver onto the hook. She swiveled her chair around to face me and smiled. "Miss Holly, I presume?"

I plastered a winning smile on my kisser. "Yes, ma'am. I apologize, but I couldn't help but overhear your phone conversation. Boy, I hope I *never* get you mad at me."

Anna blew out a perfect smoke ring and smiled. "Sugar, only two things in life we pedal that matter at all are our time and our reputation. If you don't waste my time and don't screw with my reputation, then we're gonna get along just fine. If you make me a promise, you better deliver or I *will* make you pay. And that, Miss Holly, *is* a promise."

I nodded my head up and down like a bobblehead doll.

Anna took a fresh cigarette out of a leather case and lit it with the butt of the one she'd smoked down to the filter. Anna smiled. "So, before we get started, tell me? Is your daddy just playin' golf now?"

I wished that daddy was here right now. This is one buyer who ate salesmen for lunch. "No, he's still on the road, only traveling Florida now. He'd drive my mother crazy being home all the time. My mom always says the secret to their successful marriage is half the time he's away. My dad is a force of nature."

Anna's raspy smoker's voice sounded like sandpaper scratching wood. "God's truth! Hell, it used to take me a day to recover from workin' with him. Your poor mama." She took a dress off a wall grid across from her desk and smiled devilishly. "I've gotta show you somethin' I've been practicin' in anticipation of our meetin'. Here is my interpretation of your daddy presentin' the line." She performed a wicked imitation of Dad waving a dress like a muleta and took a pass with the dress at her side. She held the hanger under her nose exactly like he does and stared. She dipped her head and grinned. "So, pretty good, no?'

I about wet my panties.

She glanced at the wall clock. "We'd better get started. Where are your samples?"

I pointed to the hall. I rolled the rack in, and she yelped, "Good God Almighty, child! Did you drive here in an eighteen wheeler?"

I gulped. "I'm sorry. Is something wrong?"

She smirked. "I see your daddy trained you."

Who did she think? Oscar de la Renta? I didn't want to blow a big account before I took the first style out of the garment bag, so for once in my life, I kept my smartass comments to myself. "Yes. Why?"

Anna softened her tone. "Your daddy is a wonderful guy and a fantastic salesman who knows his product inside and out. But I'll tell you the same as I tried to tell him. You can't present a line to a major department store the same way as to a small specialty store. First off, I don't have time to sit and go through four bags of samples. But more important, I don't want to." She waved the cigarette towards her open office door. "Did you walk my floor?"

I racked my brain for an instruction to do this from Dad. Nope. Abashed, I answered honestly. "No."

Anna jabbed a red polished talon at my rolling rack to make her point. "Then, how the hell do you expect to know which styles to present with no idea what I already carry?"

I shrank back as she waved her cigarette in my face.

"I *expect* the salesperson to do their homework before presentin' me their lines. It's your job to go through my department comparing the items I carry to the ones in those garment bags. If it's already on my floor, do I need to see it again? It's your responsibility to figure out the *white space* missin' from my selection. Next, figure out the trends you have that I don't, and convince me I need to buy them from *you*. Bring me somethin' new, but remember, not everythin' you have new is right for my customer. But you won't know what's right for my customer without studying my department. Make sense?"

I nodded. "Yeah, it does. My dad taught me not to pre-judge a line. The way I interpreted it was that the buyer leads me. Now it sounds as if I'm supposed to be leading you."

Anna waved a hand at my garment bags. "Now don't get me wrong. You do present the line the way your daddy does to specialty stores. They buy a big variety of styles, but fewer units per style. I buy fewer styles, but more units per style."

She smiled and stood up. "Let's go out on the floor together and study it. Let's see everything I carry, discuss the items I don't have, and see who's buyin' a particular item. You take notes while we're chattin' to remember what's in the department. Then I'm gonna send you back to Atlanta. Not gonna have anything presented today."

Panic squeezed my heart. Explaining *this fine kettle of fish* to Dad would be almost as bad as stolen samples. The Garment Goddess must be punishing me for not steaming those damned samples. My eyes filled, and I bit my lip hard so as not to burst into tears.

Anna caught onto my terrified state and held up a hand. "Now don't get your tail all tied up in a knot. Lemme finish. Get back to the mart and cull down the selection you were gonna present today based on the information you learned by walkin' my department. In other words, prepare a *Pizitz-specific* presentation with the right items in your lines *for my customer*." She smiled and walked towards the open door. "Come back same time next Tuesday. But bring a presentation that fits in *one bag*, not four. Make decisions and value judgments. See the presentation through my eyes. Give me a reason to buy every style presented. Do you understand my expectation?"

I nodded yes, and Anna led the way like a teacher on a school field trip. "Let's get out on the sales floor now. Grab a notepad off the desk, and get a free lesson for the way to meet the needs of the customer." Anna poked a finger in the air. "And that, my friend, is the way a salesperson becomes important to a buyer."

Anna stood in front of a four-way display and shoved one of the junior dresses under my nose. "All the information a rep needs to make the best presentation is right here on my floor."

We walked through her entire department. She talked, preached, and pointed out the good items as well as the dogs on the markdown rack. She opined on why certain things sold and others didn't. We stood adjacent to the cash register and observed the type of customers who bought which types of styles. I observed, listened, and learned.

In retrospect, the appointment where I never opened my garment bags, much less wrote an order, proved to be the most profitable one of my entire career. The fire-breathing dragon lady who could easily intimidate Attila the Hun, and certainly had better things to do with her time, spent hours teaching a newbie the way to hone her craft.

Sometimes life is so funny. The unlikeliest person you'd ever encounter turns out to be the one willing to share answers to questions you didn't even think to ask.

Chapter Eighteen

I had some time between Anna's appointment and my next one at Loveman's. Determined not to repeat the same mistakes, I walked Barb Cooper's floor and took some notes. I raced to the car, culled down the lines, and revised my presentation. Anna might not appreciate me using the information she provided to improve my presentation to her direct competitor. Too bad. The two buyers bought different categories. So, technically, I didn't take from Peter to give to Paul. Maybe to his distant cousin. If you squinted.

**** 

After a successful presentation of our sportswear lines and receiving the buyer's promise to have my orders written by the following week, I left the prim and proper world of Loveman's Department Store and headed for the place the poster child of life in transition dwelled.

I wheeled the loaded rack past an X-rated Movie Theater, an adult book store, and a gay bar all on the same side of the backstreet as Mr. Sid's Apparel/Jody's Boutique. This part of town defied the image most people have of the south. The neighborhood appeared a lot closer to West Hollywood than Tara. This many-layered, complicated region is one of conflicting values in transition on a collision course with its history and its future on the line.

The store exterior sported a pink sign written in white script across the top of the plate glass front window: *Mr. Sid's apparel/Jody's boutique.* Mannequins dressed in frilly, girlie pink outfits enticed passersby to come inside.

The interior of the store was like a cotton candy machine had exploded inside it. The all-pink and white décor featured large framed posters of fashion styles on the walls. Six rows of packed clothing racks filled the small, narrow store. The end bars of the racks were painted striped pink candy canes. Two dressing rooms at each wall opened with pink and white stripe doors. Jody made no secret of her favorite color.

Jody wore a shocking pink one-piece silk jumpsuit with a white and pink feather boa draped around her neck. Perched on matching pink stilettos, she was a vision to behold with a diamond tiara nestled into the crown of her brunette wig.

Jody glided from rack to rack grabbing outfits. She knocked on one of the dressing rooms and handed a dozen hangers to a customer. I waved and rolled my rack into the stockroom. Jody called out in a voice that started in a low masculine tenor and ended in a girlie soprano. "I'll be right with you, Sugar, as soon as I make sure Bitsy has all she needs. While you're waitin,' help yourself to a soda from the fridge in the corner."

****

Later the same evening, I sat across from Jody in the living room of a large colonial-style house. The elegantly decorated room featured expensive antiques mixed in with contemporary furniture. I took a sip of wine and grinned. "You're full of surprises. A gourmet cook, a wine connoisseur, and an interior decorator. You're a great catch!"

Jody quirked a sardonic smile. "My chances of findin' the perfect soul mate for a six- foot-six-inch gal wearin' stilettos and sportin' a five o'clock shadow in Birmingham are slim to none."

The happiness radiated by her shining eyes stole my heart. "I'm so pleased you accepted the invitation. Remember how shocked you were when I appeared at your showroom? Since the operation, your reaction is pretty much the norm. I don't have many friends left and fewer houseguests. Your daddy is a treasure. He's been one of the few who stood by my decision and *never* wavered. His jokes over my Adam's apple bobbin' don't ever offend me. He's the most open-minded person I know. I got upset when he said you were takin' over the territory. But I hoped the apple fell close to the tree." Jody smiled and waved a hairy hand the size of a baseball mitt. "And you are just like your daddy."

My heart warmed at the compliment. "Our parents raised their kids not to judge a book by its cover. But I admit that first time, you shocked the hell out of me." I risked offending my hostess if I kept traveling down the same road, so I changed the subject. I waved an arm around the room. "This is some house. Have you lived in it long?"

Jody beamed with pride. "Yes. Bought it with my signin' bonus from the Cougars. Got drafted second round after graduatin' from 'Bama. My granny always advised you can never go wrong with real estate." Jody proudly swept her arm around the room. "It's my sanctuary."

I gushed. "Wow, I had no idea you played pro football."

The gigantic she-man giggled girlishly. "I didn't exactly take the same career route as fellow alumni Broadway Joe Namath." She waggled a sausage-sized finger. "But I can thank my pro days for the path I ultimately chose. Bein' around all those hunks with the testosterone zingin' off the locker room walls made it crystal clear I wasn't one of the guys. After three seasons, I finally admitted to myself I'd rather sleep with the competition, not tackle 'em. Growin' up in this town, in this state, with my family? Trust me. I spent a lifetime in denial. The notion of tellin' my he-man, holy-roller, bible-thumpin' daddy his football hero son wanted to be the head cheerleader isn't a conversation I ever relished havin'. I lied to the family and told them I got injured and had to retire. When I made up my mind to have the operation, the only one I told about the procedure was my baby sister. I figured if anything went wrong and I died, at least she'd get me buried. She helped me through the crazy reactions to hormone therapy. She even found clothes to fit someone in transition. I had to go to a doctor in Atlanta for the procedure, since no one in Birmingham would touch me. The transition is almost complete. The doctors say the beard will be completely gone in a few months, and the Adam's apple is shrinking as the hormones start to take over. Thank goodness, my voice will stop jumping from a guy to a gal and back pretty soon."

My heart went out to her. "At least you weren't alone."

Jody sighed. "Every choice in life comes with a price. And believe me, I paid dearly for mine. I'd recovered from the procedure and my sister convinced me I needed to tell the rest of the family the truth. She tried to prepare them. But nothin' really could. The worst they thought was I came out of the closet, which trust me, in their eyes, would have been bad enough. I started to believe, needed to believe, no matter the situation, my parents would always love me. We went to their house for Sunday dinner. Daddy answered the front door. He didn't recognize me. He got angry we didn't tell them we'd be bringing an extra guest."

Jody held out her hand. "I reached out to my father. I said, 'Daddy, it's me, Sid. Don't you recognize me? It must be a shock, but I'm finally happy. I'm a woman now. I'm who I was always meant to be. My name is Jody.'" Jody's voice cracked. "I went to hug him, and he shrank away as if I had a contagious disease."

Jody took a sip of wine. "He stared at me square in the face with a flicker of recognition in his eyes. He screamed '*oh, my God no,*' and fainted. Mama ran out of the kitchen and shrieked '*You desecrated yourself. Now God will strike you dead.*' And then she threw me out of the house." Jody spat bitterly. "A regular Ward and June Cleaver moment."

I struggled to find something positive to say. "At least you have your sister."

Jody shook her head. "No. I managed to mess up her life too. Our parents forbade her any contact with me. We come from a very religious family. We were raised in the pure fire and brimstone of the Pentecostal Church."

Jody smiled the saddest smile I'd ever seen. "They sent her away to a boarding school in Switzerland. I'm sure they threatened her with being disowned, disinherited, and goin' straight to Hell if they caught her ever contactin' me again. At first, she sent a few letters.

But you can bet our parents had her mail monitored. After the first year, her letters stopped comin'. I figured I'd done enough to mess up her life, so I stopped writin' too."

And my family behaved overzealously? I will *never* complain about Dad's nosiness again. "Considering all you've gone through, do you think you made the right choice?"

Jody held her head high. "Which way to go? Either lie to myself or everyone else? I made the *only* choice. I pass a mirror now and am finally proud of who I see. I'm who I've always been, who I was always *meant* to be. You can't lose what you don't have. You can never escape the truth, no matter how far or fast you run."

After Nana, this was the wisest person I'd ever met.

Chapter Nineteen

I had an action-packed, exhausting first day filled with a cafeteria of mixed expectations and emotions. I drove east on Oxmoor Road early the next morning and hoped the second day turned out to be more normal. Of course, I had yet to figure out whatever *normal* might be.

I parked in front of a charming stucco bungalow painted white with a shake roof six buildings down from the corner on the north side of the street. A white background rectangular sign with red script letters in the window announced: *Maggi's Boutique*. A serpentine-shaped brick pathway led from the sidewalk to the bungalow's bright red front door.

A thin older woman with gray hair pulled back in a tight bun stood behind the cash register. Maggi Thompson greeted me with a beautiful smile as I walked toward the counter. "You must be Holly! It is so nice to make your acquaintance."

I offered my right hand and smiled. "Hi, Maggi. Yes, I am Holly."

A lovely woman. No wonder Dad thought so highly of her. She took my extended hand and cradled it between her two. She pointed to a mug next to the cash register. "I'm ready for a refill. Do you fancy a coffee or soda? We've got almost everything."

I held up a hand. "Thanks for the offer, but nothing for me...I've drunk enough liquids already to float away." I snapped my fingers. "Oh, before I forget, my dad sends his love."

Maggi beamed. "Your daddy is one of my special fellas. If I was ten years younger, I'd have chased him all over the store."

A disembodied deep male voice coming out of one of the dressing rooms boomed. "Ha, ten years younger, my Aunt Gussie's donkey! You only wish!"

Maggi hooted back without missing a beat. "Big Jim Thompson, get your sorry butt outta the dressing room this instant! Miss Frances don' need none a your help. Besides, we got company. Mike Schlivnik's daughter Holly is in the shop to present the lines."

The dressing room door swung open to the back of a tall, white-haired man. He stood right up against a middle-aged woman's back with his arms looped over her shoulders. His long, bony fingers pulled down on the collar points, making the top she had on much more revealing. He pulled his arms back, patted the woman on her fanny, and turned around to face Maggi and me.

Sporting a neatly trimmed white VanDyke beard, Colonel Sanders' swaggering twin brother sauntered over to check me out. As though they were undressing me, Jim Thompson's hungry gray eyes traveled up and down my body. He licked his lips while lewdly appraising me as though eying a tasty treat, and simpered as evilly as Snidely Whiplash. "My, my, who do we have here? Hell-o! Good golly, Miss Holly. I like your daddy just fine, but I'm gonna fall *in love* with you." He waggled his come-hither fingers toward his chest and winked. "Come over here, sugar and give me some love."

The dirty old man gave me the willies. No shame to

the guy. And in front of his wife yet.

Maggi wagged her index finger at the Colonel and warned. "Big Jim Thompson, you old fool, don't dare start your crap with Mike's Schlivnik's daughter unless you're hankerin' for a world of trouble from her daddy. Do somethin' helpful for a change." Maggi waved an arm at the leering man. "Holly, this dirty old man is my husband, Big Jim. Give him your keys and let him bring your samples in."

Maggi caught my squirrelly glance and flicked her wrist. "Don't worry. Big Jim is harmless. Matter of fact, he used to be an apparel rep way back in the day. Big Jim supplied General Lee's men with their uniforms. Right, Big Jim?"

Jim pointed his index finger at Maggi as he took my keys. "I mighta been sellin' 'em, but you were sewin' 'em, honey chile." He gave me another wink and pointed to the back of the store. "Lemme bring your rack and bags right in. I'll put 'em in the back office so you and her Majesty can work where it's quiet."

Maggi rolled her eyes. "He wants us workin' back in the office so he can stay out here and '*help fit*' a few more of our customers in the dressin' room." Maggie waved her finger at Jim. "I swear, it's a wonder you haven't been slapped silly by one of those ladies, or beaten within an inch of your life by an angry husband."

Jim pursed his lips and shrugged. "Hey, I help make the cash register sing any way I'm able."

I managed to fend off Big Jim's tacky advances and left Maggi's with my virtue intact and a fistful of orders three hours later.

****

Being vertically challenged at only four-feet, nine-inches in my stocking feet, I developed my own method for pulling the rack. I stood next to the center and wrapped my right arm around the middle bag to keep everything balanced. Next, I turned sideways so I faced the garment bags. Then I put my left hand on top of the rack over the middle bag. I duck-walked while pulling the rack from the middle instead of the front. Even wearing platforms, I still couldn't see over the rack. Every few minutes I leaned around the bags to avoid hitting something.

The section of 18th Street near Pizitz sat on a slight downslope. As I progressed down the street, the rack gained some speed. I picked up the pace considerably to maintain control. I tightened my grip on the top bar as the memory of the runaway rack fiasco in the Atlanta Mart loading dock flitted across my memory.

I pulled on the rack and couldn't move it. I dug in my heels, pulled it again, and moved only five feet. I danced this rolling rack cha-cha for another twenty feet. I checked under it for something stuck. Nothing. Hmm. Does a rack have a mind of its own? Maybe it got tired of all the rolling around town, or wanted to skip the next appointment? Nah. But, nonetheless, *something* gummed up the works. I walked around the other side of the rack and found a short, middle-aged man with his hands tightly clamped around the vertical bar of the back of the rack. I yelled, "Hey, let go before I call a cop!"

The man let go of the rack and held his hands up. "Now, hold on, Missy. It's not what you think. I'm standin' across the street mindin' my own business and all of a sudden I see this rack rollin' itself down the street. I figure it's either gonna roll into the street and create one helluva an accident or hit someone. So, I run across the street and stop the damn thing, but every time I got it stopped, it starts rollin' again. Now I see you pullin' the rack. Please accept my apology. I was only tryin' to help."

The man gave me the once-over. "Hey, don't I know you? Something about you is mighty familiar." He pointed to the garment bags. "These are garment bags. You a rep? I had no idea the industry had lady reps."

"No shit, Sherlock. Nothing gets past you." I clucked my tongue. "You *really* called me a *lady* rep? So, whether I pee standing up or sitting down is the criteria as to whether or not I'm capable of doing the job?" I rolled my eyes and pulled on the rack. "Now if you'll excuse me, I need to get to an appointment."

I turned on my heel and started to pull the rack. Once again, I'm walking, but getting no place. Now, I'm professionally pissed. If he didn't cut out the crap, this joker would make me late for my appointment. "Get outta my way before I roll over your damned feet."

The man snapped his fingers and slapped the garment bags. "Now I remember who you are! Mike Schlivnik's daughter. I'm Chase Kaplan. One of your daddy's good friends!"

I narrowed my eyes. No way could this social Neanderthal be a friend of my open-minded father.

"I haven't seen your daddy since the Atlanta market. I heard you were workin' for Mike, but I didn't make the connection." He rubbed his chin. "When I heard Mike hired you, I asked myself, 'what kinda daddy lets his *baby girl* go on the road by herself'?"

Mavis Thornberry made the same stupid comment. Do these yahoo southerners all talk to each other? I drilled him with a death ray stare. "You really ought to catch up to the twenty-first century. Haven't you heard the news? Women now have the right to vote."

He had the grace to be abashed. "Guess I deserve that. Let's start over. As a *friend*, may I still help you with the rack?"

I clucked my tongue, and he let go of the rack, held out his palms, and backed away. "Better try to pull my foot outa my mouth now. Tell your daddy I said hey."

I grumbled goodbye to the chauvinist jerk and rolled the rack to a surprisingly large store on a side street. I opened the door and entered Superfly Central. The interior walls were painted a bright purple and decorated with posters of Jimmy Hendrix, Lou Rawls, The Temptations, The Four Tops, Little Richard, Fats Domino, Chubby Checker, Michael Jackson, and Prince.

The shop came alive with strobe lights flashing neon colors and gave the posters the optical illusion of people dancing to the beat of loud pulsing music that made your fingers snap and your ears ache at the same time. It was like being on a trip without taking drugs. Which to do? Run for my life or shake my booty? Nah. Everyone knows white people have no rhythm. Picture your father doing the frug.

A hip brother strutted out from the back of the store to greet me. The dead ringer for Huggy Boy from Starsky & Hutch wore a perfectly tailored lavender suit with a purple shirt and sported a purple plumed fedora. We made one another's acquaintance and got down to work. MO'rice sold to a specific clientele, and chose the sexiest, most revealing dress styles in the Climax line. The plunging necklines and skirts slit above the hip left little to the imagination. The streetwalkers who shopped with MO'rice were the best-dressed hookers in town.

"You still want to work the same way as you did with my dad?" I set his selections aside. "These are the styles you want." I held up an order book. "If you do, I'll write up the order and send you a copy."

MO'rice grinned, and a diamond embedded into his front tooth sparkled off the strobe lights. The reflection almost blinded me when he opened his mouth to talk. "Yessim. Your daddy always made shore I got everthin' I need. I trust you'll do the same."

He made no move to help me pack the samples, but after I finished, MO'rice motioned to the door. "Need help gettin' your bags to the car? It be gittin' dark out in a few minutes."

I shook my head no. "Nah, I parked in the lot you suggested. Once I cross Eighteenth Street, I'm good to go."

MO'rice held open the door, and I wheeled the rack out. I made my way down the side street past a couple of tough kind of guys eyeing my garment bags. I wished I'd taken MO'rice up on his offer. I glanced over my shoulder and picked up the pace with the two of them not far behind. My bravado sank along with the sun. Going back and admitting to being a weenie wasn't an option. I squared my shoulders and rolled the rack down the dark side street to the corner of Eighteenth Street.

I got to the end of the intersection and stopped in my tracks. An ocean of people jammed the bus stop. As the crowd grew, it spilled over from the narrow sidewalk near the bus stop into the lot I parked in. I stood rooted to the spot through three traffic light cycles trying to decide what to do. I couldn't stand there forever. I had to do something. There was no way to get around the crowd or through them, so getting them to move out of my way was the only option. I crossed the street and pulled the rack towards the crowd. Time to test drive Dad's theory. I cupped my right hand into a megaphone and yelled at the top of my lungs. "Coming through, coming through, and coming through right now! Please step aside and let me through. Coming through, please step aside!"

I rolled the rack through the cleared path ala Moses parting the Red Sea. Miraculously, I made it to my car with the bags still on the rack and my body in one piece. I keyed the trunk open, heaved the bags and rack into the trunk, and jumped into the driver's seat.

All righty then. Not so bad. Proof positive that image often trumps ability, and if you act like you know what you're doing, people assume you do. I giggled myself silly back to the hotel.

****

The next afternoon between appointments, I listened to the voicemail message and almost dropped the phone. I replayed it over and over in my mind's rewind loop, relishing it. "Holly? This is Tina Braun? From The Parisian in Birmingham?" She coughed nervously as she struggled on. "I-I seem to find myself in a bit of a p-pickle, and I-I'm hoping you can h-help me out. P-please give me a call."

If nothing else but out of curiosity, I returned the call. After she detailed her situation, I said, "Let me see what I can do." An idea percolated, but I needed to call the company to confirm it doable. I hung up and called the owner of Sweet Inspirations. "Hello, Yuki? Hi, this is Holly Schlivnik. I'm fine, thanks. And you? Good. Listen, I received a call from the Parisian buyer. Yes, you're right. She usually shops us in New York. I guess she called our New York office trying to find some immediate goods and they weren't too helpful, so she called me. She has a problem and I am calling to see if we can help her. No, not anything due to us. Apparently, another supplier shortshipped her, and she's in trouble. She's been able to replace some of it, but she still needs 1200 more units. The style I want to offer her is…."

Once I made the call, the buyer was mine. "Ms. Braun? This is Holly Schlivnik. I've got good news. I found 1200 units of a great style for you. I'm actually in Birmingham. I'll be in your office in an hour. Yes, I'll bring a sample of the style. I've already spoken to the office. They're holding the goods for you. All I need is your order. Once I call it in to customer service, the style can be shipped today. Yes, really. You're quite welcome. No worries. I'm sure we can figure out *some way* for you to thank me."

Dad's voice reverberated inside my head. "Don't get mad, get even. Get even by selling them."

Roger on it, Dad. Loud and clear.

Chapter Twenty

Despite it having been an extremely productive week, I was anxious to get back to Atlanta. I finished working in Birmingham and spent the last two days of the week working my way back home and calling on accounts in every small town off of Interstate 59.

The mountainous two-lane road east of Guntersville made the drive slow and tedious. I kept my speed at 30 miles per hour on the winding, steep road. Downhill from the summit, the car behind me sped up on a short straightaway and zoomed past me as though I was standing still.

I crossed the state line at the sign "*Cave Spring, Georgia: 2 miles. Rome, Georgia: 6 miles.*" Hidden behind the bushes on the outskirts of town, the Georgia Highway Patrolman pulled behind me, siren blaring, bubble lights flashing. I checked the speedometer. I wasn't speeding, but the triumphant week evaporated until the patrol car flew past me.

I slowed to a crawl as I approached the state trooper's vehicle parked behind the car that passed me like a bat out of hell on the mountain road. The patrolman got out of the cruiser and swaggered to the speeder's car. I eyed the cop at about thirty years old and around six-foot-two. He was a rocket of testosterone packaged in a snug-fitting tan uniform that showcased *all* his best features. He had washboard abs. His muscles were ripped, and his biceps rippled as he bent his arm to push his hat to the back of his head. He wore mirrored sunglasses hiding his eyes. A nightstick swung from the left side of his belt, and handcuffs dangled on the same side. He wrapped the fingers of his right hand around the grip of his service revolver. Holy crap.

My eyes widened appreciatively as the patrolman got to the other guy's car. I resisted the urge to try out a wolf whistle as he leaned into the guy's open window. "My, my, *officer yummy*."

I giggled, but this was *so* not funny. It just as easily could have been me getting that ticket. Oye vey. Dad's warning about not getting in trouble with southern cops rang like an alarm inside my head. Between a costly traffic ticket and jacked up auto insurance rates, I'd be in the hole so deep, that I'd *never* dig my way out. I counted my blessings and went on my way well under the speed limit.

Maybe Dad's suggestion turned out not to be so dumb after all. The next day I headed straight to the Dixieland Electronic Shack and bought a CB radio. I sat in the car and pressed the microphone button. "Breaker, breaker 1-9 do you copy? This is the *California Rag Lady askin' for a bear report*." If my college roomies only heard me since I morphed into a regular Georgia cracker, they'd wet their panties.

\*\*\*\*

Given the minimal amount of time I spent in Atlanta, the apartment seemed closer to the world's most expensive closet than to an actual home. It's impossible to become rooted in a city if you're not around often enough to plant the seeds. Rarely were my roommates and I ever home at the same time. So sitting together in the living room and catching up on one another's lives was a treat.

It wasn't the beginning of the month yet, but I wanted to give Karen my rent check before I left again. Karen took it with her left hand, and my eyes zoomed to her ring finger that sported a large diamond engagement band. A surprising jab of jealousy stabbed my heart as I grabbed Karen's left hand and squealed. "Oh my God! When did you get this? It's gorgeous!"

Karen grinned and waved the ring back and forth like a pendulum. "Last Sunday night. You already left town Monday before I got off duty. David and I went to Aunt Fanny's Cabin. He'd been acting kind of nervous, but I figured the issue was his big trial coming up. It's his first as lead attorney, and he's been uptight. Anyway, David asks me to give him a piece of cornbread. I reach over to pass him the basket, and he says, "No! You give it to me. Pick out a small one, and leave the basket on your side, out of my reach. If I take one myself, it'll be the biggest, and I'll keep taking more, and won't leave any room for the chicken. I've got no resistance."

Karen glowed telling the story. "No resistance? He was right. When it came to that cornbread, David had no control. He'd fill up on cornbread and then not leave room for anything else. I grabbed the basket and lifted the smallest piece, conveniently sitting on top of the other bigger pieces." She caressed the ring and grinned. "As I lifted it to put on his plate, *this* lay beneath. I let out a scream, and two waiters and a busboy rushed over to the table. I guess they were worried I found a bug in the basket. Anyway, David grabbed the ring from my hand. He dropped to one knee, put the ring on my finger, and asked me to marry him. I threw my arms around his neck and shouted yes. Then the whole restaurant broke into cheers. It was sort of embarrassing, but still like in a movie!" Her happiness radiated as bright as the sun shining through the living room window.

A surprising lump formed in my throat. "You're so lucky. David is a great guy. Have you set a date yet?"

Karen smiled shyly. "Not yet. It'll probably be in the spring. David's big trial will be done, and he'll be able to get time off." Karen checked her watch and stood up. "I'm on duty in an hour, and I-75 will be jammed." She rolled her eyes. "When isn't there traffic on that highway? I've come off duty in the middle of the night, and I-75 had bumper-to-bumper traffic in both directions. Hard to imagine why all those people are out at 3:00 in the morning."

I cracked up. "Are you kidding? This is nothing. Do you want traffic? One month in LA on the 405, and you'll beg for I-75." Karen left, and the aura of contentment followed her out the door.

I turned to Ellen. "Wow. Karen certainly had pretty exciting news. She's so happy she glows. We should be so lucky. It's Saturday night. Let's go over to Time Out, the sports bar on Ellison, near the bridge on the northwest shore of the Chattahoochee River. It's supposed to be a great place to meet guys. Maybe our Davids will appear tonight. If not, at least we grab a burger, enjoy a glass of wine, listen to music, and people watch."

Ellen shook her head and stood up. "Nah. I'll pass. I've got a ton of schoolwork. Besides, I don't want to meet my David, at least not now. Karen and David are so settled that their engagement was so, so inevitable. It seems as if they've been married for years. They're already on their path, and I haven't even considered which path I want yet. I don't want to be tied down. I don't want to live my life in terms of someone else, making someone else happy."

Ellen bent down and rubbed Max behind his ears. "Right now, Max is the one guy I want in my life. Aren't you, Maxie boy? If hitting a bar does it for you, go for it, but leave me out." She patted Max's head and walked down the hall towards her bedroom. "Come on, Max. We've got a lot of work to do."

Chapter Twenty-One

Dad and I spoke to one another on Sunday mornings for a weekly post-mortem. I took it as a sign of his confidence in me that such a genetically predisposed busybody didn't require a nightly recap. If he wanted us to speak daily, I might as well go on the road with him.

I was depressed and out of sorts the Sunday after Karen's big announcement. Her week ended with an engagement ring, and mine with a bunch of orders to write up. But you play the cards you're dealt, so I was anxious for our Sunday confab. I had a great week and couldn't wait to brag. I guess you never outgrow wanting a parental pat on the back.

I flushed with embarrassment as Dad whispered. "Are you alone? If not, call me back after he's gone." By now, his opening salvo should entertain, not infuriate me, since he started our conversation the same way every week. A clever way of demonstrating his parental coolness and being nosy at the same time.

That Sunday I needed no reminder, least of all from my father, that cloistered nuns probably did the horizontal hula more often than me. So, I took my jealousy out on Dad. "A pretty inappropriate question for a father to ask a daughter. Not that it's any of your business, but every Sunday, it's the first thing you ask. And if I had company, do you honestly think I'd tell you? Get real, Dad."

In my mind's eye, I pictured his bushy eyebrows rising. "All right! Take it easy. I'm just trying to be respectful. You don't need to jump down my throat."

Respectful? Ha! Not a chance. "Respectful? My Aunt Gussie's donkey! You're being your usual nosy self."

Dad chose to miss the point. "Who's Aunt Gussie? Must be on your mother's side. Someone in our family owns a donkey?"

Now he pissed me off big time. "You know we don't have an Aunt Gussie, and no one owns a donkey. Although if you ask those kinds of stupid questions, you are acting like an ass. We've established I'm alone. Let's get to the weekly review."

Relieved to drop the hot potato subject of my erstwhile lack of a sex life, Dad agreed. "Fine, Miss Sensitive. Go on."

I grabbed my notes out of the briefcase. "I had a pretty good week. Let me give you the rundown by account: …. Now she owes me. I will get her to work with me if it's the last thing I do…."

Dad cheered me on. "Atta girl. You'll wear her down. And what about Anna Wellington?"

"That meeting is one I'll *never* forget! I got to her office, and she was on the phone chewing out some poor salesman. Holy guacamole. Man, she let the guy have it with both barrels. She never raised her voice. But, boy, I'd never want to piss her off. She scared the pants off me. She rings off, and we exchange pleasantries as though her prior conversation never happened. Then she picks up a sample and does a wicked imitation of *you* presenting the line. I found her take on you hilarious although you might not appreciate it."

Dad growled his impatience. "Fine, but what about her reaction to the lines? Which styles did she pick? Is she writing the orders next week? Any idea how big the orders will be? She's one of our biggest accounts, so we've got big numbers to hit."

Ding, Ding. And now for the bonus round. "The thing of it is, I never got the chance to open a garment bag."

Dad croaked like a bullfrog. "Holy cow. Do you have a problem working with her? Do I need to fly up?"

"It had nothing to do with me. I wheeled four garment bags into the office, and she kinda flipped out." Crap, this next part would really sting. "I don't want to make you feel bad, but she told me not to sell her the way you did. Not to present every style in every line. She took me onto her sales floor and made me mentally dismantle the department. After we finished, she sent me back to Atlanta to prepare a culled-down presentation fitting into one garment bag and to present it to her next Tuesday. I got a crash course in retail school, but honestly, I learned a lot. She spent over two hours teaching me the way to sell big stores." I held my breath, expecting him to explode.

"Good old Anna. She's got such a big set of balls. Do you need any help putting the presentation together?"

I breathed a sigh of relief. "Nope. This is one project I need to do by myself."

Amazingly, I got no argument. Good thing one of us thinks I am up for the task.

He asked, "Anything else?"

I eyeballed the items on my list. "Yes. I'm having a repeat problem. Whenever I present the Climax line to a specialty store in a small town, I get a lot of flak regarding the lips on the sew-in label and worse, the order form. Those small-town conservatives see *'Climax: Every girl should have one'* on the order form, and they throw a fit. Mavis from the Fashion Hut almost stroked out. She only agreed to write the line after I suggested cutting off the hang tags before putting the dresses on the floor. You might not be having a problem, but I am. We have to do something, or I'm not going to sell anything from that line to most of my accounts."

He sighed. "Not much we can do. It's not our company."

I pitched a solution. "We need to use our own order forms instead of the ones provided by our companies. We can put a blank space for the vendor's name and use our order book for all the lines. It cuts down on the number of order books to schlep around, and more importantly, it gets our own brand out in front of our accounts. We *are* a sales organization, and we need to promote our own name. We also need business cards. A lot of buyers ask for one."

He said, "It sounds like a good idea. Do you have a company name in mind?"

I reasoned. "I work for you, and you're my dad, so, the company name ought to reflect us. How does Daddy N' Me Associates strike you? You'll be the Daddy and I'll be the N' Me."

"The perfect name. Can you do a mock-up? Bring it down with you when you come in for the trade show. If we rush it to the printer, everything can be ready for the Miami market. By the way, when are you planning to drive down? This is going to be a big market, so bring your samples. That way, we don't have to go back and forth sharing them with the models."

I yelped. "Driving down? I'm not planning on driving. I assumed I'd be flying."

Dad tsked. "You do know what the first three letters of assume are? Travel the way you want, but I hope you have money for airfare. I'm only willing to pay for your gas and meals to drive down. If you wanna fly and don't have the money for the ticket, I hope you're able to sprout wings."

I squeaked. "Are you nuts? Don't you remember *your own* first rule of business? Do the most amount of business in the least amount of time. It's a ten-hour drive. It will take me days to recover from doing it alone. You want me comatose presenting the lines during market?"

Dad stuck to his guns. "Sorry, Hol. If it's good enough for me, it's good enough for you. I'm not paying a bucket of extra bucks to fly you and all those samples. If you insist on flying, I'll advance you the money, add it to your tab for the rolling rack, garment bags, and hangers, and deduct it from your first commission check. It's your choice."

I sniped, "If you're going to be a tightwad, forget it. I'd see my first commission check after I'm in the old age home. Fine. Remember, if I fall asleep in the middle of presenting the line, it's your fault."

Dad snorted. "It's a risk I'll take. Anything else?"

I threw in the towel. "Nope. You've done enough already. Let me talk to Mom."

"Love ya N'Me."

I couldn't help but smile. "Back at ya, Daddy."

"Hi, sweetie!" My mother's buttery voice soothed like a salve on a wound. "It seems so long since we flew to Atlanta."

I wanted to crawl onto her lap, but I gauged my

words. "I'm doing great, but I do have something I need your help with. It's Dad. The first thing he asks me when he calls for these weekly reviews is if I'm alone. Mom, it's so embarrassing for a *parent* to ask such a question. I've called him out on it a few times, but he keeps doing it. I don't want you to talk to him. I need to deal with this. Do you have any suggestions to make him stop?"

My mother's solution was delightfully evil. "Oh yeah, I do. Believe me, honey, do this and I guarantee he'll *never* ask the question again…"

My mother was a genius. Payback was a bitch. Daddy dearest wouldn't know what hit him. Springing it on him would be the most fun I've had in a long time.

Chapter Twenty-Two

Nothing is more boring than the ten-hour drive from Atlanta to Miami, especially driven alone. No matter how many times you spin the dial while heading southbound on I-75 in Georgia, you won't find the Beatles or Bach playing on the airwaves. If entertainment to help while away the time is important, you're going to be disappointed. The radio selections are still a toss-up between country and western and fire and brimstone.

If the drive to the state line seems dull, wait until you cross into Florida. Then the trek down the middle of the state morphs from tedious to downright painful. No improvement in the entertainment options and to be kind…the scenery is a snooze fest. You can only take so much endless flat, brown land punctuated by an occasional live oak before you either nod off or scream. It's a mystery how Dad drove this week after week without losing his mind. I was one crabby camper when I finally pulled into my parents' complex late at night. I grunted hello and went straight to bed.

My parents were busy the next day, so I had Nana all to myself. After a morning in her kitchen over coffee kvetching about my painful drive and Nana patiently listening, my mood greatly improved. The best way to get over the blues? Go shopping, of course.

We shared a sky-high pastrami sandwich at the

Nosh N' Nibble deli and then walked around the 163$^{rd}$ Street Mall window shopping and chatting. Nana and I went into the Purdines Department Store junior dress department and headed to a four-way with Climax dresses hung behind those of another supplier. I gave her the big eyes, but Nana offered no explanation when she handed me her purse. She proceeded to re-arrange the garments so that the Climax dresses hung prominently in front and the other suppliers were behind them. Next, she undressed a mannequin wearing another supplier's style. She took one of the Climax dresses off the rack and re-dressed the mannequin with it.

I pulled on Nana's arm and stage whispered through clenched teeth. "Nana! Are you nuts? Someone from the store management is gonna see you. You're gonna get us banned from the store for life."

Nana clucked her tongue. "Relax. No one is gonna do anything. As you get older, you become invisible. No one pays any attention to old people until they become a burden." She waved an arm around the store. "What are you worried about? All the clerks are little old ladies the same as me. Even if someone from the store saw me, they'd assume I'm another senior citizen employee doing her job."

She pointed to the mannequin. "See how much better your dress is than that other supplier's?" Nana put her arms around the mannequin's waist and gave our dress an extra fluff. "This takes me back to my days as a buyer."

Huh? I gave her the big eyes. "You were a buyer?"

Nana's eyes shined with a nostalgic gleam. "Oh, yes. As a young woman, I started as a trainee and worked my way up to a huge job as the millinery buyer at

Abramowitz & Straussmann. A&S was a department store chain in Brooklyn. Are you familiar with the term millinery? No? It's a fancy word for hats. I bought hats."

She patted her hair. "In my day, women wore hats every day for every occasion. Whether a woman was going to the fishmonger or a funeral, a hat was as essential a part of her outfit as her shoes and purse."

Nana's eyes glittered behind her glasses. "Believe me, if the millinery buyer from A&S told them to jump, those suppliers asked how high? One spring, a vendor missed the delivery of our Easter hats. We desperately needed them for the ladies' parade down Fifth Avenue. Let me assure you: I gave the salesman a piece of my mind and warned if I didn't have those hats by the end of the day, they'd never sell our store again. The president of the hat company delivered our order personally in a taxi cab. He and the cabbie brought the boxes into my office and piled them up to the ceiling. My team and I worked all night. But every one of those Easter hats got onto the sales floor in time, and we sold them all in two days."

Nana pointed to the four-way rack with my styles on it. "Back then, we weren't regulated by so many rules and regulations as now. Your dad says he's not even allowed to send some buyers a Christmas card without breaking company rules. In my day, buyers got offered baseball tickets, tickets to Broadway shows, opera tickets, the ballet, and even the circus. If I'd been the type of person who accepted bribes, I could have been busy every night of the week."

My jaw dropped. "You took nothing?"

Nana jutted her chin with righteous indignation. "Not a single thing. Plenty of buyers had their hands out, but not me. I placed orders on the merit of the product, not tickets for a Broadway play."

I asked, "And this store was in Brooklyn? I'm confused. Aren't you from Boston?"

Nana tapped her finger on the tip of her nose. "When we came to this country, we arrived at Ellis Island, but we immediately went to Boston. My parents' relatives lived in Boston, and the family helped get us settled. We had six kids in my family. I am the oldest. My sister Doe and I were born in England, the other kids in Boston. My father was a tailor, and my mother stayed home with the kids. After my brothers entered high school, the three oldest girls moved to Brooklyn from Boston. We lived with my mother's sister, Tilly."

"Why did you move?"

Nana lifted a shoulder. "For better job opportunities. We only had a few years to save as much money as possible to send the boys to college. My father worked hard, but with eight mouths to feed, he didn't have the money to put the boys through school. So, we girls made it happen."

My eyes bugged with surprise. "What about college for you and your sisters? Nana, you're so smart, I am sure you'd have been accepted."

Nana smiled wistfully. "Oh honey, in my day, only boys went to college. Boys needed the education so they'd have a profession, be able to earn a living, and support their own families. Boys had the big futures ahead of them." Nana shrugged. "Back then, there weren't many career choices for girls. Girls were expected to learn to cook and keep the house so they'd get married and be supported by their husbands. My sisters and I put both brothers through college and medical school. Of course, later on when the big war started, everything changed for women."

Her lost opportunity hit me hard. "So, you and your sisters *chose* to sacrifice your futures for the good of your brothers?"

Nana dipped her head. "Back in the day, if the parents were unable, sisters were *expected* to put their brothers through college."

Not sure if I wanted to hear the answer. "Any regrets?"

Nana shook her head. "Regret is the worst human emotion. It's the one we can usually do nothing about. So, no. I don't believe in wasting time and energy on the might-have-been. Now things are so much different. The only way to live without any regrets is to dive in and experience as much of life as possible. The only way to live life to the fullest is to put your fears aside and be willing to take a chance."

Nana let go of the past and looped her arm in mine. "Come, sweetheart. Let's walk around some more. We both love to shop. Imagine the delicious treats we'll find?"

Genetics is a funny thing. It's interesting which traits you inherit. Amongst the many things Nana and I shared is our love for perfumes and jewelry. We strolled companionably through the cosmetics department and tested perfumes before heading to the fine jewelry counter.

We stopped in front of the engagement rings and wedding bands. I pointed to a row of sparkling diamond rings. "I suppose you heard Karen and David are engaged? She's so lucky. David is a great guy and a romantic too. He hid the ring in a basket of corn muffins at a restaurant for Karen to find. He proposed at the table, and the whole restaurant cheered when she said yes! She described it like one of those Doris Day movies you used to take me to as a kid. Karen is so happy, she glows. I'm happy for her, too…."

Nana never missed anything. "But…"

I couldn't meet her eye. "No but."

Nana arched a brow and peered over her glasses. I sighed and threw in the towel. "It's seeing her ring and listening to her making plans. It made me examine my own life. She and David are already on their path together. They're planning a wedding, shopping for houses, and furniture. Nana, Karen and I are the same age. She's an RN. David is a lawyer, and on track to be a partner in his firm. They're this perfect couple. They've got it all. Me? I've got a rolling rack, and Dad owns it until I pay it off with my commissions. I love my job, but it's my whole life. I gaze into the future and see a blank."

Nana waggled an arthritic finger under my nose. "You can't blame not having a personal life on your job. If you want something bad enough, you find a way to make it happen. Are you on the road seven days a week?" Without waiting for an answer, she shook her head. "I don't think so. You come home on Thursday nights now. So, you're in Atlanta three days a week."

She held up seven fingers. "There are only seven days in a week, and you're home over forty percent of the time. How do you spend your free time? If you don't make an effort, nothing happens. People don't fall out of trees for you to meet."

My whine came out as cranky as a toddler's needing a nap. "Nana, it's hard. I don't know anyone in Atlanta except the girls. Karen is engaged, and Ellen made it clear she's not interested in meeting anyone."

Nana shrugged. "So?"

I clucked my tongue. "I don't see myself going to places to meet people *alone*."

Nana rolled her eyes. "Why not? You travel alone, eat alone, and stay in a hotel alone. You're alone more than you're with others. Going out to meet people alone shouldn't be a big deal. You can waste time having a pity party and blame anything and everything for the situations you're in. But the reality is, it's up to *you* to make your opportunities. Either choose to sit home and guarantee you'll be alone, or choose to go out and discover the adventures life has in store for you. If you think I'm going to let you off the hook for not taking control of your path, you've got another thing coming."

I groused, "What happened to the sympathetic Jewish Grandmother you're supposed to be? You must have missed the line the day they handed out the Nana Guidebook."

Nana grinned. "I was in the line for teaching you the way to make your own breaks."

I flipped her the bird and pecked a kiss on her velvety cheek.

We moved to the next display section with watches. I pointed to a designer tank commander's style. Nana motioned for the clerk to take it out of the case. I tried it on my right wrist and twisted it around for Nana to see. "Oh, Nana, isn't this fabulous? It's so sophisticated."

Nana nodded and smiled at the clerk. "What's the price?"

The clerk checked the price tag inside the box. "$325.00 plus tax."

Nana took out her charge card. "We'll take it. She'll wear it out. Put the box in the bag with the receipt."

I squeaked like a toy mouse. "*Nana, are you nuts*? My mother will kill me when she finds out."

Nana smirked a combination of annoyance and amusement. "I don't need her permission to spend *my money* the way I see fit." She winked. "If your mother's your problem, don't tell her."

I groaned. "Nana, my mother is neither blind nor an idiot. She'll see me wearing it and know I couldn't afford such an expensive watch. She'll know you bought it, and I'll catch hell."

Nana twisted her lips into a devilish grin. "When you were twelve, CD players were the newest thing out, and you wanted one in the worst way. Do you remember how you got it?"

I smiled at the memory. "Yep. You bought it and financed it for me. You gave me a weekly allowance of fifty cents from which you deducted twenty-five cents till I paid the debt off. What does it have to do with this watch? Last time I checked, you haven't given me an allowance in a long time."

Nana patted my wrist. "Let me buy it for you today. I wanted to buy you a gift to celebrate your new job, and this is it. And it's between you and me. As far as your mother is concerned, I am financing it for you? Okay?"

My conscience stepped in front of a reply. As much as I wanted the watch, lying to my mom? An uncrossable line. Nana didn't wait for my answer and signed the charge slip. Well, maybe a lie sounds a bit too strong. Better a slight rearrangement of the facts. Yeah, I could live with that. I wanted this watch since the second day of forever, and poof, now it was strapped on my wrist. I threw my arms around her neck. "Nana, you're the greatest! Thank you so much!"

Nana hugged me back. "Sweetheart, may you always enjoy good times when you wear it."

We walked back out into the mall and bought ice cream cones from a cart vendor and sat at a table across from the movie plex. Nana pointed to the movie posters. "I always loved movies, but as kids, my parents couldn't afford to send all six of us. We were poor but we kids had no idea that we were. My cousin, Jenny Weinstein, had a job as the organist at the local silent movie house. As an employee, she got a discount at her theater, and she gave it to us. My mother alternated sending the two oldest kids. Me one week, and my sister Doe the next. Whoever went to the movie came home and told the story to the other kids."

Nana's eyes went dreamy as she nostalgically disappeared back to her youth. "It was a serial, so you had to remember the story details from one week to the next. The other kids loved the weeks I went. I'd make popcorn, sit them in a row of chairs, play background music on the victrola, and dim the lights, the same as the movie house. I'd tell the story real dramatically. I'd pause at the high points of the drama until my brother Murray yelled, 'Go on, Rae. Don't stop now!'"

Nana pursed her lips. "The younger kids hated the weeks it was Doe's turn. She never made popcorn or played music. She'd give a three-minute synopsis and say, "That's what happened."

I applauded like you would at the end of a show. "Oh, Nana, what a great story. I love all your stories."

Nana's owlish eyes sparkled behind her glasses. "Now it's time for you to gather the stories making up your life. And someday, you'll tell them to your grandchildren."

"I hope they enjoy hearing my stories as much as I do yours." I narrowed my eyes. "You said you had no idea you were poor? How could you not?"

Nana shrugged. "You don't miss anything you don't know you don't have. It's different today. With television and telephones, the world is a much smaller place now. No television existed back then to advertise all the things my parents couldn't afford to buy us, so we weren't exposed to all the things we didn't have. No one we knew had either a car or a telephone, so we didn't feel bad being without them."

Nana's story reminded me of my drive on the way to the Fashion Hut. "A few weeks ago, while driving in rural Georgia, I passed some shacks with outhouses and no running water. I was heartsick. I've never seen such poverty. The children wore hand-me-down rags, and the adults wore such hopeless expressions on their faces. The way these people lived made the Watts housing projects seem like Beverly Hills. The vision stuck in my mind. It's hard to believe people live under such horrible conditions in our country, and no one does anything to fix it. Between the southern accents, the local expressions, the food, the music, the religions, the bigotry, the poverty, the clash of people changing but wanting to stay the same, I'm like a foreign tourist in my own country."

Nana tapped her index finger on the tip of her nose. "Keep a journal. Get all your experiences down on paper. Maybe this is the reason you're in the rag biz." She arched her brow. "This must be the story you're destined to write."

Chapter Twenty-Three

The Jewish High Holidays were a time for family gatherings, and ours was no exception. Pots and pans covered Nana's stovetop to cook the Rosh Hashanah meal. A cast-iron hand crank grinder sat on the countertop. The kitchen table held a set of brass candlesticks, china, silverware, and cloth napkins stacked on it. Bags of groceries, pink bakery boxes, and bottles of kosher wine jammed Nana's kitchen counters.

I did a one-eighty around the crowded narrow kitchen. "Where do you want me to start? We'd better get going or dinner will never be ready in time."

Nana pushed a stuffed shopping bag into my hands. "First, help me put all the groceries away to make room to work on the counters. Then I'll prepare the gefilte fish. Your dad already made the horseradish from his grandmother's recipe. He is so excited to contribute something from his family."

I pointed to the grinder and held my nose. "Nana, I don't understand why you insist on still making gefilte fish from scratch. It's so much work, and the house is gonna stink for a month. Why not just buy the prepared fish in the jar like everyone else?"

Nana smiled indulgently. "Because, sweetheart, our traditions are handed down from mother to daughter. They must be continued, so we Jews never forget who we are. The only way we never forget is by remembering the place we came from."

I rewarded her with a major eye roll. "Nana, how buying prepared gefilte fish diminishes Jewry is beyond me. Believe me, the family tradition of making gefilte fish by hand is gonna die with you. I can assure you, my mother is not gonna do it. And if you see me or Sandy doing it, you really are blind."

Nana stood her ground. "It might not be something worth continuing to you, but let me tell you something. You stop doing one thing, and then another, and each time, it gets easier. Over time, being a Jew will have little or no meaning at all with no Jewish traditions to fall back on and get us through tough times. Why celebrate the Jewish New Year at all since we already celebrate the New Year on January first?"

Nana's voice rose several octaves, and her cheeks flushed bright pink. "*Six million* of our people, including many in *our family*, were murdered at the hands of the Nazis. To stop practicing our traditions is to say every one of those lives meant nothing at all." Nana shook her head. "Sorry, kiddo, not on my watch. Maybe on yours. You'll have to make that choice for yourself, and then you'll have to live with it."

I arched my eyebrows at the intensity of her retort. "Nana, we're talking grinding fish. Not forgetting the Holocaust."

Nana shook her head and sighed. "Let's just say I prefer the way my ground fish tastes." Nana dipped her head. "Anyway, lucky for you, only one person can make the gefilte fish. Peel and dice the carrots and potatoes while the oven is preheating for the brisket. After you're finished cutting up the vegetables, polish Mama's candlesticks. The polish is under the sink."

I surveyed the packed counters and grinned. "We'd better move our tushes, or we'll be sending out for a pizza, and it won't go too great with your gefilte fish."

\*\*\*\*

My sister, Sandy, a court reporter in Tampa, arrived at noon. In typical male fashion, our brother Jerry, a Blackjack dealer on a three-day cruise ship casino, arrived in time to eat. In addition to the grandkids and my parents, Nana also included her cousin, Minnie, and her husband Moe. Minnie is one of my grandmother's last living cousins, and a treasured tie to her past.

Sandy and Jerry took one step into Nana's apartment and wrinkled their noses. No words were necessary. The three of us broke into hysterics. Minnie's and Moe's expressions asked: "What's so funny?" How to explain? Clueless, we merely shrugged.

Minnie called into the kitchen, "Rae, do you need any help?"

Nana's disembodied voice replied, "Absolutely not. Holly and I finished everything today."

\*\*\*\*

Nana's dining room table was gorgeous. Fit for a king set in its splendor with her good china, sterling silver, and crystal for the holiday meal. Once everyone got seated, Nana tied a scarf on her head, lit the candles in the gleaming candlesticks, and waved her hands over them as she closed her eyes and chanted the prayer. She finished, beamed a beautiful smile around the table, and clapped. "Good Yuntif, everyone!"

We all chorused back, "Good Yuntif!"

Loosely translated, happy holiday.

I pointed to the candlesticks. "Nana, how old are the candlesticks? They must be antiques."

Nana nodded. "My grandparents gave them to my parents as a wedding gift. They were the only personal things my mother could take with her when she left Warsaw."

"They're not very big. She must have had a really small suitcase."

Nana gazed at the candlesticks, and the memory brought a wistful twist to her lips. "A beautiful young woman, my mother. She was like a Jewish Sophia Loren, and crazy in love with a handsome man. She wanted to marry for love and fought her parents against an arranged marriage. They finally relented, but Mama was devastated after being jilted at the altar. No one ever discovered the missing groom's fate. Had he run away with another woman or been killed in a pogrom? He disappeared into thin air."

Nana surveyed the table. "In those days, to be supported, a young girl had to marry. My father is the man Mama's parents arranged the marriage with. He was a tailor. His profession made him a desirable catch. After Mama was left at the altar, the community considered her damaged goods. But my mother was so beautiful that even after she had rejected the arrangement, my father still agreed to marry her."

"Once they married, things became even worse than ever for Polish Jews. After one of the bloodier pogroms, my parents decided to leave Poland via the Jewish underground. This was a network of brave souls throughout Eastern Europe who helped Jews escape. My father went first. He made his way across Europe and then north to Birmingham, England, where he took a job sewing the coal miners' uniforms. He saved his money, and after two years, he sent for my mother. She received word and had to be ready to leave quickly. Can you imagine saying goodbye to your parents, siblings, and friends, realizing you might *never* see them again?"

My heart clenched as I glanced at my parents and siblings.

"Anyway," Nana continued, "A man came to their shtetel at midnight on a moonless night. My mother could only take one small knapsack that held some clothes, a family photo, and the candlesticks. She bid her family goodbye, and the man took her to the narrowest part of the wide Warsaw River, which was infamous for its dangerously strong currents. If you weren't familiar with the way they ran, you'd be pulled under by the current and drown. My mother climbed on the man's back, and he swam her across. On the other side, he handed her to the next underground person. She slept in forests and caves during the days and traveled either by horseback or on foot at night. It took her over two months to travel this way across Europe. She arrived at Calais and boarded a freighter to England, and finally reunited with my father."

I applauded like I would at the end of a play. "Oh, Nana, what a story. It could be a movie or a play."

Nana smiled. "Yes, it has all the drama of a film or a play. Most of all, it's a story of choices. The fabric of our lives is woven by the choices we make, and our lives are defined by them. To make those choices, you must have the wisdom to understand when a window closes on us, God opens a door. But you must also have the vision to see the door, the courage to grasp the handle, open it, and step across the threshold to the next stage in your life. God provides us with the signposts, but it's up to us to take the steps, and travel down our own path of life."

I pointed to the candlesticks. "Nana, when I get married, I want those candlesticks to be your wedding gift."

Nana patted me on the cheek. "Consider them yours."

**** 

The unmistakable smell of Gefilte fish wafted from the kitchen as Nana brought the platter to the table. Nana pointed the serving fork at Dad. "Mike made the horseradish special for us tonight. It's his grandmother's family recipe." Nana focused her eyes on me. "Another family tradition is adopted."

Jerry snickered at Dad. "So how many days did it take you to make it? If it's anything like your *world-famous pasta sauce*, it must have taken all week."

Sandy cracked up and pointed at Dad. "And Mom must have hired an industrial cleaning crew afterward since you always leave the kitchen as if a bomb hit it." She waggled a finger at Dad. "Don't dare deny it. We've all seen you in action in the kitchen, and it isn't pretty."

Dad gave Sandy and Jerry an indignant purse of his lips. "No, Mr. and Miss Smarty Pants. It took a day, not a week, to prepare, nor did I destroy the kitchen. Mom bought the recipe ingredients while I was away, and I made it once I got home."

Sandy fluttered her fingers at Mom. "Tell the truth. You called in an industrial cleaning crew, right?"

Mom dipped her head. "Nope. Considering the chef, the kitchen survived intact."

Jerry snickered, "How much did *you* do?"

Mom smiled. "Other than buying the ingredients, not a single thing. This is *all* Dad's doing. He gets one hundred percent of the credit."

Nana passed the fish platter to Dad. He took a portion and passed the platter and soon everyone helped themselves. Dad slathered the fish with the horseradish and lifted his fork. "All right, smart alecs. The proof is in the cooking. So, cut the wisecracks and dig in."

We all piled the horseradish on top of the fish, forked a piece, and chewed. Everyone but Dad spit the fish into our napkins and ran for the kitchen screaming for water, pushing one another out of the way.

We recovered from Dad's fire-breathing hot horseradish, but of course, my siblings and I have never eaten the stuff again.

Chapter Twenty-Four

After the holidays, the nonstop busy Miami market was a rousing success and wiped me out. The idea of driving back to Atlanta made me dizzy, but I couldn't put it off any longer. As I approached the state line sign *"Welcome to Georgia,"* it still didn't read welcome home. I passed another sign a few miles up *"Valdosta 20 Miles"* next to a billboard *Welcome. There are no strangers in Valdosta.* What to do? Stop and call on accounts, or drive through to Atlanta? No doubt Dad would stop and call on accounts, even without appointments. My conversation with Nana floated in front of me on the road ahead. Time to take her advice and make a life for myself. I drove past the Valdosta exit and headed north.

****

I gulped standing at the exterior of the singles bar and considered a U-turn. I shook it off. I was too ashamed to go home. I grasped the door handle, but big girl panties or not, I stood rooted to the spot. If I stayed in front of the door long enough, someone might mistake me for a greeter. This seemed like a much better idea while I was driving back from Miami. Now, it's just cheesy, cheap, and desperate. I headed back to my car, but something made me stop and notice all the people my age entering. The consequence of regret Nana warned of weighed heavily on my mind. If I never went in, I'd never know one way or the other. What's the worst thing to happen? I don't meet anyone or feel like a two-bit floozy? Natalie Schlivnik's Philosophy 101 bubbled up. "So, who cares? I'll never see these people again."

I made a bargain with myself. Go to the bar, drink a glass of wine. Listen to music and try to fit in. After an hour, if I hated it, I'd go home. Then I could say I'd given Nana's idea a shot, and it sucked. As if she stood behind pushing me to the entrance, I muttered, "Fine, fine. I'm going. I'm going."

No fool, I walked in with my right foot first and spied a packed bar. The din of conversation buzzed loudly like a swarm of angry bees. Music played, but it was impossible to hear it above the white noise of chatter.

Despite being jostled and shoved to the side, I pushed my way to the bar. I leaned over the edge and yelled to flag down the closest bartender, but either he didn't hear me or chose to ignore me. Two other bartenders tossed bottles back and forth to one another and slid drinks down the bar center. I put my purse on the bar as a catcher's mitt to stop the slide of any more drinks until one of the bartenders noticed me. Remarkably, the closest bartender still ignored me as three full mugs of beer careened their way toward my purse.

The crowd surged, and I lost my balance and a grip on my purse. A hand reached from behind my back and moved my purse out of the way of the beers. I recovered my balance and slammed my fist down on the hand. I turned around to see the culprit attached to the appendage. I yelped, "Hey! You better get your damned hands off my purse right now, or I'll call the cops!"

A clean-shaven guy of medium height, slight build, with dirty blond curly hair yanked his hand back. He cradled his paw and yelled over the din. "Hey, for someone your size, you pack a helluva wallop." He flexed his fingers and grimaced. "You may have broken my index finger."

I treated him to my death ray glare. "Serves you right. What the hell were you doing?"

He gave me an industrial-sized eye roll. "Obviously, trying to save your purse."

I sniffed my annoyance. "Neither my purse nor I required saving."

He grinned, and two cute dimples cratered his cheeks. "Cudda fooled me. I'm Peter. Can I buy you a drink?"

Chapter Twenty-Five

Between going to Miami and traveling my territory, I hadn't been home much the last few weeks. My roommates and I normally passed like ships in the night. I enjoyed the rare pleasure of sitting in our living room sharing a glass of wine with Karen and David. My heart clutched as they sat close together holding hands. We toasted their engagement, and David smiled. "Karen and I are having a little get-together at my apartment next Saturday night. Casual. A group of both our friends to share food, drink, and some music to celebrate our engagement. No gifts, no party games. Just a few friends getting together. We'd love you to come."

While my singles bar adventure ended up better than expected, bar hopping as a means to meet people turned me off. Beyond a twinge of being a floozy, one of the biggest obstacles is I don't care for the taste of most liquor. So, if a way to meet people without hanging out at a bar existed, count me in. "It's so nice of you to include me. I'd love to come. Tell me the address, what time to show up, and what I can bring."

Karen seemed genuinely thrilled. "Oh, Holly, we're both so glad you'll come. I wish Ellen would too, but she's not interested. Party starts at 7:30. Just bring your smile and a big appetite. David is barbequing his world-famous ribs."

\*\*\*\*

I left my car in the guest parking lot and made my way to the outside of a two-story stucco apartment building on a tree-lined winding street almost a duplicate of ours but on the other side of the Chattahoochie river. A short flight of six steps led to David's second-floor apartment. A sign taped to his front door read: *Welcome party animals. The door is open.*

I waved to Karen and David outside on the small patio. She held a platter filled with raw meat while David slaved over the grill.

Smooth jazz played in the background as I walked into the living room past a group of twenty people I didn't know milling around, all holding drinks and chatting. This might be a short stay after all.

The self-service bar was set up on the pass-way counter separating the living room and kitchen. There were no soft drink options. So, I poured two fingers of Chardonnay into a paper cup and took a seat on the sectional sofa in the corner.

A tall, thin, nerdy, clean-shaven guy wearing wire-framed glasses sat down at the other end of the couch. A large tray of finger food, paper plates, and napkins rested in the center of the coffee table. We grabbed the same piece of celery at the same time. We both dropped the celery and offered it to one another.

I pointed to the celery stalk. "Please, take it. I'll grab another."

Mr. Nerdy smiled tentatively. He seemed as out of place as me. He pointed to the tray. "No, don't be silly. Ladies first." He grinned and awkwardly stuck his right hand out. "I'm Charlie Wright, by the way. And you are?"

I shook his hand. "Holly Schlivnik. It's nice to meet

you. Which are you? A friend of the bride or the groom?"

Charlie pointed to the patio. "Groom. David's brother and mine were college roommates. I didn't know a soul in Atlanta when I moved here from Boston. My brother put me in touch with David. He helped me settle in, and we've stayed in touch. And you?"

I pointed to Karen standing next to David at the grill. "Karen's one of my roommates. I've never been to Boston, but I hear it's a cool city. My grandmother grew up in Boston. Wanna hear something funny?"

Charlie answered quickly. "Sure." Apparently, he was as happy as me to have someone to talk with.

"My nana's accent is interesting. She was raised in Boston but spent much of her adult life in Brooklyn, New York. She says the United States of Ameriker like the Kennedys and in the next breath pronounces coffee the same as a native Brooklyner. My grandfather's name was also Charlie. But, until I graduated college, I thought his name was *Cholly*, not Charlie because my nana pronounced it Cholly. If you don't mind me saying, you don't sound as if you're from Boston."

Charlie dipped his head. "I *was* born in Boston and spent some of my youth in Beantown, but I am a Navy brat. We moved twenty-seven times when I was growing up. We were never any place long enough for me to develop an accent." He grinned. "My parents are an interesting combination. They are the poster children of opposites attracting. My dad's family is Southern Baptist, and are from rural southern Georgia. My mother is Jewish, and her family has been in Boston for over a hundred years."

And my parents were as different as night and day? "Holy cow! Your holiday gatherings must be pretty interesting. How'd they meet?"

Charlie smiled. "Dad was stationed in Boston. Mom volunteered at a Canteen. They met at the Canteen and married six weeks later." Charlie rolled his eyes. "You can imagine the way the marriage went over on both sides. My dad's retired now, and my parents settled in Boston. They've been married thirty-nine years. And after all this time, they still can't get enough of each other."

"Wow. That's one heck of an interesting combination. I'm curious. What made you move to Atlanta?"

Charlie steepled his fingers. "After I earned my master's degree from MIT, Georgia Tech made me an offer. An attractive salary came with a great benefits package." He made a ta-da with his hands. "*And here I am, y'all!*" He wiggled his eyebrows. "My dad's brothers love to hear me talk southern. What brought you to Atlanta?"

I tipped my head. "I'm from LA. My folks live in Miami. After I graduated from college, I came to stay with them before starting grad school. Long story short: My dad's a sales rep in the apparel industry. He had a trade show in Atlanta and a family emergency in Cleveland came up during the market. He talked me into pinch-hitting for him. I wrote so many orders, that he offered me a job. The thought of more school didn't thrill me, so I accepted the job offer. And the rest is history."

He asked, "What is it you do for your dad?"

"I took over part of his territory. I'm a manufacturer's rep. A traveling saleslady."

He seemed charmed by my answer. "No kidding. Sounds pretty cool. Do you like it?"

I shrugged. "It has its good and bad points. The job itself is not difficult. It's fun most of the time. I meet interesting people, stay in hotels, eat out, and get paid for it. Sort of a paid vacation, if you squint."

He widened his eyes. "Wow. That sounds like a dream job. Sign me up." Charlie raised an eyebrow. "Which part don't you fancy?"

I dipped a shoulder. "I'm away most of the time. It's hard to have a personal life."

Charlie frowned. "Are you away for weeks at a time?"

I shook my head. "No. I'm usually gone during the week. I try to be back in Atlanta by Thursday night. If I'm not at a trade market, I'm usually home on weekends."

Charlie pursed his lips. "It doesn't sound too bad. Most people work during the week and only have weekends free."

I narrowed my eyes. He made the same observation as Nana. When had he spoken to her? "Yes, but if you're in one place and not traveling all the time, you meet people during the week. So you *have a life* during the weekends. I am home on weekends, but my roommates, David, our showroom model, and the lady in the mart sundry shop are the only people I know in the whole city."

Charlie pointed an index finger at his chest. "Now you can add me to your list." He brightened. "Say, by any chance are you a football fan?"

The nerdy guy didn't exactly have jock written across his forehead, but you can't tell a book by its cover. I nodded. "Yessir, I am. I never missed a home game in school."

Charlie rubbed his hands together. "Outstanding. The Georgia Tech team is pretty good this year. The faculty gets free tickets. We sit in our own part of the stadium, so we don't get beer spilled all over us by any crazy, drunk students. I have tickets for next week's home game against Georgia. It's going to be a great match. If you're interested, we can go to the game, and grab a bite afterward."

Maybe this engagement party would turn out interesting after all?

Chapter Twenty-Six

At the time, only two ways existed to get from Atlanta to Memphis by car. The safer route involved all interstates. But that way took eight hours going north from Atlanta all the way up to Chattanooga, continuing northwest to Nashville, then turning southwest across half of the state into Memphis.

The shorter route went northwest over the Georgia and Alabama mountains, into the flatlands of northeastern Alabama, across the north central part of the state, through the western tri-cities, and west across northern Mississippi to Memphis by traversing a series of two-lane roads the entire trip.

Coming from California, the thought of stepping foot in Mississippi for any reason scared me to death. But the more time- conscious and comfortable on rural highways I became, the braver I got. A year into traveling the territory, I chanced the shorter route on my next trip to Memphis.

I made it over the west Georgia mountains from Rome into Guntersville, Alabama, and drove down the mountains, and then through Huntsville. Going west, I picked up US 72. I drove through the tri-cities, and headed for the border. My heart hammered against my chest as I read the sign: Iuka, Mississippi 39 miles. Memphis, Tennessee 148 miles. Who came up with this dumb idea? It didn't matter. By then I had no other way to get to Memphis. I'd be at the Mississippi state line in a half-hour. Gulp.

Two signs greeted me at the border: "*Welcome to Mississippi, the Magnolia State.*" "*Welcome to Iuka, Mississippi Tishomingo County Population 3,059 home of the world-famous Iuka Mineral Hot Springs. Spend your next vacation at our restorative mineral hot springs.*" Spend my vacation? As if. I wouldn't be buried in the place.

I soon entered the *greater Iuka city limits.* While stopped at a red light, I checked out downtown. The biggest building in town, the First Redeemer Church, was built in a beautiful Greek Revival architectural style with imposing columns and a large steeple with a bell tower. My blood turned cold as I read the Wednesday event posted on the marquee on the front lawn that listed the upcoming Church activities:

All this week: Bible Camp Sign-Ups: Church office

Sunday 4:00 PM: Potluck Dinner: Church Social Hall

Tuesday 8:00 PM: Adult Bible Study Class: School Auditorium

Wednesday 10:00 PM: *KKK Meeting: Church basement*

\*\*\*\*

I obeyed the speed limits and made no stops and managed to make it through the Great State of Mississippi to Memphis without getting either arrested or lynched. The next morning, I headed to the mid-town section of Memphis.

I parked in the guest lot and entered the Casual Connection Stores lobby. I continued to the vendor reception area to sign in and get a visitor's badge. The receptionist read my name on the sign-in sheet and picked up the paging phone. "Rufus McLennan, please come to vendor reception. Vendor waiting."

The receptionist handed me a badge and a slip of paper with my meeting room number. "Rufus will be right up, Ms. Schlivnik. I've already let Pam and Cindy know you're in reception." My eyes widened in alarm. She smiled and held out a palm. "Don't worry, they'll give you enough time to set up. Give Rufus your keys and parking space number, and he'll bring your garment bags and rack into the showroom."

I thanked her and turned to see an older, stately black man with a slight limp walking slowly towards me. Clean-shaven with a full head of kinky white hair, he wore black dress pants and a black blazer with the Casual Connection logo embroidered onto the left breast pocket.

Rufus flashed a big grin with a set of bright, white teeth resembling a string of pearls. "Hello, Miz Holly. Nice to see you again. Is your daddy doin' okay? Please tell him I sent my regards. Your daddy is one of the nicest men alive. God's truth."

I smiled back, "Hi, Mr. McClennan. My dad is doing great. I appreciate you asking. I will give him your regards. He speaks highly of you too."

The older gentleman raked his white hair, and without a scintilla of irony, grinned. "Please call me Rufus. I'm too young to be called Mistah. My daddy was Mistah McClennan." Rufus held out a gnarl-fingered hand. "Let me have your keys and parking space number. Then you just go on to the meeting room. Won't take me long to fetch your garment bags and rack."

I took my keys out of my purse as we walked together. I pointed to the visitor parking lot. "Rufus, I can bring all my stuff in. I appreciate the favor, but I don't mind doing it at all."

Rufus stopped walking and said, "I'm not doin' you any favor. Bringin' your bags and rack in is *my job*. Mistah Israel and his daddy before him been payin' me to do the job for a long while now. Thanks to my job, I've been able to put food on my table, a roof over my family's heads, and my three chillen through college. My family lives a good life thanks to dis job, so if you don't mind, I'd prefer to keep doin' it."

I'd been chastened, but having this dignified older gentleman around my nana's age schlepping all my heavy stuff just seemed wrong. "I get it, Rufus. But at least let me come out and help you. I've got *a lot* of garment bags."

Rufus smiled indulgently but was firm in his reply. "No, ma'am. Folks start helpin' me, I'm gonna be outta work. Where's a man my age gonna find another job?" Rufus wiggled his index finger. "How about you give me your car keys and lemme do the job I get paid to do?"

I handed him the keys, but as I opened my wallet, Rufus put his hand out like a traffic cop. "No tips. They'se the rules, but even so, Mistah Israel pays me just fine. I've *got* a job to do if you'll just let me get on with it. I don't need handouts or special favors." He wore a grave expression and gave some good advice. "It's always best to leave a man his dignity."

Chagrinned, I pointed to my car. "All the bags except the one in the far-left corner of the trunk come in."

We went our separate ways, and I headed toward the meeting rooms past the executive offices. A disembodied voice called out my name as I walked past the largest office. "*Holly Schlivnik*! Are you trying to sneak past my office? Get your tush in here."

I entered the well-appointed office of a medium-build man in his mid-forties with the start of a small paunch. He stood and walked around his desk to greet me. He had receding, dark curly hair with a touch of gray at the temples. He possessed mischievous green eyes, and the confident smile of a successful life plastered on his full lips. I gave him a quick hug and grinned. "Hi, Marvin. No, I wasn't sneaking past your office. I planned to stop by after my meetings."

Marvin smiled warmly. "It's always good to see a Schlivnik in the building. Your dad living the good life in Miami since you're now in charge?"

I slapped the corner of Marvin's desk. "My dad might take umbrage at my being in charge. But no, he's still schlepping. Now exclusively in Florida. He's good. Probably driving my mom bonkers by being home too much. I'm sure he's cutting into too many of her opera and ballet performances with her friends."

Marvin pointed to a visitor chair in front of his desk. I took a surreptitious glance at the time and sat down. Marvin asked, "So, which lines do you two carry now?"

"The same package as last time." I held up an index finger. "Oh, I almost forgot. Dad added one line, but we don't have it for Memphis."

Marvin gave me the big eyes. "Let me get this straight. You have a line for your *entire* territory, *but not for this one particular city*?"

I dipped my head. "Since the area had no local rep before we took the line, the Dallas rep asked for Memphis, and they gave it to him. I guess it isn't fair to take it away now."

163

Marvin asked, "What line is it?"

I squirmed in my seat. "What difference does it make?"

Marvin cocked a bushy eyebrow. "I'm curious if it's one we buy or not. If it isn't, maybe we need to see it."

It wasn't a state secret. "It's a hot sportswear line, so I'm sure you buy it. It's Sweet Inspirations."

Marvin grinned. "It's one of our best-retailing lines. You bring it with you?"

I treated him to one of my perfected *duh what do you think* expressions. "Of course, I did. I have appointments in Nashville later this week."

Marvin waved an arm. "Bring it in."

I grimaced. "Marvin, I told you. *We don't have the line for Memphis.*"

Marvin ignored my reply. "I'd say you're in our office around every four weeks. We're a big account, and you take excellent care of us. We've been buying that line in New York for three years. The Dallas rep never once so much as picked up the phone to thank us for the huge orders we write, let alone come here to work with us. He demonstrates zero interest in our stores. Never once inquired how we're doing with the line, or if there are any issues or problems. The only thing important to him is his commission check." Marvin pursed his lips and pointed to the open office door. "*Bring in the line.*"

Crap. This type of situation wasn't covered during training week. "Marvin, for *crying out loud.* You're gonna get us fired. My dad is *not* gonna be happy."

Marvin swatted my concern away with a wave. "We'll see about that. Ask Rufus to bring the samples in. By the time you work with the girls, this will be all straightened out."

Oh, boy. Me and my big mouth. If we get fired, the conversation with my father would be right up there with stolen samples. Oy vey.

Three hours later, Marvin and two buyers sat facing me at a conference table. I stood next to a grid with twelve knit tops merchandised by the color story. Marvin spoke to the buyers as he pointed to three samples on the top left side. "Yes, I agree. Those three embellished styles are definitely an ad group, so make sure they're an all-chain buy. The two groups on the bottom of the grid go to the A, B, and C stores. The last grouping is quite fashion-forward. Let's test them. They go to top volume stores only."

Marvin turned to me. "When do you need these orders to make the delivery you quoted?"

I snapped out of my daze at the strange turn of events. "ASAP. If possible, all chain orders today. If you're using them as ad styles, I want to make sure they ship on time. Everything else, by next week."

Marvin stood and spoke to the women. "Make sure Holly receives the one group of ad orders today. Pam, bring the written orders to my office. I'll sign them and adjust the open to buy. Everything else on this line, and the orders for the other vendors we buy from Holly, all get written by the middle of next week." He turned to me. "Holly, come see me while Rufus is loading your car."

\*\*\*\*

I sat across from Marvin and nervously smiled. "Okay, Marvin, time to fess up. Exactly what just happened?"

Marvin shrugged and smiled like the cat who ate the canary. "Nothing much. I asked Pam's assistant to get

165

the total dollars at the cost the entire Casual Connection chain gave Sweet Inspirations for the last three years. Next, I asked for the total dollars at cost the Memphis division gave them for the same time frames. Turns out, our division wrote forty percent of the total chain dollars at cost. I called the Sweet Inspirations owner, and we enjoyed a friendly owner-to-owner chat. I explained the way the Casual Connection concept works. All divisions buy individually, but we all buy the same lines to maximize buying power and consult with each other often regarding what items and lines we are doing well with or not. I gave her the volume figures I compiled, explained we'd never met her Dallas rep, and that he'd never lifted a finger for us. I explained how splendidly you take care of us. I said that if we can't buy her line from you, we will not be buying it at all going forward. Being the astute businesswoman, Yuki said to buy her product from whomever we chose to, and she'd deal with her Dallas rep internally." Marvin grinned. "The way I see it, it all worked out great for everyone concerned."

I funneled my lips. "Everyone except for the Dallas rep. I hope you didn't get him fired."

Marvin dipped his head. "If he got fired, he can blame himself." Marvin stood and handed me my orders to indicate our meeting had concluded. "Anyway, I need to get to another meeting. Give my best to your dad. See you next time you're in town. Thanks for everything, Holly."

For the first time a customer, in fact, a powerful and important one, recognized *my* value and *demanded* to work specifically with *me*. That was the day everything changed, and there was no turning back. I crossed an invisible line, and my fledgling career shifted from newbie to standing on my own. I no longer needed a magic genie running interference for me.

****

I walked to my car still in a daze, not paying any attention to a dark-haired man around my age walking towards the Casual Connection visitors' entrance. He smiled and stopped. I smiled back. I recognized the face. But from…?

I cringed internally as he greeted me by name. He had kind brown eyes the color of chocolate candy kisses. He returned my smile, and two deep dimples cratered his cheeks. Crap, I run into a really cute guy who seems quite happy to see me, and I had no idea how we knew one another, let alone his name. I had a sinking feeling he knew it too. "Hey, Holly. Do you remember me?" Without waiting for my answer, he tapped his chest. "I'm Buddy LaValle…" I still didn't respond, so he went on. "We met at the Miami market. I work for my Uncle Miles. I'm his junior rep. I work under him the same way you work under your dad." He did a ta-da. "Don't you remember? I'm from the other LA? You're from Los Angeles, and I'm from Loosiana."

The fingers inside my memory snapped in recognition. "Hello, Buddy. Yes, of course, I remember you. We shared a good joke calling ourselves the junior schlepper brigade."

Buddy hailed from near Baton Rouge, Louisiana. His mother's older sister Pat married Dad's friend Miles in Miami. When we met at the Miami trade show, Buddy explained that he traveled the same territory as me, but we had never crossed paths on the road before.

Buddy pointed back to the Casual Connection building. "Are you finishing up or just getting started?"

I grinned. "Finished. Finally. I've been in meetings for hours. You?"

Buddy smiled. "Just finished too. I've got to go back to get a couple of my samples. One of the buyers is having her assistant take some photos. Are you finished for the day, or do you have a late appointment with another account?"

I swiped a wrist across my forehead. "I'm done for the day, thank goodness. I'm wiped out. They buy all of my lines, so coming here is always an all-day event. Are you finished for the day too?"

Buddy nodded. "Done too. Too wiped out to go for a drink? If not and you're game, let's meet up at the Peabody hotel."

I'd heard of the hotel but never been in it. "What makes the Peabody so special?"

Buddy clapped his hands. "Oh my! You're in for a real treat. The Peabody is famous for its daily late afternoon duck parade."

My jaw dropped. "Do you mean a live duck parade? Quack, quack kind of ducks?"

Buddy nodded. "Oh, yes, ma'am. Live quackers in a row. It's a real kick in the pants. A group of trained ducks comes out to the lobby every afternoon and parades in line. It's the cutest thing. Oh, come on. Say yes. It's a lot of fun."

I arched a brow. "This I must see." I pointed to my car. "I'll wait for you to get your samples and then follow you to the hotel."

I didn't know it then, but Buddy and I were destined to spend a lot more time together.

## Chapter Twenty-Seven

After we left the Peabody, Buddy and I were famished and went for barbeque at Top's, famous for its pulled pork. The storied landmark sat on the banks of the Mississippi River, nestled between the string of jazz clubs on Beale Street downtown.

I had intended to give Dad the whole Marvin/Sweet Inspiration story that night, but I arrived back at the hotel too late to call him. I figured I'd ring him in the morning, but Dad beat me to the punch. Yuki called him early the next morning. My stunned father gushed. "N'Me, you done good." Of course, in typical Dad form, he asked, "So how big was Marvin's order?"

****

Since you're only as good as your next order, we concluded our conversation, and I headed for my early morning appointment. I slowed down as I approached the outside of a large, handsomely-appointed store mid-block in the heart of funky Overton Square. Mademoiselle Shoppes was written out in bold red script above the wide plate-glass front window filled with mannequins dressed in sexy dresses.

I drove around back and rang the receiving door buzzer once, twice, three times. Maybe it was broken? I pounded on the door. Still no answer. I stood on tiptoes to peer into the tiny window on the top of the delivery door. To my surprise, the place was pitch black. I checked the appointment date and time. Right on time, to the minute. To add insult to injury, I'd confirmed this appointment with the owner herself. Twice. I rechecked the time: 8:30. I paced like an expectant father. I rang the buzzer each time I walked back to the receiving door and grew angrier by each unanswered buzz. My frustration grew with every tick of the clock.

This ditzy woman stayed in business despite herself. Lucky her husband's money had money. An oil baron, no less. Who else buys his wife a chain of clothing stores for a hobby? Maybe Letty Schopman didn't need these orders to pay her bills, but Holly Schlivnik certainly did. And I was not leaving without them. They had to open *eventually*. Dad's reminder played inside my head. *Don't get mad, get even. Get even by selling them.* An excellent game plan, Dad. Unless I strangled Letty Schopman first.

I checked my watch again. 9:20. I jabbed the buzzer again and jumped back as a young woman opened the door. She eyed me strangely and asked if I needed any help. I hid my anger with a smile. "I'm Holly Schlivnik. I had a 9:00 appointment with Letty today. She instructed me to park next to the receiving door in the back of the store at 8:30 and that someone would let me in to set up. I've been standing around for almost an hour, and now I'm late for our appointment. If you hold the door open, I'll wheel my rack in and get set up."

The woman's eyes widened. "You had an appointment *when*? We don't *ever* get in before 9:15 and Letty *never* walks in a minute before 10:00. "She dipped her head. "Are you sure this is the right date? Letty never mentioned a word. I'm so sorry you've been waitin'. I'd a come early to let you in if she told me to expect you."

I seethed with barely restrained anger, but kept my

tone civil. Don't kill the messenger. "Yes, I'm sure. Letty confirmed the appointment with me herself. Twice."

The woman tittered nervously. "As to being late, don't give it no never mind." She motioned behind her into the store. "Letty's not here yet, so you've got plenty of time to set up. By the time you're ready, she'll probably mosey in."

The woman stepped aside to let me in, and I followed her to the back of the store. Even though we were alone, she surreptitiously peered around, as though afraid of being overheard. She whispered conspiratorially. "I'll tell you somethin', but you didn't hear it from me. Letty's mind is like a sieve. She don't remember most things from one minute to another. She manages to come to the store most days, but we're always cleanin' up her messes. She places orders and don't recall where she left the order copies. Goods arrive, and we have no paperwork to check them against. We've refused shipments, and then had to pay extra for them to be re-shipped after she'd find the order copy a week later in one of her purses." She covered her mouth to contain a nervous giggle. "Good thing Mr. Schopman is so rich. Anyone else would be out of business by now."

Good grief. Judy Holliday armed with a big pencil and an endless supply of money to spend. Crap. I shook my head sympathetically. "That's awful. Hopefully, she'll arrive by the time I'm ready. Where do I set up?"

The woman shrugged. "She has no room in her office, and the stock room is packed. The only place to set up is on the sales floor. We're usually not too busy before noon, so it will be fine." She pointed to the back of the store. "Wheel your rack to the back corner."

At 10:30, a woman in her early thirties strutted towards me with a level of confidence only buckets of money buys. She sported bleach bottle-blond big hair and a figure built like a brick shithouse. Hers came equipped with a stacked rack, tight little ass, and a set of curvy swivel hips. A smokin' hot sexy package all accentuated by skin-tight, expensive clothes. Every inch of her sexy body advertised she earned her money on her back.

She waved her hand impatiently as though I'd been the one who'd kept her waiting. Letty Schopman picked up the order book, sat in a folding chair, and smiled guilelessly up at me. Channeling Marilyn Monroe, she greeted me in a breathlessly soft voice. "Good morning, Holly. I've got a busy day, so I'm glad to see you're ready to work."

I resisted the urge to take the order book out of her elegant hand and smack it over her head. The only thing preventing me? Dad's voice inside my head. *"Don't get mad, get even. The only way to get even is to sell them."*

I muttered back to him. "All right already. I got the message loud and clear, so put a cork in it."

I beamed my brightest smile and swallowed back a snarky retort. "Then let's get to it."

Dad's voice made a repetitious loop in my head as Letty constantly interrupted my presentation. She took every phone call, answered every employee question, took clothes to customers in dressing rooms, and rang up every sale. Since she appeared to do everything herself, what did she pay her employees to do?

I finally finished the Climax presentation at 12:25. I packed up the Climax samples and moved the Infinity line to the center bar. At this rate, I'd be finished presenting the lines around the time we'll be shipping the orders. I presented the first Infinity group, and Letty casually glanced at her diamond-studded designer watch. She stood up and walked towards the back of the store. She called over her shoulder, "Holly, excuse me. I'll be right back." Then she disappeared.

Annoyance tied my stomach in angry knots. But I managed to quell them by acknowledging that everybody's entitled to a potty break. I fiddled with the samples as I waited, and waited and waited until I grew tired of pacing again. I checked the time: 1:30. Must be one helluva potty break. Did she fall sick or just fall in?

I stalked to the back of the store and found the woman who'd let me in earlier. I shouldn't have taken my anger at Letty out on her employee, but I couldn't control my temper any longer. I growled. "Excuse me. Where the hell is Letty? First, she's an hour and a half late for our appointment. She has a bazillion interruptions, and it takes almost two hours to go through my first line. I present the first group from the second line, and then she excuses herself. She said she'd be right back an hour ago, and then she's never to be seen again. Did she get abducted by aliens?"

If her mouth dropped open any farther, the poor woman's jaw would have hit the ground. She squawked. "Good gravy! You're still here? She said she'd be *right back*? Letty left an hour ago. She and her husband have a standing lunch date every Wednesday at 1:00 at his club."

**** 

Back at the hotel that night, I called Dad to relay the story. But through my guffaws, I could barely spit the words out. "Nope. I swear I'm *not* making this up. The woman *really* left me standing in the store in the middle of us working to meet her husband for lunch. Yep. She was gone over two and a half hours. You're damned right I waited for her to come back to the store. No, I didn't leave the store without them. Of course, I got mad. But I also got even. You won't believe the size of these orders."

Chapter Twenty-Eight

*Two Months Later*

Catching an elevator in only twenty minutes gave cause to rejoice while fighting the mob of buyers that invaded the Atlanta Apparel Mart the first day of spring market week. Buyers packed the aisles so tightly that the floors appeared covered by a human carpet. All vying for coveted seats in showrooms so jammed, you'd think the reps were giving the stuff away.

When the Slinky showroom filled to the rafters with no place to sit or even stand, dozens of Teddy's customers spilled into our showroom. By mid-afternoon, I'd lost count of the number of stores we worked with. Lunch or a potty break? Not a chance.

With buyers crammed in as snug as sardines in a tin, individual sample requests were impossible. Cora Lee took a play out of Teddy's gamebook and scheduled the three other girls to come out in a continuous loop modeling pre-set styles.

With the chaotic hoopla drowning out normal conversation, no one paid any attention to Chase Kaplan standing in front of our showroom door until he cupped his hands into a megaphone, and shouted. "Mike Schlivnik, scrounge of the Earth, the dog of all dogs! You should be ashamed of yourself."

The crowded showroom went from a loud buzz to as silent as a cemetery. Everyone turned around in lockstep to face him and stared gape-mouthed as the guy panned the room and rambled on. "I'm in downtown Birmingham. I see a runaway rollin' rack across 18th Street. So, I spring into action. Run across the street and stop the rack in its tracks. I'm tryin' to find the owner, and all of a sudden, the rack starts movin' all by itself again. I say, 'How in the hell?' and grab the rack tight an' stop it again. No sooner does it stop, it starts rollin' again. I grab it tighter. Next thing, some little gnome comes around and starts yellin' to get my hands off her rack, or she's gonna get a po-liceman!"

A flush of embarrassment crept up my neck as Chase pointed his index finger at me j'accuse style. "And Mike Schlivnik, do you know *who* the little gnome was? None other than your daughter! I ask her what kinda daddy lets his little girl go out on the road alone? And lemme tell you what she answered. She called me a male chauvinist pig who ought to come into the twentieth century." He slapped his knee and snorted. "Don't it just kill all?" He waved an order pad at Dad. "You're the most brilliant sumbitch in the mart. Stroke of genius puttin' your daughter on the road." Chase applauded Dad, saluted me, took a deep bow, and walked jauntily down the aisle. All the buyers stood and gave Dad and me a standing ovation.

Well, shut my mouth.

****

To put it mildly, what a freaking crazy day. The models were exhausted, and Daddy N' Me might as well have been run over by a bus. I fought the conflicting emotions of being delirious the day finally ended, and yet sad it came to an end.

Jody and Buddy sat with us. Jody was a woman

176

now, and not the she-man like the first time we'd met. Or, maybe I got used to her? The fading Adam's apple and five o'clock shadow no longer seemed weird. Now, only her inner beauty mattered.

Teddy donated a bottle of champagne and cups embossed with the Slinky Fashions logo. The day certainly warranted a celebration. Dad lifted his cup and toasted the room.

We clinked cups and I said, "Daddy N' Me is the talk of market thanks to Chase Kaplan."

Jody clapped her baseball mitt-sized hands. "Chase sure makes one helluva an entrance! And people say *I'm* the flamboyant one! Ha. I'm gonna take some lessons from the boy."

I dipped my head her way. "It's hard enough for a six-foot-six-inch man or woman not to stick out like a sore thumb." I held out my hands in supplication. "Maybe it's better to be low-key."

Jody appraised me over the rim of her cup. "So, it's better to turn tail and run from who I am? Not say I'm proud of myself and make everything I've gone through all a waste of time?"

I had no intention to hurt my friend, but soft-soaping beliefs wasn't my style. "Eventually times will change, and people will too. Even in the south. But considering *where and the way* you live your life, *right now*, an *in-your-face attitude* is not the smartest way to go."

Jody tipped her head to the side as she considered my comments. "Time will tell. But right now, I've got to live my life the way I see fit, whether I fit into society or not."

She smiled at Buddy and me. "So, on a lighter note, when are y'all coming to B-ham?"

We chorused. "End of the month."

She asked, "Are y'all travelin' together now the way some of the other reps are startin' to do? I hear they help each other packin' lines, save money by sharin' rooms, and it's nice havin' someone to eat with on the road."

Buddy and I answered in unison. "No!"

I kept my eyes averted from Dad. This conversation ought to go over like a fart in church.

Oblivious, Jody tittered on. "Lots of reps are travelin' the same way." Jody finally caught on. She giggled and patted her cheeks. "*Travel* together, not *sleep* together! Y'all are either a couple of real prudes or tryin' not to give Mike a heart attack! So, which is it, hmm?"

Buddy cocked a brow in my direction. "Lowerin' travel expenses isn't a bad idea. Remember, it's not what you earn, it's what you keep." He held out his hands. "In the last few months, add up all the times we've run into one another. We've helped each other with our bags, met for dinner, and it was nice."

He had me there. "You're right. We do seem to travel the same routes. And it is nice eating with someone. But we have *our own rooms*. No one will believe we're only friends sharing expenses if we shared a hotel room."

Buddy's stare bordered on incredulous. "Do you make it a habit to discuss your hotel accommodations with your buyers? And who cares?" He snorted. "This coming from the same tough cookie who told Chase Kaplan to get into the twentieth century?" He smiled slyly. "Maybe you ought to take your own advice. Why not try it? The worst is it doesn't work out, and we don't do it again. Where's your next trip to?"

"Georgia coast. And you?"

Buddy nodded. "I've got no appointments yet, so the coast works fine for me. You make the hotel reservations." My eyes widened and he grinned. "Two double beds, *one room*. Let's meet at the mart early Sunday. We help each other pack, caravan to Savannah, and if we get in early enough, with all the money we're savin' on rooms, we splurge and eat at the Pirate's Paradise at the Wharf. Sound good?"

Such a dirty fighter. I loved the Pirate's Paradise, and he knew it. Put up or shut up time. I turned to Dad for direction. Not surprisingly, Dad sat tight-lipped and mum. So much for my open-minded daddy. Bet he won't ask me if I am alone during our confab at the end of *that* week. I was on my own for this one. I gulped. "Fine. We try this once and see if it doesn't weird us out. If it does, count me done. Let's be on the road by noon, so we get in before the restaurant is too crowded." I pointed my cup at Buddy. "By the way. Since this is your idea, the wine is on you."

****

I was as nervous as a long-tailed cat in a roomful of rocking chairs as Buddy and I entered the hotel room. Even if I wanted to back out, it was too late. With two conventions in town, every hotel in the city was booked solid. After we got all the samples situated in the room, Buddy changed first and came out wearing a Southwest Louisiana State University T-shirt and gym shorts. Who'd a thunk? The guy had great legs. I went in next and put on a University of California sweatsuit with the jacket zipped up to the neck.

I walked out of the bathroom, and Buddy's back was to me as he channel-surfed the TV. Typical man. He turned around and cracked up at my outfit. "Good Gawd Almighty, girl! Why not wear an overcoat in case I might see something?" He glanced at the clock radio on the nightstand that separated the two beds. "Aren't you roastin'? Past nine o'clock and it's still hotter than Haides outside. It took the air conditioner blastin' on high almost an hour to get this room cooled off. Don't you have anythin' cooler? I don't know about you, but I can't sleep if I'm hot."

I nervously fingered the neckline of the sweatsuit jacket. Crap. I sniffed. "No, it's not my normal sleep attire. But I don't normally share my hotel room with a strange man."

Buddy grinned. "I'm, not a strange man. Maybe little odd, but not strange. Besides, I'm not a stranger. Go change into somethin' cooler." Buddy held up his hand with his fingers poised like a boy scout. "I promise to close my eyes till you're in bed covered up to your eyeballs. Come mornin', you take the bathroom first and I'll close my eyes till the door is locked."

I sniffed with righteous indignation. "This is so not funny."

I almost throttled him as Buddy the jerk almost busted a gut with his guffaws. "Only thing funnier? If you were wrapped up in a garment bag."

I gave him my death ray glare. "Finally, you've come up with a good idea."

****

The end of another action-packed day. Too exhausted to go out to eat, we ordered a delivery pizza when we got into the hotel room. After we devoured the pie, Buddy channel surfed while I wrote a journal entry. Ricky and Lucy relaxing at home after a busy day.

Buddy pointed to my journal. "Do you make a journal entry every day?"

I nodded. "I try to. Some days I don't. If I'm too tired…or if nothing happened to write about. Of course, that doesn't happen too often."

He asked, "Did you write as a kid?"

I nodded. "Yes. I joined our high school paper as a freshman, and made it to Editor-in-Chief for my junior and senior years."

Buddy asked, "So you majored in journalism at university?"

Buddy turned out to be a pretty good reporter. He was doing a helluva good job interviewing me.

Pride filled my heart. "Yup. I worked my way up from cub reporter to the first female Editor-in-Chief. I won several prestigious national awards for investigative reporting on a campus test-cheating scandal." I pursed my lips. "Hard to believe I could be so naïve. I was certain that I'd be the first female editor-in-chief of a major west coast city newspaper."

My sigh came out bitter as burnt toast. "Never a possibility. I took this job with my dad after a disastrous interview with a big city paper." Buddy winced when I recounted the horrible experience. "After the managing editor explained *all the girls start in the secretarial pool*, I snatched my resume and walked out." I smiled sardonically. "So, instead of writing my Pulitzer Prize acceptance speech, I'm schlepping schmatas."

I might have been selling, but Buddy wasn't buying. "But every night you record your experiences in those journals. I'm guessing someday, you're gonna write stories based on them."

When did he talk to Nana? I shrugged. "My nana says everything happens for a reason. We'll see."

Chapter Twenty-Nine

Almost three years into the job and I hadn't taken any personal time off. Before fatigue morphed into burnout, I took a week between seasons to meet up with my west coast girlfriends. When my vacation ended, I flew to Miami to prepare for the upcoming trade show. Dad greeted me at the airport as though I'd been in the depths of Africa for two years instead of a week in San Francisco. Nice to be missed, but huh? While waiting in baggage claim, he joked. "It's time to start earning money for next year's vacation. And to help the cause, I've been busy while you were away. We took on a new line. Ditsy Swimwear." He gushed. "You're going to love it!" He gave me the big eyes and hiccupped a nervous cough when I failed to join in the celebration. "Come on. Besides a bad sunburn or drowning, no one has a bad time in a swimsuit."

This is one man who can never be left unsupervised. A swimwear line? Gee whiz. Big whoop. Fine for him. His customers were almost all near water. But me? Quite another story. Dad could hardly miss my underwhelmed glare. But just in case he did, I made my position crystal clear. "Swimwear? Are you nuts? You've got Florida. Goody for you. I've got Hooterville. I have a tough enough time selling Climax dresses and not getting arrested for pedaling indecent exposure. Now string bikinis in Bible-thumping land? Good luck."

**\*\*\*\***

Two days later Dad and I sat in our Miami showroom as a man in his early thirties demonstrated the correct way to hang and merchandise bikinis. A spreading bald spot on the crown of his head highlighted his thinning, light brown curly hair. With a full beard, Rob Bachmann appeared older than his years. He wore chinos, a polo shirt, tasseled expensive loafers with no socks, and sported a pompous ass to go with his superior attitude.

He talked in a slow, condescending, annoyingly nasal tone of voice as he lectured, like he was explaining Einstein's theory of relativity to a couple of preschoolers. "*We present the line by silhouette. This means we hang all the bandeau bras together and present them as one group. We hang all the triangle bras together and present them as one group. We hang all the slide bras together and present them as one group, we...*"

Merchandising the line in such a fashion made no sense. A slow burn of righteous indignation churned in my gut. I disliked the arrogant jerk before he opened his mouth. Now I despised him.

He droned on, talking down to us in a patronizing tone, as though teaching a couple of toddlers how to build blocks. "*So we remember, we do...? We hang each piece individually, not together on one hanger, so the buyer sees all the features of each bra and trunk and...*"

I heard enough and interrupted the condescending clown midsentence. "Rob, we get it. You present the line-by-body style. You don't need to name each silhouette and repeat the same procedure over and over. This isn't rocket science. We're not landing a guy on the moon. Move on to some history already. Give us some background, some context. Which bodies retailed best? Which colors sold best, and which colorways are new? Discuss the sizing. Information we might *actually need* instead of regurgitating the same damned crap. We're a lot smarter than we look."

Dad turned white as a ghost.

The vein in the middle of Rob's forehead danced the macarena in a moment of fury. The arrogant putz couldn't fathom being interrupted by someone so obviously inferior. His anger morphed into astonishment. I not only had the nerve to talk back, but the ability to think. The man was a professionally self-absorbed jerk.

I glared at Dad. What the hell were you thinking?

Rob wisely waited for a beat to get his temper under control. Dad almost fainted with relief as Rob unclenched his fists and his vein stopped pulsing. "So, the rumors are true about your reputation for speaking your mind. You're absolutely right. It's not that difficult. Instead of my lecturing, ask your questions, and I'll do my best to answer."

Once Rob pulled the enormous stick out of his ass, he proved to be quite knowledgeable, and we learned a lot. After the first day, Dad and I were confident enough to present the line. I worked with Mariel Levine from Laurie's. Mariel and Rob shared an uninterpretable moment as she gave him her thumbs up.

\*\*\*\*

The reception to the line went great in Miami, but once I got back to my territory and presented it to my buyers as instructed, their responses universally stunk. I had high hopes when I worked with one of my best accounts, but they were dashed when the Alabama boutique buyer shook her head emphatically no. "Holly, this here is a small town in the middle of no place with no lake, river, or stream, much less an ocean for a hundred miles. Where will our girls wear these little bitty bikinis to, even if their mamas let 'em out of their houses wearin' one in the first place?"

I couldn't argue the point. "You're right. The only water in town is at the high school swimming pool." I arched my brows. "But spring break and vacations do happen here. Do you want your customers to buy their swimsuits at another store *after* they get to their vacation spot, and *not* from you?"

Doreen rifled through the samples and shook her head. "This is too small a town to stock too many of the same styles. My customers don't want to see themselves comin' and goin' in the same things, especially the young girls."

It was obvious by his idiotic merchandising style, Rob had no clue how to sell to my accounts. But I did. "The problem is with the way the line is merchandised, not the product itself. Give me a minute. I've got an idea." I quickly rearranged the line into groups by print instead of by silhouette. "What if we do it this way?"

Doreen fingered the line and smiled. "Much better. Which groups are good?"

\*\*\*\*

A year made all the difference in the world. I couldn't wait for the next swim season to start. I finished hanging the new line just as Dad and Rob walked into the showroom. After Rob gave me a warm greeting, he went to the rack and started re-arranging the line by silhouette. "Let me help you put the samples in the right order."

I stood next to him and rearranged the styles he moved around. "Actually, Rob, the samples are in the right order for me. I presented the line all last season by fabric group."

Rob replied in the same condescending tone as last year. "In *Los Angeles,* we present it by silhouette. I made it perfectly clear that was the *proper way* for the line to be presented."

It took every ounce of control not to shove a bikini top down his throat. I dripped sarcasm as I mimicked his condescending tone. "Well, Rob, I presented it to my accounts the way you do in *Los Angeles,* and guess what? My accounts out in *Hooterville* hated it. If I held a gun to their heads, they bought a few tops and a few bottoms presenting it your way just to shut me up. The orders were so small, they didn't meet your minimums, let alone add up to enough dollars-worth of my time to open the garment bags." I jutted my chin. "Rob, are you happy with the business I wrote this past year?"

Rob's face lit up bright as a Christmas tree. "Are you kidding? Your numbers are off the charts." I rewarded Rob with my sweetest smile. "Then if you're so damned happy with my business, it shouldn't matter to you if I present the line in my bathrobe and slippers swiveling a hula hoop, as long as I keep writing huge orders. Now, should it?"

Dad's expression turned apoplectic as he waited for Rob to pack up the line and walk out.

Rob took a couple of beats before answering. "Holly, you're one hundred percent right. Present the line with the bras upside down and trunks inside out if you want. Just keep those orders coming."

Dad fanned himself with an order book.

Chapter Thirty

Nana turned seventy-five on October 21st. Hard to believe she'd been alive three-quarters of a century. A thrilling milestone to reach, but shocking that she was so old. With her gray hair and age-spotted hands, outwardly she appeared the same as your typical Miami senior citizen, but my sharp-as-a-tack nana was no doddering old lady.

Because this one celebrated a landmark birthday, my parents planned one helluva party. Nana and I sat in her kitchen drinking coffee and kibitzing the morning of her big bash. What went through her mind? I tried to ask the question subtly. "So, are you excited about your party? This is quite a milestone."

Nana smiled sardonically. "Yes and no. I'm certainly happy being around to celebrate seventy-five years of living, but to tell you the truth, it's also kinda sad. I'm now at the age your mortality hits you over the head every day." Nana waved her hands like a magician doing abracadabra. "One day you're in the supermarket squeezing the cantaloupes and the next day, poof, you're gone."

She was right, but I softened the blow. "All the more reason to celebrate life every day."

Nana sighed. "Ethel Cohen's husband died last Sunday night. They had the funeral Tuesday. You get to be my age, you expect your peers to start dying off. But when it happens, it still comes as a shock."

A twinge of pity twisted my heartstrings. Ethel is a nice lady, and now she is alone. "Gee, that's awful. Had he been ill?"

Nana dipped her head. "No. He was the picture of health Sunday morning. But by Sunday night, he was dead as a doornail. He folded with a losing poker hand. He threw his cards down, fell face-first into the stack of chips, and keeled over dead." She snorted. "Maybe he tried to take it with him." She covered her mouth with a napkin, as if she could shove the words back in. "Oh, my God. Listen to me making jokes. The poor guy is dead, and I'm making fun. Only a terrible person finds it funny hearing someone died. "

I bit my lip not to join her since I reacted to death the same way. "Oh, Nana, you're not a terrible person. Death is the unknown, and it's so final. You're a person so full of life that the concept of death is scary. Making jokes is a nervous reaction to it. It's a way to control something uncontrollable."

Nana stopped to wipe her eyes. "You must be right. At the funeral, all of Ethel's friends sat together. Her daughter gave a moving eulogy. Everyone else was crying, and I had the giggles."

Nana rolled her eyes. "Naturally, I sat right in the middle of the row. So, getting up and leaving as if I needed to go to the ladies' room wasn't an option. I was trapped like a rat. I had no idea what to do. I tried everything imaginable to distract myself enough to keep my reaction under control. First, I opened the prayer book and pretended to pray. I fidgeted in my seat. I bent over as if trying to find something I dropped. I tried focusing on a spot on a wall. I tried moving my eyes up and down, but nothing worked. I was drawn to this eulogy like a moth to a light bulb. The same way you can't take your eyes off a really bad car accident, even if you want to."

Nana cackled again, only harder. I bit my cheek so I wouldn't too. She threw her head back and howled. "Oh, my God. Listen to me! I can't even tell the damned story without cracking up!" She took off her glasses and swiped at the tears dribbling down her cheeks with the back of her hand. "I'm trying to be respectful, but the only thing in my mind's eye is Mary Tyler Moore standing on the podium eulogizing Chuckles the Clown." Nana asked, "Do you remember the episode?"

I nodded. "I'll never forget it. One of the funniest TV episodes I've ever seen. Mary got two words of the eulogy out and collapsed in a hysterical fit. She'd try to apologize and, instead, she howled even louder."

Nana tapped her lips. "At first, I giggled once or twice. But, once the image of Mary giving the eulogy lodged into my head, it was all she wrote. I stuffed a handkerchief in my mouth. Once the part when Mary sang Chuckles the Clown's theme song: *a little song, a little dance, a little seltzer down your pants* stuck in my head, I swear, I almost wet *my* pants. All my friends must be convinced that I lost my mind. With no way to explain myself, thank God Ethel and her family had their backs to me." Nana stopped joking and shivered. "I've never told this to anyone. The idea of dying without a clue of what happens next or where I go terrifies me."

That my fearless nana was afraid of *anything* stunned me, let alone the specific fear. We never discussed it, but I was afraid of the same thing. Crap. Genetics are not what they're cracked up to be.

Nana chuckled. "So, I am scared to death of death. The old children's song, the worms crawl in, the worms crawl out keeps playing in my head. Please promise me when I die, you'll make sure…"

Whoa! This is not a subject I wanted to discuss. Not then, not *ever*. So, I maturely put my hands over my ears and started singing out loud. Nana pried my hands off my ears and put her index finger on my lips. I resisted the urge to bite her finger. "Nana, I do not want to discuss this. Tell my mother your wishes, not me. In my mind, you're going to live forever, and you'd better. I can't imagine surviving your death. I don't want to live without you."

Nana put her arms around me and kissed my forehead. "While I hope to live to be a hundred years old or more, when I do go, believe me, you will survive. Kiddo, life goes on even if you can't imagine how. Remember, we Jews believe life is for the living. We mourn our dead quickly and resume living our lives. We honor and remember our dead, by living."

Nana smiled. "Listen, let me tell you the way I want things done now since it's too late once I'm dead. Promise you'll make sure they bury me with my glasses on, my false teeth in my mouth, lipstick on my lips, and make sure I'm wearing a snazzy outfit…something in red…" Nana patted her hair. "My beautician advised that bright colors like red are great with my gray hair." I crossed my eyes, and Nana gave me that over-the-glasses stare of hers. "Hey, dead is forever, and I wanna be my best for the long haul. Oh and before I forget, there's one more thing. I want *you* to give my eulogy."

Whoa. I sputtered like a car engine running out of gasoline. "M-Me? Isn't the eulogy for Mom to do? She *is* your daughter. after all."

Nana gave me the big eyes. "Are you kidding? First of all, your mother will be too much of a mess to get in front of a crowd and talk. Second of all, I trust you to make sure they celebrate my life, and not mourn my death, by reminding them how great it is to be alive. How important it is to love and laugh, and how much a gift life is. You're the perfect one to give my thoughts a voice. Accomplish that, and I promise I *will* be with you forever."

So much for a bottle of Tabu. Gee, Nana. How do I tie a bow around *that* birthday present?

In retrospect, I understood the reason she chose me to do the honors. I *was* her in so many ways.

Party on!

Chapter Thirty-One

With Buddy in Louisiana for a family bash, I'd be traveling on my own all week. After a wildly successful three-hour appointment, I left Abboud's Department Store in La Grange, Georgia with a huge stack of orders. I couldn't have asked for a better meeting or outcome than the one with Freddy Abboud, yet my heart ached as I left his office. Why? My breath caught with how much happier the times were when Buddy and I were together. Oh boy. Thank goodness for a packed schedule with no time to wander into *that* dangerous territory.

Just under an hour later, I passed the highway sign *Welcome to Columbus, Georgia Home of Ft. Benning*. I cruised through downtown to the Casual Connection Columbus division corporate headquarters housed in a new industrial park on the outskirts of the city.

I signed in at the vendor registration desk and received a visitor's badge. Then I went down the hall to the executive wing and entered a fancy office decorated with framed photos of Casual Connection store locations on the walls. A short, slightly-built man in his early fifties stood up from behind a large mahogany desk and greeted me more like an old friend than a sales rep. Impeccably dressed Sam Sechler stood ramrod straight with the confident posture of a successful man.

Sam impishly grinned. "Holly gal, I talked to Marvin Israel. He said he called the owner of Sweet

Inspirations while you were in his office, and now you're handlin' the Casual Connection account for all our divisions, including his."

Such a bunch of Yentas. No wonder Dad loved them. These guys were all cut from the same cloth. I gave him the big eyes. "It turned out fine, but he just as easily could have gotten us fired! Imagine me having *that conversation* with my dad?"

Sam smiled warmly. "It's quite a compliment. Your daddy must be so proud. Listen, come on back after you're finished workin' with my buyers. Still comin' over for dinner tonight, right? Becky's been fussing in the kitchen all day. Our boy Junior came over from Troy this afternoon, so he'll be joinin' us."

I nodded. "I'm planning on it."

Sam rubbed his hands together and smiled like a shark. "Junior is right pleased to finally be meetin' you. He's heard a lot about you."

Internal alarm bells rang loud in my head. Mike Schlivnik's signature of interference was all over it, but I didn't want to be disrespectful to Sam, so, I plastered a smile on my kisser. "It'll be nice meeting him too. He's coming in from Troy? Is he there on company business?"

Sam smiled wistfully. "No. Junior isn't with Casual Connection." Sam sucked in his cheeks as if he'd swallowed a lemon. "He's a math instructor at Troy State."

Huh? Junior is the heir apparent to a huge, successful company, and he'd rather teach math at a second-tier university in a dipshit town in Alabama? The guy had to be crazy. My heart went out to Sam. I struggled to come up with something positive to say. "Wow, math instructor. He must be pretty smart. I was doomed after long division." I smiled. "Maybe he'll end up company CFO."

Sam shook his head ruefully. "I'm afraid it's not in the cards. He's never been interested in the store. The only thing important to him is gettin' tenure. But since it's my own fault, I can't complain. Raise your children to be independent, a parent can't turn around and penalize them when they do what you taught them to do, just because they choose a path you wish they hadn't gone down."

I dipped my head. "Funny, my mother says the same thing."

****

The next night my report to dad regarding dinner with the Sechler's dripped sarcasm. "My evening last night was utterly *fascinating*."

"Oh really? A fascinating evening? Doing what?"

Even though he couldn't see me, I still rolled my eyes. "Oh, don't play dumb. My dinner at the Sechler's that *you and Sam* arranged. You two Yentas conspired to throw his son and me together in a rather transparently pathetic effort to fix us up."

He sputtered his denial, but I interrupted with a snicker. "Don't bother denying it. I've been to this rodeo before. Let me tell you something, Mr. Nosy. If Sam's son and I ever had even a remote interest in one another, last night sure killed it. Junior has a personality as exciting as tapioca pudding, but he seems like a nice guy. I'd be able to tell more about him if he uttered more than three sentences all evening."

I quipped, "Of course, it required his father to stop answering my questions for his son. Picture conversing with Paul Winchell and Jerry Mahoney. No wonder

Junior ran away to Troy. I'm surprised he didn't keep going. With a pushy father like Sam, an ocean between them wouldn't be far enough. Sam's son and I have nothing in common but nosy fathers who can't mind their own business. Believe me, Junior is no more interested in me than I am in him." Annoyance crept into my tone. "Do me a favor, and let me be in charge of my love life. I don't need any help from you. You trusted me enough to hire me. Trust me enough to run my own life."

\*\*\*\*

Nothing but peanut farms as far as the eye could see. Most of southern Georgia is a string of small towns connected by 4H Clubs and silos.

I pulled into the Junior Junction parking lot in Albany, Georgia mid-afternoon. One of the larger regional burgs, compared to other places in the southern part of the state where I had accounts, Albany appeared as cosmopolitan as New York City. Once I finished working with Warren and Jack Mossman, the southern Georgia swing to the "Jewish Mafia" as Dad called them, would be complete.

Hopefully, Yenta Schlivnik didn't ask Warren to introduce me to one of his cousins. I wouldn't put it past my nosy dad to suggest Warren set me up with the only Jewish peanut farmer in the state.

\*\*\*\*

After packing up my samples, I popped into Warren's office to thank him for the humongous orders his buyers wrote. He motioned me to take a seat. A stab of fear pierced my gut. Buyer's remorse? As it turned out, my business with Warren was on the line. But for a completely different reason.

Out of the blue, Warren announced he, his dad, Sam

Sechler, Marvin Israel, and the other Jewish merchants in the South had a big charity fundraiser planned in two months. and that as soon it was finalized, he'd be discussing it with all his suppliers. He gave no details. He made no donation request, nor did he reveal the name of the charity. Nothing to set my alarm bells off. Yet I left Warren's office with an inexplicable uneasiness churning in the pit of my stomach.

Several days passed since the last time I spoke to Peter. Guilt squeezed my heart. But after we greeted one another, I regretted dialing his number. "Peter, I'm sorry. I do know this company dinner means a lot to your career."

Peter whined, "You promised."

I sighed. "No. I said I'd try."

Peter's voice dripped sarcasm. "Like you even tried."

I rolled my eyes. "Of course, I tried." With some effort, I pushed the annoyance bubbling up from my gut back down. "I'm sorry, but I couldn't re-arrange the rest of my week. I work with buyers when they're able to see me. It's not at my convenience. It's at theirs. Be reasonable. I'm over two and a half hours away."

Peter snapped like a cranky croc. "If I was a buyer, you'd find a way to make it happen."

"I'm sorry you feel that way." Exasperation laced my tone of voice. "For crying out loud. You act as though I *purposely* tried to ruin this for you."

He spat. "Obviously, I'm just not that important to you."

It was time to end the conversation before I said something I'd regret. "My day is packed tomorrow, and I've gotta get some sleep. I'll call you when I'm home."

Peter snapped. "Do that. We need to talk."
No kidding. "You're right. We do."

Chapter Thirty-Two

*Two Months Later*

I stood next to Warren Mossman in the Junior Junction showroom as he fingered the Ditzy swimsuits on the grid. "This fashion show fundraiser is gonna be a huge event. The Jewish Federation, The Anti-Defamation League, and The United Jewish Appeal are just a few of the organizations gettin' behind it. Our local B'Nai B'rith, and Hadassah are providin' models. The southern Georgia Jewish Retailers Association is workin' with suppliers to provide the apparel we're gonna auction off after the fashion show. Food and beverages are bein' provided by The Fetterman Catering Company. Liquor and wine has been donated by Schwartzman Spirits. The affair will be held in the Temple Emanuel Activity Center."

I pointed to our samples on the grid. "We're pleased to be a part of it. I'll make sure the LA office sends all size seven bikinis by the beginning of next week, so the models can try them on and trade around to see which styles are best on which models."

Warren bunched his shoulders. "Those organization models are not professionals. Will you work with them backstage the night of the event? You're the only female rep we work with. We need an industry pro makin' sure the girls don't come out on stage with the dresses inside out or the swimsuit tops on upside down!"

I raised my brows. "Believe it or not, I've seen professional models do the same thing. No problem, Warren. I'm glad to help."

Warren grinned. "Wondaful. Sam and Marvin are donatin' gift bags. This is gonna be one of the biggest fundraisers in the history of the state."

I asked, "Which charity is the fundraiser for? If retailers from outside the state are pitching in, it must be a national."

Warren eyed me strangely. "Holly, you're confused. This isn't for any *charity*. It's a *political* fundraiser. We're tryin' to raise money for the State of Israel."

Oh, Boy. Nana always said what the first three letters of *ass*uming make you. How would Rob take this? Crap. What if he backed out? "When you asked if we'd participate in a fundraiser, I assumed it was for charity, and that's what I told my boss." I held out my hands in supplication. "It's one thing asking for a donation to a charitable event. It's quite another asking to donate money to a country. I'll see if he still wants to participate."

To my utter astonishment, Warren asked, "Is your boss Jewish?"

Huh? "Yes he is, but so what? This is a political fundraiser."

Warren smiled slyly. "You're dead wrong. It has *everything* to do with being Jewish. We better take care of our own because no one else is gonna. *Never again* means we Jews gotta stay strong with a strong Israel. What's the best way to keep the homeland strong? Cash is king. So, call your boss and explain to him the reason we're tryin' to do our part."

It made sense, but I was only the hired help. "I'll do

my best, but it's not my company."

Warren made the consequences clear. "Lemme be blunt. The suppliers who support this effort are the ones we'll be supportin' with continued business."

Crap. Being a rep just became a lot more complicated.

\*\*\*\*

My eyes bugged as I peeked out of the closed stage curtain to check the crowd size. Jack Mossman, Marvin Israel, and Sam Sechler roamed the standing-room-only packed house, glad-handing the attendees and collecting donations as fast as the envelopes were handed out.

The house lights dimmed and the music stopped. Dressed to the nines in an expensive tuxedo, the television game show host wannabe jumped on stage and grabbed a microphone. "Hey, y'all! I'm Warren Mossman! Welcome to a spectacular evenin' of fashion, food, and fun brought to y'all by the southern Georgia Jewish Retailers Association. I promise, y'all gonna enjoy yourselves tonight."

Warren held his hands up, rubbed his index fingers and thumbs together, and grinned. "We hope y'all know the *best way* to demonstrate your appreciation!" He waved to the closed curtain behind him. "Without any further ado, let's get the show on the road!"

Pulsating disco music blared through the loud speakers as the spotlight beam lit the place up like the fourth of July. That was my cue to shove the first three models out onto the stage. They strutted down the runway, and the audience went absolutely wild.

\*\*\*\*

Three weeks later, I made another road trip to southern Georgia. I had more business to get from one of my biggest customers, Renfrew's Fashions in Valdosta, as well as work with many of our accounts located in little towns who never attended the Atlanta markets. I left home before dawn and deadheaded to Valdosta, a good-sized town close to the Florida state line. Three and a half hours later I exited I-75 South and drove east a mile down the road from the sign: *"Welcome to Valdosta, Georgia. There are no strangers in Valdosta"*

The corporate offices of Renfrew's Fashions were located in a newly-built industrial park down the street from the Sinai Temple. I glanced at the Temple, and almost crashed my car into the curb. Yellow crime scene tape was draped around the building, and police sawhorses blocked the entrances from the street. The side of the Sinai Temple had been defaced in huge red letters: *Keep America American! Jews Get Out Now! Go to Israel and Be with Your Own Kind!* A burnt cross on the front lawn of the Temple drove the hateful point home.

I left Renfrew's three hours later and spent the rest of the afternoon with the Bellew's Department Store buyers. Valdosta is a college town populated with mainly open-minded people. The incident at the Sinai Temple was the talk of the town. Frightened by the hate crime that hit too close to home, I couldn't wait to leave.

I took US-84 and headed west to Cairo. Unlike the city in Egypt, the Cairo in Georgia is pronounced as though it were spelled Kay-ro. I approached the outskirts of Cairo after dusk happy to see the sign: *Welcome to Cairo, Georgia's Hospitality City.* It had been a long and disturbing day. I wasn't in an adventuresome mood for local fare, so I checked into my usual hotel east of Cairo's downtown and ordered room service. I picked at my meal and called it a night. I was exhausted, but the image of the defaced Sinai Temple replayed like a scene from a horror movie every time I closed my eyes. A few hours of fitful sleep was all I could muster.

****

After a restless night with a modicum of sleep, I checked out and packed the samples into the car. I drove the three miles to Main Street to see Al Cohen. Al and I had chatted briefly at the charity fashion show. Naturally, he left his appointment calendar at home that night, but he said I didn't need an appointment. Just to come into the store whenever I got into the area, and he'd make time for me. I don't usually travel without appointments. But with Al? I never worried. He was *always* in the store. He spent so much time in it, his wife Miriam joked he really lived in the store and only visited their home.

I slowed down at the art deco Zebulon Theater. Cohen's was two doors down. I pulled up to the curb in front of the store, and my jaw dropped. The shell of Cohen's Department Store stood as an indictment of the times. The abandoned store sat completely empty. No racks, no mannequins, and no merchandise inside. A hand-written sign hung haphazardly in the window: *Prices slashed. Everything Goes. No Offer Refused. Store Closing. Lost Our Lease*. A message written in angry red letters scrawled on the side of the store: *Keep America American! Jews Get Out Now! Go to Israel and Be with Your Own Kind!*

I tried calling Al, but no one answered at his home. I prayed he and his family were safe. It was impossible to imagine Cairo without Cohen's Department Store. It was one of the oldest retail stores in the state. Al Cohen's family had been in southern Georgia continuously serving the retail needs of the citizens of Cairo decades before the Civil War. Cairo is a small town, and Cohen's was my only account. I couldn't bring myself to prospect a replacement. The open wound throbbed too raw.

I drove north on U.S. 319 headed to Tifton. Seymour Friedman might be able to see me earlier. I drove under the I-75 overpass and headed east. On the outskirts of Tifton, the sign read: *Welcome to Tifton, Georgia. The Friendly City*. It begged the question: Is Tifton still friendly? I drove past the Abraham Baldwin Agricultural College Campus and took the downtown exit east.

Friedman's Department Store anchored all the other stores on Main Street. I pulled in front of the store at the end of the block and burst into tears. The only thing left of the burnt-out store was the foundation and a couple of mangled mannequins laying on a bed of broken glass like corpses on a funeral bier. The remnants of a scorched cross embedded in the foundation along with a sign on a post hammered into the grass in front of the store read: *Keep America American! Jews Get Out Now! Go to Israel and Be with Your Own Kind!*

Why bother calling Seymour? I doubt he'd answer his phone. Besides, what would I say? I had no adequate words. I drove past the once Friedman's Department Store and asked myself why I ever moved to the south?

I took the U.S. 82 west under the I-75 overpass and headed for Albany. I needed answers. What kind of Pandora's Box had Warren Mossman and his cronies opened? An armed guard stood in front of the newspaper kiosk outside Warren's corporate office. The headline above the fold of the Albany, Ga. *Times Herald-Examiner* screamed *Rash of Anti-Semitic hate crimes terrorizes Jewish communities of southern Georgia!*

I bought a paper and went into the lobby. I didn't bother checking in at the reception desk for a badge. I marched into Warren's office unannounced, and my jaw dropped. Inside of a month, he'd aged a decade. I slapped the newspaper on his desk. Warren stared at me through haunted eyes.

Every Jewish-owned store in southern Georgia small towns had been hit, some worse than others. Sam Sechler lost two locations. Warren was one of the "luckier" ones. Six of Warren's stores had been vandalized, but none burned down. Warren reported that the few Jewish-owned stores still standing were closed until further notice and being guarded twenty-four seven. With no business to keep me in southern Georgia, I left Warren and headed back to Atlanta.

Man plans, and God laughs. Considering the catastrophic reaction the fundraiser had unleashed, never had Nana's words of wisdom rung truer. If I ever doubted it before, I had no doubts now. *This* is not the America I grew up in. Way beyond sad, way beyond frightened. I'd been shaken to my core.

****

Our business in the Carolinas and Virginias grew substantially enough for a permanent presence at the Charlotte Apparel Center. Those states weren't part of Buddy and his uncle's territory, so I'd be going to Charlotte for market week alone.

Traffic flowed relatively light heading northbound on I-85. I jolted out of the kind of reverie you easily fall into during the monotony of a solo long-distance drive by a large billboard on the south side of the interstate past the first Greenville, South Carolina exit. The billboard read: *Trouble finding reasonably priced gas and oil today? Thank the Jews. Take our country back from those who do not share our American values. Don't spend another day overpaying for gasoline. Take action.*

Fingers of fear mixed with outrage twisted my heartstrings into knots. How does one remain living in a place with hate such an accepted part of society that it is advertised on a billboard on the side of an interstate highway?

****

I was weary from the disturbing drive, but too wired to slow down. I put the pedal to the metal and arrived in downtown Charlotte about two hours later. I checked into the hotel and then went to the mart. I hung all the samples and started some market décor, when a monster headache almost felled me. I pawed through my purse for some aspirin but only found the remnants of one crushed tablet. Fabulous. Before my head exploded, I walked down the hall into the first open showroom. A young woman around my age stood hanging samples and talking to an older man.

"Excuse me," I interrupted their conversation and pointed down the hall. "I'm Holly Schlivnik. I'm in the showroom four doors down. I hate to bother you, but can you possibly spare a couple of aspirin? I've got a beastly headache, and my cosmetic case is back at the hotel."

The young woman's eyes widened. "You're *Holly Schlivnik?*"

I nodded. "Yes."

She flashed a hundred-thousand-watt grin. "Wow, this is so cool. We were just talking about you!"

I narrowed my eyes. Familiar face? Nope. "I'm sorry. Do I know you?"

She stabbed an index finger into her cleavage. "No, you don't know me. But I know *all about you*."

Now she had my attention. Should I be gratified or horrified? God forbid, had a customer complained about me? Hard to imagine what I could have done to precipitate such an action, but you never know. I studied her more closely. She didn't seem like a nut or a stalker, but then again they don't come equipped with an announcement sign, so, how do you tell..?

She extended her right hand. "I'm Harriet Kaplan."

The best description of Harriet Kaplan is a persona in beige. Her light brown frizzy shoulder-length hair gave the impression that an unruly bush had grown on top of her head. She hid behind clunky brown plastic frame glasses. The thickish lenses made her doe brown eyes appear large and out of focus and reminded me of the way Nana's eyes are. Harriet was thin, flat-chested, and on the tallish side. She had a gangly frame with the slightly stooped posture of someone uncomfortable inside their own body. She wore khaki pants, an oversized beige slouchy pullover, and oxblood penny loafers. A lusty laugh started in her toes and worked its way up to a beautiful smile that lit up her face and gave a glimpse into her possibilities.

She pointed to the middle-aged man beside her. "This is my Uncle Herb. While I've been helping him get ready for the market, I've been telling him I am interested in getting into this business and being a rep. My uncle said if a woman wants to be a rep in the southeast, you're the lady to talk to."

I squelched down a snort.

Harriet led me by the elbow. "Let me get you those aspirins. Maybe we can grab a cup of coffee and chat while they start to work?"

Chapter Thirty-Three

Buddy and I scheduled our appointments in tandem so we blocked out a good deal of a buyer's time. Even though we were competitors, some retailers considered us as a sales team and requested our joint participation for in-store promotional trunk shows and vendor fairs.

Jody asked us to create a trunk show extravaganza with all our lines. We made plans to work out the details together after I returned from the Charlotte, North Carolina market.

I deadheaded for Birmingham from Charlotte and met up with Jody and Buddy. The night before her big event, Jody, Buddy, and I toasted the upcoming extravaganza with several rounds of Margaritas at El Palacio del Rey Mexican restaurant. Of the one hundred invitations sent out, only four RSVP'd no. Jody went all out. She hired a DJ and catered a lavish spread with caviar and champagne for the event set for Saturday evening at 8:00. My heart filled with joy as Jody beamed with excitement at being on the road to acceptance. No one deserved it more.

**** 

Buddy and I wheeled our samples into Jody's store at dusk. The lights were on, but we found nobody home. Not a soul in the store. Weird. The big event started in three hours, and there were a lot of preparations still to complete. Where was Jody? She'd never leave with the store-wide open. Not even for a mani and a pedi two doors down from her place.

We called out her name like a couple of kids searching for a lost puppy. God made up for my height deficiency by blessing me with a strong set of pipes. With both of us yelling at the top of our lungs, it would be impossible for her not to hear us. We yelled loud enough to wake up the dead. No response. A mixture of annoyance and unexplained dread settled into the pit of my stomach as we searched the dressing rooms, stock room, and even the bathroom. The store wasn't that big and in no time, we'd run out of places to search. How do you misplace a six-foot-six-inch tall woman? You don't. Nevertheless, she was nowhere to be found and had seemingly disappeared into thin air.

A cool breeze in the back of the store rattled the delivery door ajar. Buddy cautiously opened the door. I leaned out into the alley and screamed. She wore one of her pink frilly dresses, and the silly tiara and wig sat askew on her head. She lay sprawled on her back, legs splayed, drenched in a pool of blood. A large splotch blossomed red at her heart and stained the front of the dress. Garbage from the dumpster had been heaped around her body, framing it like a perversely displayed painting. A number 50 University of Alabama football jersey draped over Jody's legs. A cardboard sign made of cut-out magazine letters lay on top of the jersey: *Freak! God Made You a Man! Don't Mess with God's Will!*

Bile gurgled up to the back of my throat, and I fought to keep it down. The creepy scene was positively macabre. Naturally, I burst out laughing. Buddy's stunned expression at my response said I'd lost my mind.

Maybe I had. Between guffaws tinged with overwhelming grief, I tried to explain my crazy genetic reaction to death to an incredulous Buddy. Not sure if he believed me. I wouldn't blame him if he didn't. Afterall, if it made no sense to me, how could it make sense to him?

I reached down to throw all the crap off her, but Buddy kept a tight grip on my arms and held me back. We could do nothing more for Jody but call the police. With exquisite timing, the DJ and caterer arrived at the same time as the cops. The EMT rolled the covered gurney away, and I took solace in Jody was finally in a place where she'd be accepted for who she is at last.

*The Birmingham Star News-Gazette* headline above the fold the next morning screamed in boldface letters: **Ex-'Bama Linebacker Murdered; Suspect at Large**. How hard would the police search for the killer of a misfit southern society was so willing to discard with the same regard as yesterday's trash? If I only knew how, I'd investigate on my own. God knows I'd dig a helluva lot deeper than the Birmingham Police. I'd be relentless until I found the killer and gave Jody the justice she deserved.

****

The irony of the name of the place amused me as we drove past the sign *Eternal Peace Cemetery* to an open grave in the back corner with a plain wooden coffin set on a funeral bier. My heart ached at how few people came to say goodbye to our friend. I searched their faces to see if any of them resembled Jody, but I recognized no one. I dabbed my eyes as I placed a single pink rose on the coffin. Dad and Buddy stared at the coffin, as if willing her to pop out and say, "Surprise, Sugar."

We sat in the front row as the minister droned his few canned platitudes. His memorized spiel made it painfully obvious he'd never met Jody. From his cookie-cutter comments, he might just as easily have eulogized a departed Dalmatian. I scanned the sky for answers. None lurked behind the clouds.

Chapter Thirty-Four

As Nana wisely predicted, life goes on even when it seems impossible to imagine how. So, early the next Monday I arrived at the mart preparing to hit the road. I'd spoken to Dad on Sunday, so my stomach dropped when the phone rang and it was him.

"Hol? Yeah, it's me. No worries. Everything's fine I'm really glad I caught you. Listen, where are you gonna be Wednesday?"

I glanced at my calendar. "I'm leaving for Nashville right now. Why?"

"Good. You can be back in Atlanta by Wednesday. Rob wants to talk to both of us. It's something so important, he's flying us out Thursday morning for a long weekend in LA. We land within an hour of one another, so we'll meet in baggage claim."

I tried to tamp down my annoyance. An hour ago, I made a week's worth of appointments I now had to reschedule. The buyers will be thrilled. Not.

"Why the big rush to drop everything and hop on a plane across the country?"

Our sales were on fire, so it couldn't be anything bad. Besides, Cluck-cluck de Grande Rob hated confrontation. He'd never fly us out to fire us. The gutless chicken couldn't face us in person and let us go. He would do the deed over the phone.

Dad answered, "He's being very cagey. I tried to pin

him down, but all he would say is it's all good, and we'll be extremely happy. No point speculating. We'll find out soon enough."

****

Damned irritating how much Rob enjoyed the drama and mystery. He grinned wide as a Jack O'Lantern. "I guess you two are pretty curious why I flew you out here."

I gave him the stink eye. "Nothing gets past you, Sherlock."

Rob smiled devilishly as he deadpanned. "The issues we need to discuss warranted a face-to-face."

Duh. I gave him an industrial-strength eye roll.

Between the hassle of cancelling and rescheduling appointments, the rush to get back to Atlanta, the long cross-country flight, and my normal lack of patience, it took every ounce of resistance not to slap him silly if he didn't get to the freaking point. I must have channeled my annoyance since he wiped the shit-eating grin off his face and moved it along.

He held his palms up with supplication. "Believe me, it's all good. It's quite a compliment to you both. But you've got some decisions to make. I am *ecstatic* with the business you brought to the company."

Rob turned to me. "I should thank Mariel Levine at Laurie's since she recommended that I hire you." He suddenly found something fascinating with his shoelaces. "Holly, I hope you don't get mad, but truthfully, I almost didn't hire your dad because of you."

I flushed with anger. The nerve of the arrogant SOB. *Did you fly me across the country to insult me?* I ignored Dad's warning hand on my forearm. I clenched my teeth and growled. "Why? You didn't even know me."

214

Rob had the grace to be abashed. "I'm kind of embarrassed now, but I worried after I'd invested time training you, being a nice Jewish girl, you'd meet a guy, get married, want to start a family, and get off the road."

Ding, ding, wrong answer, Schmuck. This was one of those times the truth isn't all it's cracked up to be. I glared my death ray stare at him. "So, the issue wasn't my lack of swimwear experience? It's because I'm a *woman?* Would you have the same worry if I *stood up to pee instead of sitting down?*"

Rob blushed from his neck to his receding hairline and found something critical that needed his full attention on the ceiling.

I shrugged Dad's cautionary hand off my arm again and answered the question myself. "Clearly not. Gee, Rob, how sexist *are* you?"

Rob waved his hands in the air, as though by abracadabra, poof, he made the past disappear. "Guilty, guilty, guilty on all counts. Fortunately, Mariel made *excruciatingly* clear everything you said. Despite my stupidity, it all ended up fine. Actually, pretty fabulous and it is the reason for our meeting. Honestly, your numbers are astonishing. You two shipped a 38% increase in volume over last season and added 25 new accounts. No other rep in any territory came close to you." Rob grinned. "Cutting to the chase, I want you guys all to myself as exclusives."

Whoa. Dad and I started to speak at the same time. Since "Daddy" is the senior member of our organization, and the one with more control over his mouth than me, for once in my life, I shut up, and let him do our talking.

Dad put his game face on. "Rob, the concept is quite a compliment but, even if we wanted to, I doubt we could afford to accept the offer. First of all, we make *a lot* of money off our other lines. Frankly, we'd be hard-pressed to make up the income going exclusive with you. Those other lines give us *year-round* incomes. Swimwear is a seasonal business, but our expenses are year-round. Secondly, with all due respect, as independent contractors, we're not at the mercy and whim of one company. If we get let go by one, or one goes out of business, or their product changes and no longer fits into our package, they can be replaced, and we still earn a living with our other lines."

Rob replied with his annoyingly condescending voice. "Mike, give me some credit. Before I flew you to LA, I considered everything."

Rob turned over a packet of face-down papers and pushed them over to Dad. "This is an exclusive contract. Let's go over the terms. Afterward, you two take the weekend to discuss it, call your family, and go over your figures. Do everything necessary to make an informed decision as to whether you'll accept the offer or decline it. We'll meet for brunch at my tennis club Sunday morning before you fly out, and you give me a yes or no."

My eyes bugged as Dad and I read over the documents. Wow, the guy wanted us bad.

Rob held a copy of the documents in front of him. "This is a five-year exclusive contract, automatically renewable unless one of the parties executes the out clause thirty days before renewal."

Rob read the terms aloud:

1. *$10,000 per month draw against commissions, 12 months a year.*
2. *Ditzy pays the rent on all your showrooms.*

3. *Ditzy pays all your trade market expenses.*
4. *Your territory includes the Caribbean.*
5. *No house accounts.*
6. *No commission splits with the New York sales force on any accounts of yours they work.*
7. *No sample charges.*
8. *Ditzy pays the health insurance for Holly, Mike, and Mike's wife.*

Rob smiled. "I want you guys, and I'm willing to pay for the privilege."

We were too stunned to immediately respond, but Dad recovered first. "Rob, this is pretty generous, but you're right. We've got some things to discuss."

Rob's smug expression said discuss things all ya want, but you two are mine. He smiled good-naturedly. "Fair enough. Let's go into the design studio, so you can preview the new line."

I cracked up at the way Rob organized the samples. He merchandised the line my way. By fabric group, not by silhouette. He turned back to face us after hanging the last sample on the rack and flashed the smile of an extremely confident man. Rob and I locked eyes as his lips quirked with the unmistakable smirk of Gotcha.

\*\*\*\*

Back at the hotel later that evening, we put the Schlivnik family decision-making process to work. Dad drew the line down the middle of the legal pad page, and we scored the pluses and minuses of taking or rejecting the offer. After tallying the score, we put our careers and livelihood on the line, our trust in Rob, and left LA Sunday afternoon with a signed contract.

As I boarded my flight, Nana's voice whispered inside my head. *Nothing turns out the way you think it will.* How prophetic Nana would turn out to be.

Chapter Thirty-Five

With Buddy in Miami for sales meetings, and afterward going on to Louisiana, I worked my way east from Knoxville and drove into Bristol, Tennessee. Eastern Tennessee is the lushly green, mountainous part of the state. The pleasant drive on I-40 going east was gorgeous. Fall in the south is nature's reward for having survived summer. The changing leaves reminded me of gumdrops. I reveled in the chill you get with a slight nip in the air. To be honest, I was just happy to no longer be drowning in my sweat. I rolled down the window and resisted the urge to howl like a hound dog. I stuck my head out and let the cold wind slap my face as I made my way east.

Bristol is another one of those annoying twin cities like Columbus, Georgia, and Phenix City, Alabama. In this case, Bristol, Tennessee, and Bristol, Virginia share the same downtown business district. The two towns and their state's borders were divided right down the middle of appropriately named State Street. Unlike Columbus and Phoenix City, at least these two towns shared the same time zone, but with different telephone area codes. I was rather embarrassed after calling one account in one state with the area code of the other…three times. Channeling Dad once again, we mock what we are to be. I need to start writing this stuff down.

****

After settling into the hotel room, I juggled the phone, paper, and pen as I struggled to write down a note from a pretty aggravating message. After I pitched my fit, I called Peachtree Travel and found out flying from Los Angeles to Europe cost less than flying from Bristol, Tennessee to Mobile, Alabama. And timewise, with two stops, it takes the same amount of time.

I called Dad next as I paced and ranted. "You won't believe the message I received. Amy Marx from McNamara's wants to work with me right *NOW*? Could she work with me the last time I came to Mobile? Oh, no. Sorry, completely booked. Able to go into our New York showroom and shop the line? Oh, no. Sorry, not shopping swimwear that trip. *Now* she says she's worked with *all* her other major swimwear vendors *but Ditzy* and *must* see me in the next two days because she needs to turn in all her swim orders before she leaves on vacation. She warned if I don't get to her now, she'd give my units away!"

Dad asked, "You call her back yet?"

"No, I wanted to talk to you first. I'm in Bristol, Tennessee. I am as far from Mobile as possible. Don't bother asking about the possibility of flying. I already checked into it. A flight to Europe is faster and for a helluva lot less money. Dad, you're a lot closer. Can you possibly work the appointment for me?"

Dad apologized. "Sorry. I wish I could help, but the Laurie's two-day vendor fair is at the same time."

I smacked my forehead. "Oh, heck. I forgot the vendor fair is this week."

Dad asked, "You want me to cancel? Mariel will pitch a fit, but I will try to get out of it."

I sighed. "No, no. The vendor fair is a big deal for

an important account, and you've got to do it. But we also do a ton of business with McNamara's. Their stores are in every town in south Alabama and all across the Florida panhandle. We can't afford to blow off that amount of business."

Dad clucked his tongue. "Then there's only one thing left to do."

**\*\*\*\***

I took a calming breath and vowed not to speak with clenched teeth as I dialed the phone. "Amy? This is Holly Schlivnik. Yes, I heard your message. That's the reason I'm calling. No, tomorrow morning is impossible. Right now, I'm as far from Mobile as it gets. No, flying is not an option. Believe me, I tried. It's at least a nine-hour drive with no stops. Thursday afternoon is the soonest. Let's say 2:00. Yes, Amy, since I can't sprout wings, it *is* the earliest possible time. Yes, of course. If I can get in earlier, I'll call you. Yep, I remember you're leaving on vacation Thursday. I'll do my best to be earlier. Unless you hear from me otherwise, I'll see you Thursday at two." Maturely, I stuck my tongue out and gave her the middle finger salute as I hung up.

**\*\*\*\***

It was an endurance test of a trip. Eight and a half hours of eating while driving and only two fuel and pee stops. I wheeled the samples into the McNamara's lobby at one-forty. I deserved a freaking medal. I announced myself to the receptionist. She handed me a badge and a slip of paper and pointed down the hall. "Showroom number three is reserved for you. I'll let her assistant know you're here."

I unpacked the line and stifled a yawn as I straightened a few samples. The clock said two-twenty.

This buyer is a real piece of work. I drove six hundred miles and managed to be on time and she can't get off her ass and walk twenty feet down a hall?

At two-thirty a frazzled twentysomething woman apprehensively walked into the room carrying a folder. I peered around her, but the young woman came in alone. She extended her right hand. "Holly? Hi, I'm Dee Ann, Amy's assistant." She flipped open the folder. "Are you sure you've got the right appointment date?"

The blood drained down to my toes. "Absolutely positive. She confirmed the appointment with me herself on the phone Tuesday. Why?"

Dee Ann grimaced. "Amy's not here. She went to a morning staff meeting, and left for her vacation right afterward."

Don't kill the messenger. I kept my voice to a low growl. "She left me a voicemail Tuesday morning saying she *must* see me before she left on vacation. I was in Bristol, Tennessee when I received her message." I snarled. "Do you have *any idea* how far Bristol, Tennessee is from Mobile?"

Dee Ann cringed and shook her head no.

I yelped. "Over six hundred freaking miles!" Controlling my temper proved impossible. My voice grew louder with each word as I visualized my hands around this buyer's throat. "When I returned her message, she *insisted* I come to Mobile before she left for vacation, or she'd give my units to another supplier. And *now,* you're telling me she left without seeing me?"

Dee Ann bunched her shoulders. "I don't know what to tell you. She's gone. She is kinda scattered, but she'd never do this without calling. When's the last time you checked your messages?"

She had me there. "Honestly? Not once. I drove like a maniac to make the appointment on time. I barely made food, fuel, or potty stops. Besides, it didn't occur to me to check since Amy confirmed our meeting herself. Can I use a phone to check and see if she called?"

Dee Ann nodded, "Yes. You can use the phone in my office. "

I played the message and went crazy. "*Oh hi, Holly. This is Amy from McNamara's. It's ten-forty-five on Thursday morning. I have to cancel our appointment this afternoon. Sorry for the short notice. I'll call you with my available dates.*"

Dee Ann shrank back as I slammed down the phone. "Unfreakin' real! Not acceptable."

Dee Ann wrinkled a brow. "I admit it's pretty awful, but what can you do? She's gone."

I waved a hand in dismissal. "I'll tell ya what I can do. I'm going back to the room. Get Mr. Brighton. He's her boss, right? Bring him to the room *now*. Amy's gone? Too freakin' bad. I am *not leaving* without my orders. I don't care if I have to see Mr. McNamara himself to get them!"

Dee Ann's eyes widened. "I can't barge into Mr. Brighton's office. I don't wanna lose my job."

I couldn't put her job in jeopardy. I made a decision that might end up costing me dearly.

"You're absolutely right. I'll go myself."

I stalked down the hall to Brighton's office, knocked twice, and opened the door to a bespectacled man in his forties seated behind a metal desk. He glanced up startled, but motioned me to come in and take a seat.

His eyes widened as I remained standing and introduced myself. "Mr. Brighton, I'm Holly Schlivnik, the Ditzy Swimwear rep. We've got a major problem."

Mr. Brighton logically asked, "Have you discussed it with Amy? She'd be the starting place. If you two are unable to get it resolved between yourselves, then bring me in."

I clucked my tongue. "Unfortunately sir, Amy *is* the problem. She left me a voicemail Tuesday demanding I come to Mobile the next day to work with her before she left for her vacation . If I didn't, she threatened to give my units away to another supplier. I was about as far from Mobile as I could possibly be at the time of the message. I returned her call and at her *insistence*, I drove over six hundred miles to work with her today. I managed to arrive on time, and Dee Ann said Amy left for vacation this morning."

Brighton sat up at attention. "You mean to say she didn't try to contact you?"

"The appointment time was set at two today. At ten-forty-five this morning she left me a voicemail at my office. Let me use your phone so you can listen to it."

He raised his eyebrows. "Fine. But why?"

I didn't answer the question. "Do me a favor and just listen. Remember, *she insisted* I make this trip or I'd lose my business. Believe me, she timed the message right. She made sure I'd be on the road and miss it. I told her how far I had to come to work with her. This is strictly a cover her ass call, so she can say she didn't stand me up."

Brighton jutted his chin. "Fine. Dial the number."

His expression darkened as he listened to the message. A muscle in his right cheek twitched as he hung up. A stab of pity pierced my heart for the guy. On the one hand, he needed to defend his buyer. But his scowl said he struggled to see how he could.

He gave me my opening, and I took advantage of his predicament. "It's not my style to go over a buyer's head. Honestly, it's political suicide. And I've never done it before. But I'm not accepting what she did. This is as rude, disrespectful, and unprofessional as it gets. I'm sure the management of this store doesn't want a reputation saying you condone this kind of behavior by one of your buyers. Believe me, all reps talk to one another. And if you don't think this kind of stuff comes into play if a store needs a rep's help, you're kidding yourself."

Abashed, Brighton dipped his head. "You're right. This is not the way we treat vendors." He puffed the air out of his cheeks. "But she's gone. What do you propose?"

If ya don't ask ya don't get. I pointed down the hall. "The line is all set up. I'll give you an overview. No one knows a line better than the salesperson. I know which styles and colors are best for your customers. Let me write the orders. You've seen the profitability reports for all your swimwear vendors. Last season we finished as one of your two most profitable swimwear lines. Based on our performance, we deserve a twenty-five percent increase. If you let me write the orders now and not wait for Amy to come back, you won't lose delivery and your competitors won't have our goods on the floor months before you."

He stood and smiled mischievously. "When you're done writing them, bring them to me for signature. Be sure to leave copies of the orders on Amy's desk so she sees them first thing on the day she gets back."

I liked this Brighton guy more every minute. Amy better be having a rip-snorter time on vacation because she's gonna have one helluva crappy first day back at work. Imagine her having to go into Brighton's office for him to adjust her open to buy dollars…. Oh, to be a fly on the wall for that meeting. Dad got it right. Don't get mad. Get even.

Chapter Thirty-Six

I walked out of McNamara's with a briefcase full of signed orders at five-thirty on a Thursday afternoon. I called Dad, and after I related the story, he crowned me the undisputed Queen of Chutzpah. I sat in the car considering what to do next. Go home? Good grief. Mobile is an awful long way from Atlanta. I'd just driven six hundred miles. The concept of another long drive almost half that distance was too awful to seriously consider. But, with no other appointments, I had no reason to stay in Mobile. What to do, what to do? I snapped my fingers. In a flash, it came to me.

I had to share the crazy adventure with Buddy. Of course. I put my travel dilemma aside for the moment and dialed his number. I reveled in the warmth of his hello as it seeped deep into my bones. I related my McNamara story, and Buddy gleefully cheered my victory. I finished the tale, and we discussed our next road trip. We had nothing else to talk about, but I couldn't bear to hang up. Did the longing in my heart come through the phone? I hoped not. How to explain it to me is a mystery, and impossible to explain to him.

Buddy took the problem out of my hands. "Hey, Holly Swimsuit, I've got a great idea. You're an awful long way from home, but it's only 90 miles to Nawlins from Mobile. Come here for the weekend. I've got some friends I'd love you to meet."

Some things are *bashert*. Yiddish, for meant to be. Things happen for a reason. I silently blessed Amy Marx. "Sounds great! Do you have to call first and see if your friends are free?"

"It won't be any problem. We'll stay in the quarter. You're gonna love it. Say yes?"

I jumped at the suggestion. "Yes! I've only been to New Orleans once as a teenager. This is gonna be great. If the westbound traffic on I-10 isn't too heavy leaving downtown Mobile, I'll be in the Quarter in time for a late dinner."

I hung up sky high and just as quickly crashed back down to Earth as I suddenly remembered Charlie. Oh boy. We'd made plans for Saturday to go up north to Dahlonega for a Bluegrass festival. He was a big fan of the genre and introduced me to it. He hadn't stopped talking about the festival for weeks.

Fingers of guilt twisted my heart. With everything happening during the crazy week, I never gave him or our plans a second thought. I put on my big girl panties and made the call. "Charlie, I'm sorry. I'm not gonna be home this weekend. No, not a trade market. I'm in Mobile. Yes, you're right. Mobile is not the place I said I'd be. It's a long story. Anyway, I'm in Mobile. After a six-hundred-mile drive to get here, I just don't have it in me to turn right around and go all the way back to Atlanta. Since it's only a ninety-mile drive to New Orleans, I'm going to Louisiana for the weekend. No, you can't come down to spend the weekend with me. I'm going to be with Buddy and some friends. I hope you understand, and I'm sorry. Bluegrass is a big thing in the south, so I'm sure there will be other festivals. I'll call you once I'm back, and we can make plans for another weekend."

****

If you spent as much time driving as me, you can only listen to so much news, C&W, and Fire & Brimstone before your mind wanders and you tune out all the radio crap. Some people did their best thinking in the shower. I did mine in the car. As I headed west towards the Big Easy, my heart steered my brain to the path it wanted me to be on. But to reveal my feelings to Buddy, first I needed to admit them to myself. I was in love with him. Oh, boy.

The French Quarter is so romantic. In my mind's eye, we snuggled close together in one of those horse-drawn buggies clip-clopping around Jackson Square. I couldn't ask for a more perfect place to tell him what was in my heart. Nana had it right. Things do happen for a reason.

****

I checked the address as I approached the apartment in the heart of the French Quarter. I buzzed with anticipation and rang the bell. Buddy opened the door and let me in. He took my overnight bag and lightly bused my cheek.

It's a miracle my jaw missed the ground as he nestled his arm around the waist of a tall, thin, honey-blond woman with a patrician nose, piercing blue eyes, and a shy smile. He brushed her cheek with his fingertips and made the introduction. "Holly, this is my fiancée, Lee Ann Weisiger." He dipped his head at me. "Honey, this is my friend Holly. I'm so tickled two of the most important women in my life finally meet."

Lee Ann leaned into Buddy and smiled sweetly as she fondly squeezed my shoulder with a door knocker-

229

sized diamond engagement ring adorning the ring finger of her left hand. "It's a real pleasure to meet you, Holly. Buddy's told me so much about you, that it's as though I've known you forever."

All righty. Nothing like being a day late and a dollar short. Nana's voice whispered *man plans and God laughs* as I stood rooted to the spot with a frozen smile plastered across my kisser. At that moment, the meaning of the old Yiddish expression *I didn't know whether to shit or go blind* became perfectly clear.

****

The excruciating weekend in New Orleans proved to be the longest two days of my life. Mercifully, Monday finally arrived, and I left the French Quarter two hours before the crack of dawn. I crawled back to Atlanta with my emotional tail between my legs. I dropped the samples and rack off at the showroom and crept into the apartment late. I was grateful no one was around to greet or question me as I dragged my suitcase down the dark hall and went straight to my room. I put my bag down, and the perfect end to a perfect weekend lay on my bed: Karen and David's wedding invitation.

Not ready to deal with Buddy or my feelings, I told him I planned to work locally. We would catch up the following week. Hopefully, throwing myself into work would keep my mind off my troubles. Tuesday morning, I went to the mart to make appointments, but my heart wasn't in it. Who was I kidding? Keeping up the pretense that everything is great as my world fell apart proved impossible to pull off. I'd pick up the phone and get halfway through dialing and hang up. I brought the samples I'd just packed and put into the car back to the showroom and unpacked the garment bags.

At the end of my training week, Dad said however I got my business done was fine by him as long as it got done. If I managed to do it with less time on the road, more power to me. I never skipped a single day of work before, but this seemed the perfect time to test-drive his theory. I grabbed a few of the duplicate bikini samples and took them home.

**\*\*\*\***

I knocked on Ellen's bedroom door. She cracked it open and squinted at me funny as I stood wearing only a skimpy bikini and a goofy grin. "Ever been up to Lake Lanier? I've got a customer in Gainesville, but I've never been to the beach. My buyer said it's fantastic. You can rent paddle boats or lay on the beach, and there's a café, as well a snack bar, if you get hungry. Wanna go?"

Ellen shook her head. "No, I've never been to the lake. I'm too wrapped up with studying for anything else." Ellen consulted her watch. "It's already eleven o'clock. It's kinda late to start schlepping to the lake now. By the time we get there, the day is already half over. Doesn't seem worth it. Besides, I've got a lot of research to do at the library."

Ellen grabbed Max by the collar as he stuck his wet snout in my crotch. "Come on Max." She pulled the dog back into her room. "We have a lot of reading to do." As an afterthought, she mumbled, "Have fun," and shut the door in my face.

**\*\*\*\***

An hour or so later, I pulled into the public parking lot a quarter-mile from the Lake Lanier shoreline. Not a cloud in the bright blue sky. Even though it was the beginning of fall, it was still warm enough for a day at the beach. The heat of the sun penetrated deep into my bones and served as a salve to my emotional wounds. If not for the ever-present humidity, it was a glorious day on the beach. Since it was a workday for most folks, I had the lake almost to myself. A half dozen small boats dotted the water, and only two dozen sunbathers were on the sand. I had my choice of spots to plop my tush down on.

I hadn't eaten anything all day, and my tummy protested loudly. I took a seat on the outside patio of the cafe, facing the lake. I treated myself to a chocolate malt accompanied by a juicy cheeseburger and a mountain of extra-crispy fries. Good old-fashioned comfort food to heal an aching heart.

I finished every morsel of my gluttonous food fest and headed for the ladies' locker room. I locked up my valuables and grabbed my towel and suntan lotion. I took a glimpse at myself in the mirror before starting to the beach. Big mistake. My lunch parked itself in my abdomen. Suddenly, my bikini was a lot smaller. It wasn't too attractive wearing a couple of bandages masquerading as a swimsuit. I slipped a cover-up over the swimsuit and hummed the words to the old Brian Hyland song of a girl wearing a yellow polka dot bikini.

I opened the locker room door and stuck my head out. I craned my neck turtle-style to survey the beach. Still only a few people on the sand. I tiptoed out of the locker room and dragged my rented lounge chair a few feet from the shoreline. I slathered on the suntan lotion and laid down. I opened a book and tried to forget my troubles by losing myself in another world. I read a few pages and let the lapping rhythm of the tide lull me to sleep.

**\*\*\*\***

As the weekend neared, I grew rather nervous. I vegged out every day, and hadn't called on an account or written a single order all week. When Dad invariably asked why I took the week off, what would I say? I'd never tell the Great God of Guilt the truth. Subject myself to the ten thousand inevitable questions too painful to explain to myself, let alone to anyone else? Not a chance. So, I never told him the reason, only that I took the week off. Oddly, Mr. Nosy never questioned why. He only asked if I enjoyed myself and *if it had been worth it*? Smart man, my dad. Happy I'd done it once when I needed to, but I never played hooky again.

**\*\*\*\***

The following weekend Peter invited me to do the semi-annual Chattahoochee River Raft Race. Glad for the distraction, I accepted. It wasn't much of a race. It was more of a social happening. Hundreds of crafts in all shapes and sizes meandered down the river filled with fun-loving entrants and well-stocked coolers. We reached the end of the race two hours later and pulled our raft onto the shore. Peter finished tying it to the roof of his car. He faced me, and even a blind guy could tell Peter had something on his mind. He took a deep breath and sighed. "I've been offered a huge promotion."

Peter had worked his ass off to move up the corporate ladder. I was thrilled his efforts had been recognized and rewarded. I squeezed his hand. "Congratulations. What will you be doing?"

Peter's eyes shone with excitement. "It's a fantastic opportunity. I'll be in charge of a new division." He cast his eyes downward, having found something fascinating on his tennis shoes. "The thing is, it involves relocation to Portland, Oregon. I've had the offer for a few weeks.

I asked management for some time to consider the ramifications and to be sure I'm good with moving so far." Peter grinned self-deprecatingly. "I'm an upstate New York boy from a small town. Atlanta is the furthest from home I've ever lived."

Peter's eyes clouded with a sadness so intense that I turned away when he whispered, "But the main reason I hesitated to accept the offer is because of *us*."

I forced myself to face him. I owed him that much. "And now?" I searched his face, but the defeat in his eyes made the answer clear.

Peter fondly brushed a stray strand of hair out of my eyes. "I've accepted the job. I'm moving next week." Peter caressed my face with his fingertips, and his voice grew husky with emotion. "I'm falling in love with you, and before I let myself fall head over heels with no turning back, I had to take a reality pill. You've made more of an effort to be around, but if forced to make a choice, your career will always take precedence over me."

I wanted to argue, but the words died in my throat.

He dipped his head. "It's impossible for me to stay. I'm not interested in meeting other women here. We'd continue seeing one another, and my feelings for you will only grow stronger. As time went on, I'd demand more than you're able or willing to give. I need someone who wants *me* as the center of their life instead of me always being an also-ran coming in second banana to a buyer. I've never met anyone like you before, and probably won't ever again. You're smart, funny, interesting, easy on the eyes, and the most driven woman I've ever met. It pains me to say it, but there isn't enough room in your life for both me and your career."

No point in arguing since I agreed with him. Yet my eyes blurred with tears for the what-ifs of a life with Peter. I'd never know how it would have turned out. Wow. They're dropping fast as flies. What kind of odds would I get in Vegas for going 0 for 2 in a week?

Peter pulled into my apartment parking lot and stopped in front of my building. We searched one another's eyes, but there was nothing left to say. I pecked his cheek, wished him good luck with the new job, and then watched Peter drive out of my life.

Chapter Thirty-Seven

Traveling with Buddy became unbearably painful. I considered coming up with an excuse and telling him it was for the best if we started traveling separately. I found nights most difficult. Unrequited love is the cruelest love of all. It took all my willpower not to slip into bed beside him and make him my own.

Men might be dense at times, but how thrilled could his fiancée be with Buddy and me traveling together, especially if he told her we shared a room? Or did he? I didn't have the guts to ask, and he didn't volunteer. She was either mighty trusting, naïve, or supremely self-confident. I envied her in so many ways.

Naturally, Buddy spent a lot more time in New Orleans. Instead of caravanning from Atlanta, we met up on the road. He called to say he'd meet me in Memphis. Dark semi-circles smudged under his eyes. I attributed the worry lines etched across his face that made him appear tired and drawn to the long drive. We met at Tops and ordered our usual favorites, but from the way he pushed the food around his plate, it was obvious that he had something on his mind. For a thin guy, especially if the menu was barbeque, Buddy always cleaned the plate. I pointed to his dish. "So, you planning on actually eating the pulled pork or just shoving it around?"

He pinched his lips into a wan smile. "I guess I just don't have much of an appetite. I've got somethin' to tell you, and it's not gonna be easy." My heart clenched as he sighed. "I've resigned from my uncle's organization and quit goin' on the road."

I bought myself a few moments by glancing out the window at the mighty Mississippi roiling its way down to the gulf. Life is indeed a circle. Buddy and I started our relationship in Memphis, and now we'd end it in the same place. Nana's warning to be careful what you wish for floated up to the shoreline. Fate played tug-of-war with my emotions. Relieved or upset? Either way, I had to ask. "Why? You love being a rep."

Buddy took the issue out of my hands and shrugged with a nonchalance that irked me. "At first it was fun and I had me a real adventure, but the constant traveling started to get to me. I don't fancy bein' a gypsy all my life. Besides, Lee Ann says it's time for me to settle down since we're engaged."

Now we got to the heart of it. Lee Ann. The question of whom was the mastermind behind his change of heart no longer remained a mystery. A measure of victory. A chink in her armor. Maybe she wasn't so confident after all. So, winning a skirmish and still losing the war is sufficient? Apparently, yes. I found my voice. "So, since you're off the road…?"

He smiled his lopsided smile that still pulled at my heartstrings. Damn him. "I'm goin' on the other side of the table so to speak. I'm gonna be a buyer at Westerly Brothers, her daddy's operation. If you get Loosiana as part of your territory, will you call on me?" He smiled, but the smile never reached his eyes. He joked, "I promise to be on time for appointments, not get ugly if I don't fancy a style, and give you a big order."

I ignored his graceless attempt at levity and got

down to brass tacks. "When do you start?"

Buddy dipped his head. "I already started. I gave Uncle Miles notice two weeks ago and, he's already hired my replacement. He's sent out letters to my accounts they'll be gettin' any day now."

Anger trumped a broken heart. I was so pissed that I could have slapped him. "You resigned two weeks ago, and you're *just now* getting around to telling me? Imagine my embarrassment if a *buyer* gave me the big news first? You didn't have enough respect for our relationship to tell me once you decided to quit?"

Buddy winced. Too bad. He whined. "I wanted to do it in person. This is the first time we've been together in a couple of weeks."

Wrong answer. He could have told me when I was in New Orleans. Two can shuffle the inconsideration deck and draw the indifference card. I asked coldly, "So, who took your place?"

Buddy flinched as though I'd slapped him. "That's it? You got nothin' else to say?"

I was hurt and angry, and not in a charitable mood. Only one way to get past him. Cut him out of my life as completely as a cancerous tumor. I chose my words with the same precision as a surgeon's scalpel. "I'm a big girl, Buddy." I choked back unshed tears. "The world won't fall off its axis with you out of my life."

Buddy came around, scooted close to me in the booth, and reached for my hand. "You gonna be all right?"

I slapped his hand away and spat out my words with the lethalness of a round of ammunition. "Don't flatter yourself. I managed to live without you before. I'll survive without you now just fine." Tough talk. But the truth? I'd expire being so close to him another minute. I tossed my napkin on the plate and threw a twenty down on the table. I grabbed my purse and stood. I stomped toward the exit and called over my shoulder. "Be sure to mail me a wedding invitation. I'd love to send a gift."

I turned for one last glance at the man I loved. Buddy's stunned expression gave me a hollow measure of consolation as I stalked out the door.

****

It was a miracle I somehow managed to concentrate while working with my Memphis accounts. I finished my last appointment an hour before dusk and couldn't get out of town fast enough. With the passing of each mile marker on eastbound I-40, my heart hurt a little less as the distance between Buddy and me grew. Not a lot of civilization between Jackson and Nashville. Having skipped lunch, I was famished, but not in an adventuresome mood to chance the kind of meal choices I might find further down on the highway. I stopped for dinner before leaving Jackson at a familiar roadside diner and sat in a booth facing the one in front of me. It had been a long, difficult day, and I still had a good distance to go. I sipped a cup of strong coffee hoping to fight off fatigue.

A professionally-dressed black man walked into the diner and sat in the booth in front of me. Two white men in overalls came in a few minutes later and slid into the booth opposite the black man. The trio smiled as they bid one another with a warm hello. Old friends? Maybe even around these parts, times had started to change.

The worn booths of the small diner sat squished closely together, so, I easily overheard their conversation.

White man #1 smiled at the black man. "Hey, Luther. How ya doin'? We wanna reserve the barn and the land for all Friday and Saturday nights this month. Same price as the last time since we're repeat customers, right?"

My ears perked up. Hmm. Two white guys renting land from the black man. Things do change.

Luther nodded. "Yep, the same price as last time. Eight thousand dollars plus security deposit of one thousand. Deposit returnable upon inspection of the barn and land for damage. Cash only, boys."

Wow. This was some expensive event they planned.

White man #2 pulled a stuffed, sealed manila envelope from the pouch pocket of his overalls and handed it to Luther. "Wanna count it while we're here?"

Luther grinned at the two white guys and waved off the question with a flick of his wrist. "Nah. I know where to find y'all if it's short."

White man #1 pointed to the envelope. "Then I reckon we're done here. Don't worry none about the barn and land. We'll clean up and close the gate after us."

White man #2 rolled a toothpick to the side of his mouth with his tongue and smiled. "Nice doin' business with you, Luther. See you next month."

The two white men stood up to leave. They extended their right hands to Luther, revealing the KKK cross with a drop of blood in the center tattooed on each of their wrists.

Did Luther just collect blood money from the great-grandsons of the mob who lynched his great-granddaddy? Does revenge trump history? Or maybe Luther conferred with Dad? *'Don't get mad. Get even. The only way to get even is to take their money.'*

Luther shuffled the big batch of greenbacks like a deck of cards and shoved the loot into the recessed compartment of a leather briefcase.

Ca-Ching.

Chapter Thirty-Eight

A capacity crowd filled the Temple Beth Shalom sanctuary. All eyes were focused on Karen and David standing under the Chuppah exchanging their wedding vows. Charlie, Ellen, and I joined the crowd chorusing Mazel Tov as David stomped on the wineglass. My eyes glistened with jealous, yet joyful, tears as David kissed the bride.

***** 

I turned to Ellen as we walked to our cars. "No need for us to take two cars to the reception. We'll follow you home. Drop your car off and you can go with us."

Ellen shook her head. "Thanks for the offer, but I'm gonna skip it. I went to the important part. Finals are in a couple of weeks. I've got a lot of studying to do."

Such an odd duck. This is her life-long friend's wedding reception. How do you not take part in the celebration? By comparison, Karen and I barely knew one another, but not attending the reception never entered my mind. "Are you sure? Karen will be devastated."

Ellen shrugged her indifference. "Karen will never miss me. Enjoy the reception. See you tomorrow." Ellen waved to my date as she headed to her car. "Nice seeing you, Charlie."

**** 

Twinkling   lights   entwined   through   gorgeous

arrangements of lush flowers transformed the elegantly decorated ballroom of the Druid Hills Country Club into an enchanted fairyland fit for a princess.

Everyone watched as David held Karen closely during their first dance. Charlie stood behind me and wrapped an arm around my waist. "You're kinda quiet. Is everything okay?"

Peachy. This was the sixth wedding I've been to in the last five years. I was happy for Karen and David. Honestly. I'd been so sure Buddy was my David, but Buddy belonged to someone else. Charlie was a nice, decent guy. And if given half a chance, this might be us. I've tried, but there just were no sparks. I wished with all my heart it had turned out differently, but Charlie was not *the one*. Being a nice guy isn't enough. It's gotta be sparks or nothing.

I smiled. "Everything's fine. I'm enjoying the party."

A prisoner of my mind, I was relieved when Charlie pointed to the crowded dance floor. "Wanna dance?"

****

Charlie pulled into a parking space close to the front of my apartment building and killed the engine. I turned to face him and smiled. "Professor, I had no idea you were such a terrific dancer!"

Charlie took off his glasses and cradled my hand in his. "You don't know lots of things about me. Besides being a wonderful dancer, I play a vicious game of handball, whip up a great omelet, make a mean margarita, and I'm crazy for you."

Oh, boy. I stiffened and pulled my hand away. "Charlie, please…"

He put his index finger on my lips. "Holly, let me

finish, okay? With all your traveling, we haven't seen as much of one another as I hoped we would. And I heard I have competition, so that's another reason why we aren't together every weekend. Despite all that, it didn't take me long to fall for you." I widened my eyes when he said, "I know you don't feel for me the way I feel for you."

He said self-deprecatingly, "Don't be so surprised. For a geek, I'm actually pretty observant. It doesn't matter to me. Maybe over time, you will. A blind guy could see it in your face tonight. You were picturing yourself as the bride. I've wanted to tell you something for a while, and this seemed a perfect time. I've received an offer from the Naval War College in Washington D.C., to teach the brass the most efficient ways to use probabilities in war games. It's a dream job, and I've accepted it. It would make it a perfect dream come true if you came with me. If we were together and you weren't always traveling, we could see if we can take our relationship to the next level."

Charlie held up his hands in front of his chest. "Don't give me an answer tonight. If you do, I doubt I'll like the answer. Please, give my proposal serious consideration. I need to be in D.C. by the end of this month. I'd love it if you're part of the adventure."

I hated to hurt this kind and gentle man, but I had to. It pained me to step on his heart, but it would be far crueler to lead him on than nip this in the bud. Fond of him? Yes. But try as I might, my feelings for him were not the same as his for me, and never would be.

I brushed my fingers across his cheek, hoping to soften the blow. "Charlie, you are the nicest, kindest man I ever dated. And I do care for you. But you're right. My feelings for you are not the same as yours are for me. But

I care for you too much to short-change you. You deserve someone who loves you and is *in love* with you. I'm not her. I'm comfortable with you and trust you never to hurt me. Believe me, I wish it were different, but it isn't enough for me. Over time, you'd expect more from me. More than I'm able to give. And you'd come to resent me. Or worse. Believe me, this would never work out. The right woman is waiting for you to find her. And you will." I shrugged. "I need sparks. Warm and cozy just isn't enough."

I kissed Charlie on the cheek and got out of the car without letting him walk me to my apartment. I'd hurt him. But if I didn't walk away then, I'd only hurt him a lot more.

The pitch-dark apartment had not a single light on. Self-absorbed Ellen has never been the most considerate when it comes to anyone else but Max. Thinking about Charlie and not paying attention, I stumbled over Max while trying to turn on a light. I walked into my room and the light bulb in my head turned on.

By late Sunday afternoon, I sat in the Riverbend Apartments rental office signing a lease. It took no time to pack up my things. I didn't have a lot to pack. Monday, I used my very first credit card at Rich's Department Store, and in less than three hours, I bought myself an instant house. By Wednesday afternoon, all my new stuff had been delivered. By Wednesday night I finished unpacking, and for the first time since I'd moved to Atlanta, I was finally home.

## Chapter Thirty-Nine

Going exclusive to Ditzy proved quite challenging for Daddy N'Me. We'd taken a huge financial and professional risk for a one-season line with no screw-up factor figured in. Exclusivity put me in harm's way more than Dad. He traveled Florida, the sunshine state. Tourist central, and a state surrounded by an ocean and one with a legion of homes with swimming pools. By contrast, I got the land of Billy Bob and barbeque. No bikini haven on a good day. But we'd made the decision together, and I played the cards from the deck of life I'd chosen to draw from.

With the additional territory, we revised our geographic responsibilities, and more territory became mine. Dad concentrated on the Florida high volume accounts from Orlando south and the Caribbean. In addition to my original territory, plus the Carolinas and Virginias, I took over the Florida panhandle to Jacksonville. Even with only one line, it spread me out quite thin. I could easily fall hopelessly behind with only a single misstep.

While driving to an appointment, the perfect solution came to me. This situation couldn't wait for our weekly Sunday confab to discuss. I pulled off the highway and called Dad. "Since we went exclusive, there aren't enough days in a week for me to get my job done. It made geographic sense for you to concentrate on mid and south Florida and the Caribbean and me to take over the Florida panhandle. But now with the panhandle in addition to the Carolinas and Virginias, it's too much. I need help, or I'm gonna drown. Between the initial orders, the reorders, preview line orders, tracking retailer's weekly sales reports, the fashion shows, trunk shows, and teen boards, I'm never caught up. We better do something before every account of mine gives our business away to another supplier better equipped to meet their needs."

Dad's frustration came through the phone line. "I hear ya kiddo, and feel your pain, but it's still only the two of us."

I asked, "Want to adopt another daughter?"

\*\*\*\*

I tried not to stare. I'd been raised better. Extremely impolite, but hiding it proved impossible. Like I've said: I'd never earn a living playing poker. Talk about your Cinderella syndrome. Cinderella sat right in front of me.

Harriet Kaplan walked into the Atlanta showroom with a transition from boring beige to beautiful so complete, I almost asked what store she bought for. She wore her hair in a cute curly afro. She ditched the slouchy sweaters, the clunky loafers, and nerdy glasses for trendy duds and contacts. Her chocolate brown eyes now shone with the brightness of light only beamed by self-confidence.

We had a lot of ground to cover. I created a crash course with no time for a learning curve. Fortunately, Harriet proved to be a fast study. I taught her my way to set up the Ditzy line and explained the selling features of each silhouette. I related my sales experience first presenting the line by body type the way Rob instructed.

I imitated Rob with his "*In Los Angeles, we present it this way*" speech, and Harriet giggled at my imitation. Between lessons in delivery dates, color trends, and sizing, Harriet clutched her sides as I regaled her with stories of Dad expecting me to steam samples nightly and my runaway rack. She mastered the technical product information and how to incorporate it into a smooth line presentation. She conquered the different sales techniques to use based on the store type in record time.

Once she completed the 'simple portion' of the lesson, the tough stuff came next. "We're gonna plan your first trip."

I had the same panicked reaction to Dad as Harriet's terrified eyes widened in alarm. I fondly squeezed her arm. "Relax. I'm going with you. I'll call the buyers and set up the appointments so you see the way it's done. At each appointment, I'll introduce you as our newest associate and that you'll be the rep working with them going forward. And then I'll pass you the baton."

I pushed a map under her nose. "Plan your first road trip and the route you'd take. Remember, the goal is to do the most amount of business in the least amount of time." With a minimum of prompting, Harriet mapped out her first road trip.

We drove on I-85 north to Charlotte. Before we rolled our samples into the Ivory's Department Store buying cube, we walked the sales floor. I blessed Anna Wellington once again as Harriet analyzed the swim department with the precision of an old pro. After I introduced Harriet to the buyer, I stepped aside, and Harriet presented the line.

We worked our way around the Carolinas until we

completed the circle. I left Harriet in Charlotte with her own set of samples and my advice to always go into appointments right foot first and have the answers before the buyers asked the questions.

I'd done my best to pay it back by paying it forward. As I drove back to Atlanta, I prayed to the Swimwear Goddess I'd done half as good a job teaching Harriet the ropes as Dad taught me.

Chapter Forty

It had been two years since Nana's Leukemia diagnosis. While she certainly tried keeping it a secret, she finally reached the point of having become visibly deteriorated physically. It became simply impossible for her to hide her condition anymore. Stubborn independence kept her going on her own. But once she could no longer manage the treatments without help, she had to fess up. Imagine the way *that* family reunion went. We all fell apart, and Nana held us together.

Nana wouldn't go down without a fight. But with her fear of dying, she refused to acknowledge the death sentence the illness carried. And she wouldn't let any of us either. Whenever one of us wanted to, needed to, tell her what she meant to us, she brushed it off. She'd decide when her time was up, and it wasn't up now. She wasn't dying yet and refused to hear anything we had to say until the time came. And she'd tell us when the time had come. Her reaction to the disease? The grandparent equivalent of a kid putting their hands over their ears and humming to drown out anything they chose not to hear.

Nana believed life goes on no matter what, and celebrations should not be precluded by troubled times. The tougher the times, the more reason to party on. Her way of sticking a finger in fate's eye.

Our family gathered to celebrate my twenty-fifth birthday. Two days before my party, Nana and I sat in her kitchen having coffee. It was past lunchtime, and early riser Nana still wore her robe and slippers. Her skin tone cast a sickly gray pall, and dark circles outlined her eyes. Nana's deterioration was a painful thing to witness. My forever young nana appeared as old, tired, and ill as she had become.

Despite her illness, Nana still missed nothing. She read the pain in my eyes and went for levity. "My God, I caught a glimpse of myself in the mirror this morning when I brushed my hair, and I scared myself." Nana's hand shook as she rubbed her fingers over her pallid, sunken cheeks. "I'm death warmed over. I've got to get to the beauty parlor. I'm telling you kiddo, I'm gonna get my hair done, a facial, a mani and a pedi, and anything else they can do to me, so I don't scare the hell out of everyone at your party. Trouble is, I'm so damned tired, I'd need a three-day nap to get enough energy to do it all. Do you remember how fast I used to walk?"

I smiled at the memory. "Are you kidding? As a kid, I ran to keep pace with you. I was always scared you'd lose me if I didn't keep up."

Nana smiled ruefully. "Those days are long gone, kiddo. Now it takes me an hour to get from the bedroom to the kitchen. I finally arrive, and I'm too damned exhausted to cook. Maybe the girls from the beauty shop will come to the house and fix me up?"

My eyes widened with alarm. "If you're not up to going to the shop, I'll call and ask. You've been going to the same beauty parlor for years. They won't say no to you." I narrowed my eyes. "We can cancel the birthday party if it's too much for you. I'm not a little kid."

She puckered her lips into a funnel. "Nothing doing, kiddo. Birthdays are to celebrate, and that's what we're gonna do. I'm not gonna be the one to ruin it for you because I'm not feeling up to snuff. Remember, it's great to be alive. And don't you ever forget it."

****

I stayed at Nana's instead of with my parents. She was too weak to be left alone. Nana woke me around dawn. Her fingers were cold as an ice cube as she tapped my arm and joked. "You'll be a big hit if you do the Chuckles the Clown schtick as part of your eulogy. Do you remember it?" Her reedy voice came out tinny and sounded far away. She faintly sang as off-key as Lucy Ricardo. "*A little song, a little dance. A little seltzer down your pants.*" She wheezed trying to crack another joke. "Maybe do a singalong. Audience participation is always a crowd-pleaser."

I pulled my arm away. "Knock it off will ya? This isn't funny." I turned on her nightstand light, and my heart leaped into my throat. Except for the blue lips, she turned sheet white and trembled. Nana's eyelids fluttered, and she moaned low. As I reached for the phone, Nana tried to speak. I pressed my ear right up to her lips to hear her as she whispered. "Holly, dahling, I'm so scared."

My voice cracked, and I willed myself not to cry. "Nana, don't be scared, it'll be okay. I'm calling nine-one-one right now."

With effort, Nana pushed the words out. "No, don't call. It's time. Don't leave me. Hold my hand so I won't be so afraid."

No way. I cried out. "Please Nana. Let me call for help. It's not time. I won't let it. Please don't leave me, Nana, not yet. I'm not ready."

Nana twisted her lips into a sardonic smile. "Well,

kiddo, you better get over it. You might not be ready, but apparently, I am."

****

Mourners packed the memorial chapel of the Riverside Funeral Home on my twenty-fifth birthday. An unadorned pine coffin with a royal blue Star of David burned into the lid lay on a bier. The Rabbi Dovened over the coffin as he chanted Kaddish, the Jewish prayer for the dead. Dressed in black, the Schlivnik family sat stone-faced in the front row. Dad held my inconsolable mother's hand. We three Schlivnik grandchildren sat together staring at the coffin, willing Nana to come back while trying to imagine life without her.

The Rabbi finished the ceremonial part of the service and stepped up to the microphone. "Friends, now Rae's granddaughter Holly will eulogize her beloved grandmother."

I approached the stage and stepped-up right foot first. Nana made her presence known, and I drew strength from her beside me. I hoped she heard me as I hummed *A little, song, a little dance, a little seltzer down your pants* as I reached the lectern. I took a breath, held onto the sides of the lectern, gazed out over the audience, and beamed a beatific smile. I greeted the mourners by echoing the philosophy that governed Nana's life. "Good afternoon, ladies and gentlemen. It's great to be alive!"

With a glance at the coffin and upwards, I peered out amongst the mourners and soldiered on. "Today we gather to celebrate the life of Rae Hart Eiger. No one loved life more. She lived every minute of it to its fullest. Everything she did, she did it all the way. Nothing half-assed, no holding back, no holds barred for her. She saw each day as a gift, an opportunity, a mystery, an adventure, and a challenge. She laughed often and from deep within the depths of her soul. She acknowledged the humor in her own foibles as easily as the ridiculousness of others. Nana loved all the television situation comedies. When Nana babysat my sibs and me, we'd be in our rooms, and we'd hear her laughing from across the house. Mind you, we had no clue what she found so funny. But her laugh was so contagious that we'd start to do it along with her. Nana ate with gusto, and no matter the dish, it was always *the best she'd ever tasted*. Every time. She played cards with the fervor of a gambler, told a joke with the timing of a stand-up comic, and played the piano with the passion of a concert musician with more love of music than her ability to play."

I drew strength from my words, Nana's words, and spoke with a passion reserved for the righteous. Nana chose *me* to ensure her voice was heard one last time, and I wouldn't disappoint her.

"Nana was ahead of her time in so many ways. She was always her own person. Opinionated, outspoken, and always spoke her mind. She always told you what she thought, not what she thought you wanted to hear. Certainly *not* your typical doting Jewish Grandmother. Anything but. She let you get away with *nothing*. No pity parties allowed on her watch. She'd defend you to the death but had no problem telling you in no uncertain terms if she thought you were wrong. She'd help you make a decision, but she'd never make it for you."

I jutted my chin. "But she always stood up for herself and her own. Nana was brave, at times brazen, especially when it came to helping her family." I smiled at the memory. "A while back, Nana and I went into the junior dress department at Purdines. So, Nana is checking out the sales floor, and she sees a mannequin outfitted in another supplier's style instead of one of mine. She doesn't say anything, but she hands me her purse and proceeds to undress the mannequin and re-dress it with a dress from one of the companies Dad and I represented. She rearranged the whole department so our products were the prominent ones on all the racks. By then, I had a fit. I was certain she'd get us banned from the store."

My heart filled with joy when the audience applauded as they roared with delight. Somewhere out in the great beyond, Nana was in her glory.

"So, Nana shined it on and said no one would question anything. She told me to survey the department. I'd see a bunch of other old ladies working in the store, and she was just another one of them doing her job. With an open mind and an open heart, she was passionate about everything she believed in and compassionate for others. Nana's love for her family and friends was the foundation of her life. I learned everything important in life from my nana. She taught me we are responsible for ourselves, and the choices we make determine the path our lives will take. She taught me how to drive, how to care, and how to swear. And most of all, she taught me *how to live*. Anyone who knew my nana knows she would be furious if you came here to mourn her. To honor my nana as she'd want to be honored, let no tears be shed today. Instead let us laugh together and remember her as someone who relished every smile, every sunrise, every breath, every heartbeat, every embrace. Nana, you will live on in our hearts forever. It is indeed great to be alive."

**** 

After the graveside service, our family gathered in my parents' living room once the mortuary delivered the Shiva stools for the family to sit on for the week of mourning. Traditionally, mourners are not allowed to do anything except grieve. Not cook, not clean. Nothing but mourn.

Ironically, a festive, party atmosphere filled the house. Packed to capacity with those family and friends attending to the needs of us, the mourners. Deli platters and desserts naturally covered the dining room table. There is no occasion we Jews ever go hungry, including this one. People ate, drank, and laughed as they shared their favorite Nana stories. Somewhere in the Great Beyond, Nana was thrilled.

My mother came out of the kitchen holding a large birthday cake with lit candles singing happy birthday. I stared as everyone formed a semicircle around me and joined in. Was I the only one who hadn't gone around the bend? Were party games next?

My mother put the cake down on the coffee table and motioned for me to blow out the candles. I sat rooted to my Shiva stool. Had she flipped her lid? Maybe she was so overcome with grief that she didn't know what she was doing. To my horror, she came over to me, put her hands under my armpits, lifted me off the Shiva stool, and placed me in front of the damned cake.

Mom pointed to the cake. "Come on, Hol. Today is your birthday. Make a wish and blow out the candles."

I stared at her as though she lost her mind. "What's the point? My wish won't come true."

Mom jutted her chin. "Nana would be appalled if she ruined your birthday."

She had me with that one. Nonetheless, I couldn't ignore the irony of the situation. My laugh was as bitter as burnt coffee. "Too late. The ship already sailed. Sitting Shiva and celebrating your birthday is just so wrong." My eyes begged Mom for understanding. "Let's bag my birthday this year and hope my next one gives me something to celebrate."

Mom emphatically shook her head. "Sorry, kiddo. No can do. We Jews believe life is for the living. We bury our dead quickly. We mourn them for a week, and then go on with our lives. In fact, it is against Jewish law *not* to celebrate your birthday. If you were getting married and Nana died, according to Jewish law, we are *obligated* to go on with the ceremony."

She accurately described our religious laws, but I kept whining. "What is *wrong* with our people?"

Dad stood next to Mom. "The way we Jews honor our dead is by keeping their memory alive."

Fabulous. With both parents team-tagging me, I didn't stand a chance.

Dad said, "We do it by naming our children after cherished loved ones, by speaking of our departed loved ones often, and most of all, we remember them by living our lives and moving forward as they'd *want* us to. The way our faith *instructs* us to."

Dad tossed me back to Mom. My mother narrowed her eyes. "Did you mean everything in your eulogy? *Really* mean it, or did you just say some pretty words?"

I jutted my jaw with righteous indignation. "Of course, I meant every word. How dare you even ask such a question?"

In our emotional ping pong match, the ball went back to Dad. My father challenged me. "Oh yeah? Prove it."

I gaped helplessly at my parents. "How?"

Mom pointed to the damned cake again and said the only thing that changed my mind. "If you *really* meant everything in the eulogy, then you *know* what Nana would want. What Nana would *expect* of you."

I threw in the towel. "Fine. I give up. You win. You said the magic words." I glanced at the cake and widened my eyes. "But just so you know. From my spot here in the cheap seats, this gets weirder by the minute." I closed my eyes, made a wish, and blew out the candles. Everyone clapped their hands and yelled happy birthday. Next Mom brought over a pile of gifts and handed me a specific box and card. "Start with this one. It's Nana's birthday gift and card."

I gave her the big eyes. "She shopped? No way. She couldn't muster the strength to go to the beauty parlor."

My mother grinned. "If my mother set her mind to something, she would not be easily denied. Go ahead. Open it. Don't forget to read the card. It will explain everything."

I smiled and turned my eyes to heaven. *Sorry, Nana.* I bet you cringed as I ripped the wrapping paper. I pushed the tissue paper aside and stared gape-mouthed. I lifted Nana's ID bracelet, now with *my initials* inscribed in diamonds, out of the box. I held it up closer to make sure I read the initials correctly. My eyes searched my mother's as she smiled and pointed to the card.

My hands trembled as I opened the envelope. Nana's voice spoke inside my head as I read her chicken-scratch handwriting to myself. *"Holly dahling happy birthday! I can hardly believe how fast time flew by. It seems only yesterday I changed your poopy diapers. And now poof. With the blink of an eye, you blossomed into a wonderful, intelligent, funny, strong, and independent young woman successfully making her way in the world. I couldn't be prouder of you. Since you inherited my love of jewelry, I am sure this is the perfect gift. I changed the initials to yours. With this bracelet on your wrist, I am with you every day. I love you, sweetheart, more than my next breath, more than life itself. Happy birthday. Love Always and Forever, Your Nana."*

I closed the card and sensed her spirit with me as I clasped the bracelet on my left wrist.

## Chapter Forty-One

Just as life is made up of the practical nuts and bolts of going through each day, so it goes with death. Once the mourning week ended, we dealt with the painful task of cleaning out Nana's apartment. And despite being unprepared to let Nana's physical presence go yet, her death became undeniably real. I needed a tangible sense of her. Something material to keep my connection to her. The way to do it came to me in an instant. I stood in the center of Nana's walk-in closet. I closed my eyes and breathed in deeply, smelling the scent of her Tabu perfume permeating her clothes. With my eyes closed, she stood next to me, choosing which outfit to wear. My mother and Sandy walked into the closet and caught me. We cracked up as each of us set out to do the same thing.

I held the sleeve of Nana's favorite blazer under my nose and breathed her scent in. "Every time I smell Tabu, I'm gonna turn around expecting Nana to be there."

My mother fingered another one of Nana's favorite jackets. "She will be." Mom brushed her fingers over my heart. "In here forever."

I wanted to believe her, had to believe her, chose to believe her. But just in case, I pilfered Nana's perfumes.

Nana always said she couldn't guess who wanted what, so she left it to us to sort it all out. Nana left everything to my mother, but we kids could take any treasured remembrances we wanted. In addition to her perfumes, I took my grandfather's garnet and diamond pinky ring that had been Nana's engagement gift to him, and Nana's candlesticks.

Sandy took three of her favorites of Nana's paintings. Sandy and Mom divided up Nana's silverware and china. I gave Sandy my share, as it wasn't my style. Mom took Nana's diamond ring and necklace, all the family photographs, and Nana's recipes. We divided up the rest of Nana's jewelry and art.

Jerry took Nana's book and old record collections, and Dad wanted Nana's antique art deco cigarette lighter.

One could not help but be stunned by how quickly the detritus of a vibrant person's life got broken down and dispatched. But as the Jewish Family Services donation truck carted off the last of her possessions, poof, in the blink of an eye, any physical evidence of Nana having walked the Earth disappeared.

The time drew closer to the family scattering and going back to our own lives, but I wasn't ready to deal with this loss alone. Dad and I went out for a cup of coffee, and I told him I needed some time to regroup and heal. He asked me what I wanted to do. I told him I wanted to go to Los Angeles and spend time with my friends. He asked how long I needed, and I told him honestly. I had no idea. He said he understood, and I was grateful. One of the best things about working for a parent is no matter what, he is always gonna be my dad first.

****

I went back to Atlanta and asked Harriet to pick up some of the slack. Out of respect, I told Rob my plans. "Yes, you heard right. I am coming to LA to stay with friends. I need to regroup and take a breath. I'll be in Los Angeles at the end of this week. Why?"

Rob replied, "I've wanted to talk to you for a while now, but with your grandmother's death, I didn't want to intrude."

I remarked sadly. "As Nana once told me, life goes on, even if we can't imagine it will. What did you want to discuss?"

Rob answered my question with a question. "You'll be on the west coast at the end of this week? We need to talk face to face. Pick a convenient day for you to come in to see me next week."

I had no room in either my head or my heart for a business detour. "Rob, any other time, absolutely. But this time, I need to be with the girls and find a way to recover. So, if you don't mind, just tell me now."

He drew a deep breath. "Our company is growing by leaps and bounds, and you're a big part of our success. From my vantage point, you've gone as far as possible with Mike. Your talents go way beyond being a road rep. I'm prepared to offer you a huge promotion with a generous compensation package. Move you back to LA and be our Vice President of Sales. What do you think?"

Whoa. "I think you caught me completely off guard. The opportunity sounds enticing, but a decision this big involves more than just me. Give me some time, and I'll get back to you as soon as I make a decision."

Rob would not be denied. "You're coming out to Los Angeles anyway. Let me fly you out, and pick up your expenses. You consider the offer and come see me at the end of next week with a decision."

Oh no, you don't, pal. I've been down that road with you once before. Nice end-around try. "I'll consider the proposal and let you know whether I accept the job or not. But I'll pay for my expenses. That way I'm not obligated and can make up my mind independently."

\*\*\*\*

As the plane reached its cruising altitude level, the overhead movie projector came on with the preview of the in-flight movie: A classic oldie. Warren Beatty starring in *Heaven Can Wait*. I cracked up as the irony didn't escape me. I peered out the window and whispered. "Nana, did you see the movie they're showing? I bet you would have found the movie choice hilarious." I searched the clouds for an answer and sighed. "Maybe you did."

\*\*\*\*

The week I spent with my friends was the salve my heart needed to heal. We laughed and cried over coffee, ate at all my favorite restaurants, and hit all my favorite stores. As I walked alone early one overcast morning along the beach below the Santa Monica pier, my head overruled my heart. I met with Rob the next day, and we sealed the deal with a hug and a handshake. I made him pinkie-swear not to say a word to Dad. I owed my father everything. Out of love and respect, this must come from me, face to face.

Would Nana approve of my decision? As I boarded my flight, she whispered, "Always believe in yourself and trust your gut."

I buckled my seatbelt and jutted my chin. Who says you can never go home again? Once more, Nana got it right. Life is a circle. But as the plane took off, one thing was clear. I might be going home, but I wasn't the same person who left.

\*\*\*\*

As the plane touched down in Miami, the time came, as Nana would say, to put my cards on the table and show my hand. Gulp. Maybe letting Rob drop the bomb for me would have been the smarter move. Does Western Union still send telegrams? Nah. Time to put on those big girl panties. On the way to the mart, Dad chattered on about everything and nothing. I tried to listen, but drifted off. I was too nervous and preoccupied with the future to pay attention. I fidgeted in my seat. I tapped my fingers on the armrest, and ran my fingers through my hair.

Dad never missed a nuance. The concern in his eyes twisted my heart as he squeezed my shoulder. "Are you all right? You seem a little distracted. I hoped you'd come back from LA with your batteries re-charged."

"I am re-charged. I had a great time hanging out with the girls." Now or never. I took a deep breath. "Dad, we need to talk…"

He dipped his head. "Okay, sure."

It was show time, but I had a helluva time stepping out on stage. I cringed inwardly, hearing myself ramble. "With everything that's happened. So many changes. People getting married, moving away, moving on with their lives, Nana dying. All those changes forced me to take stock of my own life. Dad, I owe you everything. You gave me an opportunity I can never repay you for…" The words trailed off and I couldn't bear to see his face.

"But…" Dad prompted.

I'd dipped my toe in the water, but I couldn't dive into the pool. Pretty soon, I'd need a dentist to pull out the words stuck in the back of my mouth. I forced myself to go on. "But the reality is, I've gone as far as I can with you and, and…." So far, I'd danced all around it. A vision of Nana's scowl of reproach chastened me as she whispered inside my head. "Move it along already, for crying out loud. Before he dies of old age waiting, get to the point."

I almost cried with relief as Dad finished my sentence. "And now you want to take the next step in your career. I'm guessing you're moving back to LA."

Either Dad became clairvoyant, or loose lips Rob couldn't keep his yap shut. I'd kill the big mouth if he blabbed and broke his promise. I forced myself to turn to my father. "Y-yes. I didn't say a word to anyone, so, who told you?" I narrowed my eyes. "And why are you smiling? I've been a mess all week trying to figure a way to tell you, and *this* is your reaction?"

Dad's smile melted my heart. "From your first day working for me, it was inevitable that someday we'd be having this conversation. It was only a matter of time before you'd max out, and want, no need, to move forward to your next career step. I'm grateful I had you with me this long. I've taught you all I can. It's time for you to take the next step, whatever it is. I'll never be able to replace you. Harriet will take over, and she'll do a good job, but she won't be you. No one will ever be you."

What a kind, generous, and gracious man this marvelous father of mine is. I choked up. I had no adequate words. Once I could trust my voice, I said, "I owe you everything. How do I ever repay you?"

Dad lifted a shoulder. "By paying it forward." He smiled. "So, what are your plans?"

Holy guacamole! Rob respected my wishes. This was gonna be fun. I widened my eyes. "You know the way Nana always said things never turn out the way you think they will? As it turns out, you're not exactly getting rid of me. We'll still be working together, but differently. We're kinda swapping places."

Dad peered over his glasses and grunted. "Huh?" His deer in the headlight's expression meant he had no clue. Gotchadaddyo. I grinned evilly and enjoyed his confusion a few beats more. "You're right. I am moving back to LA. I'm gonna be the new, actually the first, Ditzy Swimwear Vice President of Sales and Merchandising." I gulped. "How *do you feel* about me being your boss?" I giggled to cover my nervousness at what he'd answer. "Pretty weird, huh? I'm not used to the idea myself."

I glanced over to gauge his reaction. He grinned as maniacally as a circus clown. Not the reaction I expected, but I'd take it. He cackled. "Are you kidding? Nothing says job security like I feed your mother. This is fabulous. My deliveries are gonna be great."

Maybe it was his gotcha after all. He wiped away an errant tear dribbling down my nose with a flick of his pinky and gave my cheek a tender love pat. His smile warmed me to the depths of my soul. "I couldn't be prouder of you."

Thanks, Daddy.

Love ya Always, N'Me.

Chapter Forty-Two

Rob wasn't a happy camper, but too bad. I promised Dad a month to transition Harriet and our customers over. Initially stunned by Dad's call, Harriet flew to Miami to work with him. Then she came to Atlanta to go over account lists, active orders, and territory maps with me. We went on an introductory road trip. The tears on both sides of the table when I introduced Harriet as my replacement gratified me beyond words.

We completed our around-my-territory-tour, and Dad came to Atlanta for a final meeting. When we finished, Dad gave us a moment. As I handed Harriet all the showroom keys, I reminded her to always walk in and out with her right foot first.

The next day I made the rounds in the mart, saying goodbye to Sadie, the little old lady who ran the Schlepper's Sundry Shop in the mart lobby, as well as the apparel center workers and showroom colleagues. Cora Lee cried her eyes swollen, and I had black and blue marks on my chest for a week from her hug.

I had a farewell dinner with my ex-roommates and David. The next day I flew to Miami. According to Jewish law, once a person's body is buried, it takes a year before the grave marker is set, and only then can the deceased receive visitors. Since visiting Nana was verboten, I pretended she was on another Caribbean cruise, and I'd see her next trip. My family and I laughed and cried a lot, and then the time came to savor last hugs and a bittersweet goodbye.

I spent the next week extricating myself from my life in Atlanta. Giving notice at River Bend, contacting utilities, turning in my leased car, closing bank accounts, and deciding which things to take with me to LA and which ones to toss. I found it remarkable how one person, rarely home, still managed to accumulate so much crap.

My mother's gift was one I neither expected nor deserved. Mom flatbed shipped her beloved, vintage bubblegum pink convertible wrapped in a huge red bow to my apartment. The car meant everything to my mother. Nana bought it for Mom when she started her first big job out of college. Mom attached a card to the bow with a note saying our family values traditions, and she hoped I'd cherish the car as much as she did. And that someday, I'd continue the tradition, and pass the convertible down to my daughter.

My life in Atlanta came full circle. I made the rounds of favorite places to say goodbye to the city I'd finally come to call home. I took a last walk-through Centennial Park, Stone Mountain Park, and the plantation. A final fried chicken meal at Aunt Fanny's Cabin, a final visit to Mary Mac's Tea Room, and a Varsity hot dog after the last High Art Museum tour. For the heck of it, I hit the Underground Atlanta, the cheesy tourist trap. I caught a movie at the famous art deco Fox theater and then ate dinner at the Pleasant Peasant. And only so I could mark it off the list of life experiences, I ordered a mint julep at Pitty Pat's Porch.

****

I made the rounds bidding farewell to all dear to me,

but I couldn't leave without seeing someone special one last time. The trees at Eternal Peace Cemetery had grown so much that I found it difficult to locate Jody's grave. I wandered from gravesite to gravesite searching for my friend. It's not as though she got up and moved. It took me a few minutes, but I finally found her. I laid a huge bouquet of pink roses on the marker. Although she wasn't Jewish, I chanted Kaddish. I dovened over her grave while reciting the prayer for the dead.

Then I talked to my dear friend as though she could hear me. The tree leaves hanging over her grave rustled in the wind, as she made her presence known. It had been a long time, and we had a lot to catch up on. I told her about Buddy, and Peter and Charlie, and Nana dying, and Karen's wedding, and River bend, and Harriet, and my big decision. After thanking her for everything, and encouraging her to find Nana, I touched the grave marker with my fingertips, told my wonderful friend how much I loved and missed her, and bid my precious Jody goodbye.

## Chapter Forty-Three

After the moving van pulled away packed with my worldly possessions, I made one last pass through my empty apartment and took my memories with me as I opened the door. I turned my eyes up to the heavens for Nana's guidance and walked out of my apartment right foot first for the last time. I fired up the convertible, and after crossing the bridge over the Chattahoochie River, I waved goodbye to Atlanta fading away behind me in the rearview mirror. I transitioned from the I-285 bypass onto I-85 south and the next station in my life.

****

Hyped up on a mixture of excitement and nervous energy, I could have driven a lot further. With the tough part of the drive still ahead, I opted for the smart choice and spent the night in Montgomery, Alabama. I checked into the Governor's House Hotel after sunset. With Montgomery part of my territory, it only seemed like another road trip, not a final departure. I took a last stroll around the beautiful antebellum buildings of the state capitol. After a catfish and hush puppies' dinner at Mojo's Fish Shanty, I turned in, hoping exhaustion trumped emotion, and I'd get some sleep.

Early the next morning, I got on I-65 south. An hour later, I approached the exit for the Waffle House. The memory of goofy waitress Betty Jean who once served me breakfast and funny stories warmed my heart. I'd passed the place hundreds of times over the years but had never been back. Butterfly jitters had invaded my tummy at sunrise, so I passed on breakfast before getting on the road. The familiarity of the highway seemed to calm my nerves, and my stomach growled loudly.

For giggles and squeaks, I pulled into the Waffle House parking lot. Betty Jean wasn't on duty to serve me, but her interchangeable clone took my order. I tucked into a waffle special with the same genuine imitation pancake syrup sans the country ham and grits, served with a cup of strong coffee and a side order of memories at no extra charge.

Back on the interstate, I glanced in the rearview mirror and bade goodbye to all the Betty Jeans I encountered over the years. My heart clenched as too many memories blurred my vision, so I tried to concentrate on the road. For someone so anxious to get going, I took my time, driving at a southern pace. I committed the live oaks, roadside motels, and small towns along the way that had become an integral part of my life to memory. Not willing or able to let them go.

I reached the junction of I-65 and I-10 on the shady side of the afternoon. I came to the sign I-10 Westbound: New Orleans, and my heart reminded me that I still had someone else to say goodbye to. The phone rang, and I prayed Lee Ann didn't answer. She won, I lost. I wasn't emotionally prepared for the sound of victory in her voice. I sagged with relief when Buddy said hello. After all that time, I still thrilled at the sound of his drawl.

"Hi, Buddy. Yes, it's really me. Good, good. Yeah, it's been a long time. It's good to hear your voice too. Listen, I'm going to be in New Orleans tonight. No, only passing through. I'm driving to LA. No, everything is fine. It's too much to go into on the phone. I'm on I-10 west of Mobile. If I leave now, I'll be in New Orleans in time for dinner. Why don't you and Lee Ann meet me at the seafood place off I-10 near Lake Pontchartrain with the great Jambalaya at 6:00? I'll bring you up to speed on everything then."

**\*\*\*\***

I paralleled the beautiful gulf with a mixture of dread and anticipation twisting my heart into knots. I arrived at the Cajun restaurant first and was shown to a booth with some privacy in the back. Buddy walked in alone and did a one-eighty searching for me. I waved to get his attention. He made his way across the dining room. While I was surprised, truthfully, it was a relief to see him alone. I had no more desire to see Lee Ann than she likely wanted to see me. Buddy smiled, leaned down to buss my cheek, and sat across on the opposite side of the booth.

I meant it when I said, "Hey, kiddo. It's good to see you." Dark circles smudged under his eyes. I forced myself to take a casual approach. I craned my neck and pointed at the restaurant entrance. "Is Lee Ann meeting us?"

Buddy smiled sadly. "I'm afraid Lee Ann won't be joining us. We broke up a while back."

Nana whispered, *"Man plans and God laughs"* in my ear. I covered Buddy's hand with mine and tried not to choke on my words. "Oh Buddy, I'm so sorry. What happened? You guys seemed so perfect for one another."

Buddy shrugged. "We were great as a long-distance relationship. Once we were constantly together, everythin' changed. It was always her way or the highway." Buddy smiled sardonically, "Fact is, she was quite jealous of you."

I speared him with an incredulous expression of shock and poked a finger into my chest. "Jealous of *me*? Why? She's gorgeous, intelligent, comes from a great family, and you were crazy over her. What threat could I possibly pose?"

Buddy grinned. "I guess your name came up a lot. Listen to her, and it was Holly Swimsuit this and Holly Swimsuit that. To be honest, she was probably right. Every time Lee Ann tried to steer me into doing something she wanted, I threw your name up at her."

Well, shut my mouth. A ridiculous surge of pleasure warmed my heart. I narrowed my eyes. "Meaning?"

Buddy held out his hands. "Meaning, you never tried to change me. You took me as I am. Once she got me back here, all Lee Ann wanted to do is change everythin' about me, and re-create me into her vision of a perfect guy." Buddy quirked a rueful smile. "At first I went along with everythin'. If you're in love, ya get kinda blind."

He reminded me of myself talking to Nana as he fidgeted with his napkin. Unfolding and refolding it over and over again. I resisted smacking his hand the way she slapped mine. Buddy kept his eyes focused on the tabletop and avoided me as he talked. "Gettin' off the road? Her idea. I know I said I didn't care for the life, but truth be told, it was Lee Ann's tellin' me that. The truth is, workin' for my uncle, and travelin' with you was the happiest time of my life. I'm not very proud of myself. I let her lead me around by the nose. She picked the place she wanted me to work, wanted to change the way I dressed, weed out my friends, and made me move into her fancy apartment. I was just becomin' an extension of her."

He had guts. I'd give him that. I bet it cost him dearly to admit everything to himself, let alone to me. "So, what was the last straw?"

Buddy smiled at the irony. "The weddin' plans. I gave her my guest list, and by the time she got done, none of my friends were invited. She actually told me since I was '*marryin' up*,' I needed to get a better class of friends. I was much better off with her friends. People who'd help *raise my social standing* and get me to the level I needed to go professionally. Like some kinda Professor Higgins and I was a bumpkin born in a barn she was tryin' to teach good manners to. When she scratched your name off the guest list, I packed my bags and moved out."

I could afford to be compassionate now, yet a selfish jolt of pleasure surged through me, and I flushed with shame. "I'm sorry for the way it ended. You really loved her."

He twisted his lips into a sardonic smile. "I did. But not the way she turned out to be, and I hated everythin' she tried to turn me into."

Put up or shut up time. "And yet you didn't think to call me?"

His eyes begged for understanding as he held out his hands in supplication. "And say what? Hey, it's Buddy. I just want to tell you how big a moron I am?" He had the grace to blush. "I'd climbed up the tree, crawled onto the limb, and sawed myself off. There was nothin' left to say."

From the punch in my heart, it was clear he'd given me my answer. If he loved me, he would have called. Better to be sure, and not spend a lifetime second-guessing myself. Maybe calling him had been a monumental mistake. Screw you, Buddy, and the horse you rode in on. Didn't reach out because his precious ego got bruised? Wah, wah. Gee, too freaking bad. Anxious to put a whole country's distance between us, I considered leaving, but brushed it off. Not that he deserved it, but how to explain? After all, I called him, not the other way around.

Buddy interrupted my mental game of ping pong with a sweet smile that still touched my soul. Damn him. "So, enough about me. I'm sorry to hear that your Nana passed. She meant the world to you."

He hit a raw spot, so I was relieved when the server stopped at our table to take our orders. I fought the urge to follow her as she walked to the kitchen.

I jumped as Buddy slapped his hand on the table. Oh yeah. Things were going just peachy. "Now what in the Sam Hill is this business of you driving to California all about?" He narrowed his eyes. "What in tarnation is goin' on with you, girl? You were mighty mysterious over the phone."

Time to put it all on the table. "Nana's death gave me a real wake-up call. I lost so many people who'd either passed away or moved on. Jody died, you left the business, and Peter and Charlie both moved on too. I guess it took losing Nana to see time had marched on...." I squirmed in my seat, but forced myself to continue. "I went to LA after Nana died and spent time with my friends. I also met with the owner of Ditzy Swimwear. He offered me a management position based in LA and I accepted."

Buddy's smile warmed my heart. "Wow. What a fantastic opportunity." He dipped his head. "Bet telling your daddy had to be tough."

I couldn't help but laugh. "A true example that things never turn out the way you think they will. I'd been agonizing over telling him. I finally get up the courage, and not only does he guess I was moving on, he says he's been *expecting it*. I'm worrying the Great God of Guilt will try to talk me out of it, and he's grinning like a Cheshire Cat. Thrilled with the great job security he just scored, since he feeds my mother."

Buddy grinned. "That's Mike, all right. So, who's gonna replace you?"

"You remember Harriet from Charlotte? She's been working for us in the Carolinas and Virginias for a while. She's moved to Atlanta, and they'll replace her in her old territory."

Another subject that was too raw to elaborate on. So, I went for a more neutral topic. "Hey, you'll never guess who I ran into in Memphis? Rufus. Did you hear that after twenty-five years on the job he retired? The Israel family threw him a retirement party at their country club and invited all their vendors. Over one hundred of us attended. Marvin gave a moving speech that choked up the crowd. Then Marvin's dad surprised Rufus with a gold watch. It was a beautiful affair for such a wonderful man. I am so happy he got the recognition he deserved. I can't imagine going to that office and not seeing him. It's gonna be weird for all the vendors. I pity his replacement. The poor guy has some awfully big shoes to fill. Anyway, Rufus has been involved with the SCLC in Memphis since he retired. He is something."

Buddy smiled. "Rufus is a measure of the way things finally changed here."

I nodded my agreement. "Living in the south, I've

learned things are not always the way they appear to be. There is no one you can't love once you know their story. When I first met Jody and Cora Lee, they struck me as freaks. Now I love them like sisters. Jody taught me not to be judgmental. She gave me so much more than I gave her. Cora Lee taught me how to make fun of myself. Both of them showed me that you can't judge a book by its cover. Everything I believed in changed over time, and I'm not leaving the same person as when I arrived."

Buddy smiled and dipped his head. "Any regrets?"

Time to put up or shut up. "Nana always said regret is the worst human emotion since it's the one you can't do anything about."

Buddy smiled sadly. "I believe she's right."

Wait a Cincinnati minute. Could *this* be my answer? If not, at least he'd given me my opening. But suddenly I developed paralysis of the mouth. Why? Either I was too afraid to reveal my true feelings, or too afraid of his response? Maybe I wanted him to tell me his? An involuntary shiver crawled down my back. Nana's reproach chilled me as I remained mum.

We filled the awkwardness of avoiding more painful issues by chatting on safe topics of news, weather, and sports. As we ran out of innocuous subjects to discuss, the server mercifully arrived with our meals. We ate in companionable silence, and Buddy insisted on paying the bill when we were done.

We walked through the parking lot, and Buddy asked, "So what are your plans now?"

"My stuff will be the last of four stops the movers deliver. I've got around ten days to get to LA and find a place to live. Then, I'll have to dive into the new job before my furniture arrives. It's gonna be mighty interesting having my dad work for me." I grinned. "But regardless of our role change, rest assured, he'll still make *me* hang the samples and brew the coffee at all the markets."

Buddy cracked up.

I stopped at the convertible, and Buddy's jaw dropped. He circled the car and caressed the hood ornament like he would a lover's cheek. He gasped. "Good golly, Holly Swimsuit! When did you get this beauty? This is one classic set of cool wheels!"

I gave him the lowdown on the car's history and opened the trunk. "Before I forget, I've got something for you." I moved a carton packed with fifty blue spiral notebooks to the front. I took out a set of folded maps on top of the notebooks. I fought to keep the quiver out of my voice. "I wanted you to have something to remember our trips by. These are maps of all the places we traveled together. I've circled all the towns and cities we opened accounts in." I unfolded the maps, and we leaned over them. The memories tap-danced across my heart as our road trips flashed through my mind.

Buddy lifted the maps for a closer perusal. "This is a fantastic gift." He pointed to the notebooks. "Are those your journals?"

I nodded. "They are."

Buddy smiled. "I reckon you kept those journals for a reason."

I pursed my lips. "Meaning?"

Buddy dipped his head. "Meaning I still believe you were destined to take the job with your daddy to write about it. It's quite a story to tell."

I narrowed my eyes. "You really think so?"

Buddy nodded. "I know so."

I mused out loud. "Funny, Nana said the same thing."

I closed the trunk and checked my watch. "Wow. Where did the time go? If I'm gonna get to LA in three days, I need to make it to Beaumont, Texas tonight. I better get going, or I'll get in awfully late."

He folded me into his strong arms and we clung to one another tightly, realizing the embrace was for the last time. How I wanted the moment to last forever, but the time to say good-bye had come. I turned my face to kiss him on the cheek. He tipped my chin up with his index finger, and I swooned as he kissed me soundly on the lips. Nothing turns out the way you think it will. His soft lips were as delicious as I always dreamed they'd be. But as he kissed me, once again, my brain overruled my heart. Buddy had to remain a part of my past and be left behind if I were to complete my life circle.

Buddy's voice cracked hoarse with emotion as he held me tightly and talked into my hair. "Then you best be on your way. I'll never forget you, Holly Swimsuit. Drive safe and be sweet now."

Buddy broke the embrace and nestled the maps in the crook of his arm. And without uttering another word, he quickly walked away. He turned his head and took one last look at me standing next to the convertible. Then he keyed his car door open and slid into the driver's seat. He turned east out of the driveway and merged onto the street. I stared after his car until the inky darkness of the night swallowed its taillights. My eyes filled as Buddy LaValle drove out of my life.

Nana's voice whispered. "Remember. God put our heads on facing forward for a reason."

I pointed the convertible west and headed home.

### A word about the author…

Born in the Big Apple, award-winning cozy mystery author Susie Black now calls sunny Southern California home. Like the protagonist in her Holly Swimsuit Mystery Series, Susie is a successful apparel sales executive. Susie began telling stories as soon as she learned to talk. Now she's telling all the stories from her garment industry experiences in humorous mysteries.

She reads, writes, and speaks Spanish, albeit with an accent that sounds like Mildred from Michigan went on a Mexican vacation and is trying to fit in with the locals. Since life without pizza and ice cream as her core food groups wouldn't be worth living, she's a dedicated walker to keep her girlish figure. A voracious reader, she's also an avid stamp collector. Susie lives with a highly intelligent man and has one incredibly brainy but smart-aleck adult son who inexplicably blames his sarcasm on an inherited genetic defect.

Looking for more? Visit her website: www.authorsusieblack.com Sign up for her reader list and receive a free swimwear fit guide. Or reach her at mysteries_@authorsusieblack.com

Thank you for purchasing
this publication of The Wild Rose Press, Inc.

For questions or more information
contact us at
info@thewildrosepress.com.

The Wild Rose Press, Inc.
www.thewildrosepress.com

Printed in the USA
CPSIA information can be obtained
at www.ICGtesting.com
LVHW021029161123
763929LV00024B/116